PRAISE FOR

THE MANY-WORLDS SERIES

"Will have your heart pumping." —*Justine* magazine

"Weds old-fashioned legends of princesses trapped in towers along with contemporary teen concerns. It's a great mix." —*Booklist*

"A solid, fun adventure." —*Happily Ever After (USA Today)*

"Jarzab succeeds with a parallel-world concept that is also an entertaining read." —*Kirkus Reviews*

"Good for fans of fantasy and intricate other-world construction." —*VOYA*

"Action and conspiracy abound." —*SLJ*

PRAISE FOR

the opposite of hallelujah

★ "At its heart, this is a story about sisters, and it's as complex and convoluted as the relationship itself." —*Booklist*, Starred

"An engaging read." —*VOYA*

"A layered meditation on family and belief that will ring true." —*Kirkus Reviews*

PRAISE FOR

ALL UNQUIET THINGS

"Confident, literary prose." —*Publishers Weekly*

"Compelling." —*Booklist*

TETHER

ALSO BY **ANNA JARZAB**

All Unquiet Things

The Opposite of Hallelujah

Tandem

TETHER

THE MANY-WORLDS SERIES

ANNA JARZAB

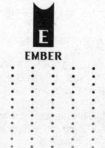

EMBER

Text copyright © 2015 by Anna Jarzab
Cover photographs copyright © 2015 by Oleg Babkin/Shutterstock

All rights reserved. Published in the United States by Ember, an imprint of Random House Children's Books, a division of Penguin Random House LLC, New York. Originally published in hardcover in the United States by Delacorte Press, an imprint of Random House Children's Books, New York, in 2015.

Ember and the E colophon are registered trademarks of Penguin Random House LLC.

randomhouseteens.com

Educators and librarians, for a variety of teaching tools, visit us at RHTeachersLibrarians.com

The Library of Congress has cataloged the hardcover edition of this work as follows:
Jarzab, Anna.
Tether / Anna Jarzab. — First edition.
pages cm. — (The many-worlds series ; book 2)
Summary: Sasha returns to Aurora, the parallel universe of generals, princesses, body doubles, and the boy she loves, Thomas, where she tries to help and find missing people and save them all.
ISBN 978-0-385-74279-5 (hc : alk. paper) —
ISBN 978-0-375-99078-6 (glb : alk. paper) — ISBN 978-0-307-97726-7 (ebook)
[1. Science fiction. 2. Adventure and adventurers—Fiction.
3. Love—Fiction.] I. Title.
PZ7.J2968Te 2015
[Fic]—dc23
2013048888

ISBN 978-0-385-74280-1 (trade pbk.)

Printed in the United States of America

10 9 8 7 6 5 4 3 2 1

First Ember Edition 2016

Random House Children's Books supports the First Amendment and celebrates the right to read.

For Françoise Bui, who made all of this possible

WHEREVER YOU ARE IS MY HOME—MY ONLY HOME.

—CHARLOTTE BRONTË, **JANE EYRE**

NATURE'S GREAT BOOK IS WRITTEN IN MATHEMATICAL SYMBOLS.

—GALILEO

PROLOGUE

Everything repeats.

It's one of the fundamental axioms of the multiverse. Every-thing repeats, over and over, again and again; throughout the universes, atoms assemble according to predetermined patterns.

Everything repeats, and so does everyone. You. Me. Your best friend. The boy at school you've had a crush on for ages. We are all one of many, connected by a tether—a strand of dark energy finer than the most delicate silk thread—to the others who wear our faces. If everything proceeds as it should, you'll never meet your analogs, your doubles in those other worlds. The universes are meant to be separate. You're meant to believe that you are the only you there is. So go ahead. Believe it. You might as well; there's a 99.9 percent chance you'll never be proven wrong.

But I know better. I've seen it with my own eyes: another world, not much different from mine, but at the same time more different than I have words to explain. I've seen *her*, too—my analog, my double. I looked into her eyes—my eyes—as she be-trayed me, as she tried to steal my life. So maybe you get it now, why I want you to think you're the only one. It's better that way. If you don't know the truth, you can take comfort in the lies.

PART I : THE LARK

FOR KILMENY HAD BEEN SHE KNEW NOT WHERE,
AND KILMENY HAD SEEN WHAT SHE COULD NOT DECLARE.

—JAMES HOGG, **"KILMENY"**

THOMAS ON THE THRESHOLD

"You see that?" The man grabbed Thomas by his hair and yanked his head so far back he thought his neck was going to snap. There was a clock on the wall, four bloodred numbers: 11:38. As he watched, one minute ticked away.

"Eleven hours, thirty-seven minutes till you're in front of the firing squad," the man hissed, digging his fingers into Thomas's scalp. When Thomas didn't respond, the man backhanded him across the face. Thomas's head rolled to one side. He didn't flinch. The pain seemed very far away now.

The past couple weeks were nothing but a smudge of memory in the back of his brain, a sickening blur of blinding lights and deafening noises. The worst had been the sound of human screaming, piped like music into his tiny cell. Sometime during those long, dark hours, he'd fallen into a waking dream in which it was Sasha screaming, as if she were being torn apart. He'd seen her as if she were really there, curled up on the floor in agony, begging him to make it stop. He tried to go to her, but his broken body wouldn't move; he tried to say something to comfort her, but his throat was so sore and dry he couldn't speak. He couldn't even cry, as if his body couldn't spare the water for tears.

Just when it felt as if it would never end, they hauled him from the cell. His knees scraped the rough concrete floor as they dragged him to another room and flung him down on a cot. He got a few hours of fevered sleep and woke up wearing chains. Shackles bit into his wrists and ankles. His lip was split and bloody, his right eye so swollen he couldn't open it. Never before had he felt so hopeless, not even when he was a little boy staring at a box of ashes—all that remained of his parents—on some faceless neighbor's kitchen table. At least back then he was too young to understand; he still believed that better things awaited him.

But the best moments in his life had come and gone. He remembered them all so clearly. His favorite was prom night, after the dance. Standing on the shore of the lake with Sasha, he'd marveled not only at the size of the universe but at the size of the space that had opened up inside of him, the realization that everything he'd always wanted—a normal life, someone who cared about him, a future of infinite possibility—was so close and yet so out of reach. He held on tight to the memory, but it cut as deep as it comforted, and very soon it would be lost forever, gone as if it had never been.

But Sasha was safe, back on Earth, where she belonged.

He'd made her a promise, and he'd kept it. He knew it would be hard to send her home, but he couldn't have imagined how sad and frightening it would be to watch her disappear, just vanish, like a figment of his imagination, there one minute and gone the next.

Even after all that, he couldn't quite let her go. He kept expecting to blink and find her beside him. When this nightmare first began, he still believed he could make it back to her; he'd attempted escape twice, determined not to give up without a fight. The first time, he got as far as the prison's outer wall; the second, slowed by hunger and weakened by fever, he didn't even make it out of the building.

The guards learned their lesson, and they took it out on him. He knew what would happen next. Bound and exhausted, he would die in Adastra Palace Prison; his body would be incinerated and his ashes buried in the yard with those of countless other criminals and spies, traitors and enemies. His only possible future was a mass grave.

His interrogator released him and sat back in his chair. "Tell us where the girl is, and we'll let you live." It was the only thing they seemed to care about. Thomas wanted to ask which girl he meant, but it didn't matter—to the man, Sasha and Juliana were the same. Not to Thomas, though. Not to him.

The guards had been bewildered when they found him alone in the cell with a gunshot wound in his shoulder, delirious from blood loss. They'd brought in the prison doctor to patch him up, to prevent his death long enough for the queen of Farnham to order it herself. The extraction he'd hoped for had never come.

Lucas and Juliana had taken off long before the sun came up. Lucas might have hesitated, questioning the decision to leave him behind. Thomas had already begun to slip into unconsciousness, so he couldn't be sure. But whether Lucas had been reluctant to desert him or not, the outcome was the same: his brother and his friend had left him on that cold stone floor to bleed to death.

"There's a war on, do you know that?" the man said, softening his tone. Torture hadn't worked, and neither had threats. Now he was trying to coax Thomas into cooperating, but that would fail, too. "You can help us end it. Tell us where to find the princess and you'll have your freedom. Don't you want it?"

"I don't believe you." Thomas's ragged, pinched voice was foreign to him. His throat ached. The man held out his hand. There was a brief flurry of movement, and then he pressed a canteen to Thomas's lips. The metal was cold, and Thomas could smell the cool, crisp water. His pride begged him not to drink, but his body needed it, so he did.

When he was finished, the canteen disappeared and the man leaned forward, his face only inches from Thomas's. "Believe this: no one is coming to claim you. They've left you here to die. Doesn't that make you angry, boy? Don't you hate them for abandoning you?"

"I'm not a boy," Thomas said in a low, dark voice. They thought he was weak, but there was power in him yet, a dangerous, animal might that was lawless and ancient. He could make them feel all the pain they'd dealt him if they only gave him half a chance. "You can't break me. You're wasting your time."

The man shook his head. "I have all the time in the world. You're the one who's running out. Make no mistake: if you don't tell us what we want to know, we will kill you."

"Then do it already! I have nothing to say." The man was right about one thing—Thomas was angry. He'd lost more than they would ever know. But they couldn't make him a traitor. He'd sworn an oath, and he wouldn't betray it, not even to save his own life.

"Come on," the man said to the guards, rising. "Let's leave him to contemplate his mortality."

And then Thomas was alone with nothing but his thoughts, and his pain, and the clock that ticked away the last moments of his life.

Eleven hours and twenty-four minutes left.

* * *

When the time came, they were quick about it. Thomas's muscles shook with the effort it took to stand. They shuffled him out of the cell and down a series of concrete hallways until they reached a large, empty yard of packed dirt where no weed or blade of grass dared grow. He'd spent so long in near darkness the light from the sun hurt his eyes, but he forced himself to keep them open, to adjust enough to look at the sky. It was bright blue and streaked with clouds, so normal in spite of everything.

He licked his lips and tasted blood. There was a lump the size of a rock in his throat; he swallowed against it and struggled to breathe his last breaths with whatever dignity he still possessed. The world began to waver before his eyes. He was so, so tired. The men and women on the firing squad were wearing masks, so he couldn't see their faces. He didn't wonder if they were good shots. They wouldn't be there if they weren't. A guard blindfolded him and asked if he had any last words.

"Aim high," Thomas said. He'd never needed to hide behind bravado before, but now he was really afraid. It was a fear that lived in a deep, unknowable corner of his heart, cowering like a scorpion beneath a rock and waiting for the darkest moment to strike. Its venom spread through him like a shock of cold water. His fingers curled up instinctively, as if someone had taken his hand. He closed his eyes, imagining Sasha's head on his shoulder, her hair soft against his neck, and his own voice came back to him on a tide of memory: *Whatever happens, this has been the best night of my entire life.* He'd meant it when he said it, but he hadn't known how true it was until now.

Thomas braced himself as the gunmen raised their weapons. He heard the shots, but he felt no pain. Was this really what it was like to die? But he wasn't dead, he realized after a few jagged heartbeats. They had fired, but not at *him*. His legs buckled, and he fell to his knees. Someone removed his blindfold, and he squinted up at the figure standing over him as hands freed him from his shackles. A familiar voice spoke his name.

"You're all right." It was Adele. She was a friend of his from a long time ago, back when he was at the Academy. She put a gentle hand on his shoulder, and he winced; the bullet wound wasn't quite healed. She helped him to his feet, and he glanced around the yard. Bodies littered the ground; all his guards were dead. He felt nothing but relief, and he wondered if something in him *had* died after all.

"What's going on?" he asked.

"You're being extracted," Adele said, indicating the rest of the rescue team. He recognized some of their faces: Sergei and Cora, Navin and Tim. Adele gave him a tentative smile and added, "Obviously."

He choked out a laugh. He had no idea what had possessed his father to dispatch a rescue squad, but he was grateful the General had thought to send his friends. Grateful—and a little bit suspicious. Adele murmured something into her comm and then turned back to Thomas. "Can you walk?"

He nodded. "What are you doing here, Adele?" The last time he'd seen them was when he graduated from the Academy; they'd still been recruits then. He hadn't spoken to any of them in over a year, not even Adele. He considered once again the possibility that he had died or was hallucinating. None of this felt real.

"It's Agent Nguyen now." She clutched a black mask in her hand. "I'm here because I asked to be. Let's get out of here. I figure we have about three minutes before someone realizes what happened, and it's a long way back to the Labyrinth."

The Labyrinth was a military compound that housed the training academy of the King's Elite Service. Thomas couldn't think of a single reason why Adele would be taking him there. "The Labyrinth?"

"That's right," she said. "The General wants to see you."

THERE WAS A KNOCK AT

the door. Selene's heartbeat quickened, but she didn't know whether that was due to the person whose appearance she anticipated or to the news she suspected he bore. In any case, she was pleased. Leonid was the only person at Home she was interested in these days. He strode into the room full of purpose, caught the widening of her eyes, and smiled. Her pulse thumped in her throat. He had it: the final piece of Terminus, the machine that would save them all.

She'd never doubted he could do it. Some of the older Learners had objected when she'd chosen Leonid, but she'd ignored them. She'd known from the moment she met him that he was the only Learner who would be able to help her decipher the prophecies of Kairos. It had nothing to do with experience or intelligence; it was his intuition that set him apart, and his open mind, unusual for a Learner. Leonid understood the nuances of Kairos almost as well as Selene did. She was lucky to have him, for that reason and so many others. Leonid was her confidant, her companion, her partner. There was so much she had to do alone, but what she could share, she shared with him.

"What does it say?" she asked.

"I don't know, exactly," he said, thrusting a piece of paper into her hand. "I believe that's your job."

She tried to hide a smile. She wasn't supposed to have favorites, but he had to know she liked him best. Perhaps more than liked him.

But she knew the dangers of being distracted from her goal, and her personal affections could not get in the way of her world's future. She unfolded the paper and turned away.

"Do you know what it means?" he asked impatiently. She liked Leonid's eagerness to get to the truth. He wouldn't eat or sleep or speak to anyone when he was working on a prophecy, not until he'd cracked it. It was a difficult job. Kairos was an encrypted text that required intense analysis and mathematics to read, only to yield inscrutable prophecies. Decrypting Kairos was the duty of a Learner; interpreting the prophecies was the duty of the oracle, the Korydallos—Selene's duty. One that meant the difference between the continuation of life in their world and its end.

"Yes," she whispered. "I think I do."

Her long white skirt swished around her ankles as she entered the chamber. It annoyed her that Leonid wasn't by her side; no one below Second Tier was allowed in the Tetractys assembly room, and as a young Learner, Leonid was stalled at Third Tier. She wanted him there, if only to lend strength to her case. The Tetractys would balk at her request. They didn't send anyone into the other world haphazardly.

The Tetractys sat at a large triangular table. Erastos, its highest-ranking member, eyed her with growing curiosity. He was a small man, old-fashioned and infuriatingly out of touch. Selene didn't like him. He never smiled, and he was suspicious of all Listeners, so he didn't much like her, either. But as the two most important people in Apeiron, they were forced to tolerate each other. Sometimes it was all Selene could do to remain civil.

She stared them down. To show fear or apprehension—or worse, doubt—before the Tetractys was to undermine the power of her position. On her deathbed, Corinna, the previous Korydallos, had warned Selene that the Tetractys would make her fight for every prophecy, force her to argue her case before acting upon anything she divined.

13

"It is their way," Corinna had said. Selene, only thirteen years old at the time, had been so afraid of her new responsibilities that she was visibly shaking. It had taken longer than she was willing to admit for that fear to go away. *"They must question you, because an oracle is a powerful thing. The people revere the Korydallos; they fear the Tetractys. The Korydallos is spirit; the Tetractys is law. There must be balance. It is the only way to prevent chaos."*

"Korydallos," Erastos said now. *"It has been many months since you graced this room with your presence. I can only assume you come bearing a prophecy."*

"I do," Selene said. *"I've come to tell you three things. First, that my Learner and I have decrypted Kairos's last prophecy. There will be no others."*

Erastos raised his eyebrows in surprise. Kairos was a mystery even to the Tetractys. Selene and Leonid alone knew how much of the text had been solved over the centuries. Selene had always known she would be the last Korydallos and that they would finish decrypting Kairos in her lifetime, but she hadn't expected the end to come so soon. Nevertheless, she was relieved. The new world was almost upon them. When it came, perhaps things would be different. Perhaps she would be allowed her own happiness. She wished again that Leonid were with her but pushed the thought aside.

"Second," she continued, *"that Terminus is complete."*

"No," Hypatia interjected. A tall, elegant woman with the dark coloring of a New Lands native, Hypatia was sitting to Erastos's right, a symbol of her status as his second-in-command. *"There's still the matter of the energy source. Terminus might be structurally sound, but it won't work without fuel."*

"I said I had three things to report." Hypatia stiffened, duly chastened. The Tetractys might not have liked Selene, but they owed her deference. *"Third, that Kairos's last prophecy concerns how we will power the Terminus device."*

The Tetractys murmured to each other in excitement. *Selene smiled; she liked shocking them. Erastos bent his head as Hypatia spoke into his ear. He cleared his throat, and the rest of the Tetractys fell silent. "And what does it say?"*

"You know I can't tell you that." Selene could communicate the meanings of the prophecies, but the words themselves remained between the Korydallos and her Learner. "What I can tell you is that the energy source cannot be found on Taiga. Or, to be more precise, it cannot be found only on Taiga."

"Meaning?"

"I need you to send me to the other world." She'd been nervous about making the request, but in the end it was easy. She was so certain of her interpretation. She hadn't always been, with the other prophecies, but each time she'd been right, as Corinna had assured her she would be.

"There is a reason each generation has only one Korydallos," Corinna had said. "It isn't something you can learn. It is something you feel, something that comes from deep within you and high above you — a true gift of apeiron. *You are blessed, my child. Do not doubt yourself, and do not tolerate anyone who doubts you." It had been difficult for Selene to believe in the supremacy of her own instincts as a thirteen year-old Fourth Tier, barely out of the crèche, but she had learned, with Corinna's guidance. It had all been in preparation for this moment, the beginning of the beginning. The Tetractys couldn't stop her.*

"Absolutely not," Erastos scoffed. "We're not going to send you through the veil."

"Why not?" Selene argued. "I know what I'm doing. I can find the energy source and bring it back, and when I do, Terminus will finally be complete. The new world, Erastos. It's within our grasp." She examined her bare wrists, imagining the left one branded with the traveler's mark.

"You're seventeen!" he protested. "You don't know what it's like over there."

"And you do?" Her eyes burned with the thrill of the challenge. Despite Erastos's bluster, she was confident that she would have her way.

"I've read the reports," Erastos continued. "It's not like Home. There are barbarians who wage war with each other, who kill each other over nothing. It's a moral wasteland. You wouldn't last a day in that world, and I will not send our Korydallos through the veil only to meet her end!"

"I'm stronger than you give me credit for," Selene insisted. "And I'm clever. You can send someone else through—send dozens if you like—but they won't find them. They can't find them. I'm the only one who can."

"Them?" Erastos's face was growing red with the effort it took to contain his anger. Selene could see that he was reaching his breaking point. She'd never been told not to speak of the veil and the world beyond; still, it was a topic not many had the temerity to broach. But she wasn't one to avoid taboo subjects. She liked being controversial. It made her feel in control.

"The fuel cells," she said. "There is more than one." Three, she thought. We need three.

"Tell us where they are and we'll send someone for them."

"I won't," she said. "I'm the only one who can successfully retrieve them." She lowered her voice. "I'm no ordinary Listener, Erastos; you know this. I see things clearly, and I have never been wrong. You must trust me."

Suddenly, she rose. The members of the Tetractys murmured in shock. It was against the rules for anyone to leave the Tetractys's chambers before being dismissed, but Selene wasn't just anyone. She was their Korydallos. And she meant to show them just how certain she was.

EARTH

ONE

For the third time since I started my shift, my phone went off. It vibrated, then buzzed to tell me I had a voice mail. I ducked into the break room and dug the phone out of my pocket. Five missed calls, one from Gina and four from Grant, plus several text messages, also from Grant, all asking the same thing: *Where are you?* I pressed play, dreading to hear what Grant had to say.

Where are you, Sasha? I've been trying to reach you for hours. If you're supposed to be my girlfriend, the least you can do is pick up the phone. Call me as soon as you get this. My hands shook as I deleted the message. I knew I should call him back. I'd been ignoring him for hours, and Grant didn't do well when left to his own devices. I took a deep breath, then exhaled, repeating my mantra—*Everything is fine*—the way my therapist had instructed me to do whenever I felt anxious. Sometimes it helped, but this was not one of those times.

"Earth to Sasha." My boss, Johnny, snapped his fingers in front of my face. I hadn't even seen him come in. "Anybody home in there? What are you doing? You already took your fifteen."

"Sorry," I said, gripping the phone so hard I was surprised it didn't break. "I just need a few minutes. I have to deal with something. It's personal."

"We've got a whole restaurant full of people, and they'd like to eat sometime this century. Your personal something is going to have to wait until you're off the clock. Move." He swatted me out of the break room and over to the hostess podium.

"I'm sorry," I repeated. A stack of menus slipped through my fingers and tumbled to the floor, fanning across the linoleum like playing cards. I bent to pick them up, stammering more apologies. "I don't know what's wrong with me. I guess I'm just a little out of it today."

Johnny scoffed. "Today and every day since you started this summer. What's going on with you, Sasha? I don't remember you being like this last summer."

Last summer. Quite a bit had changed since then.

My disappearance on prom night hadn't exactly flown under the radar in Hyde Park, the sleepy little neighborhood on Chicago's South Side where I'd lived since I was seven. It'd been headline news, and there was no end to the theories people had dreamed up to explain it. The most popular story was that Grant and I had eloped to Las Vegas in a fit of foolish teenage passion, returning only when it turned out we couldn't get married because I was underage. Grant and I had decided to let that particular rumor grow legs, to lie low and ride it out as best we could, because even if we could have told people where we'd really gone, they wouldn't have believed us. It was better to let them think what they wanted.

"I just seated someone at table twenty-three," Johnny told me. "Go do your job."

I was grateful for a reason to ignore Grant's voice mail, but if I avoided him for too long, he'd show up at the restaurant. Work was where I came to get away from him and everything he reminded me of: where we'd really been while we were missing, what had happened to us there, and Thomas, the boy from another world who shared his face. If I let myself dwell on that too much, I really would lose my mind, and I couldn't afford to be the crazy one. Grant had that base pretty much covered.

Grant had come home damaged: distant and temperamental, prone to fits of anger and bouts of impenetrable silence. He'd retreated from everyone he knew—his mother, his friends, everyone . . . except me. Maybe it was because I understood what he'd been through, or maybe it was just because I put up with him. For whatever reason, Grant trusted me. I was his touchstone, the thing that reminded him what was real, and for better or worse, he was mine. It would've been so much easier, though, if he looked like *anyone* else.

Each minute spent with Grant was a million tiny paper cuts on my heart. The slope of his nose, his golden-blond hair, his broad, well-muscled shoulders—even his restlessness— reminded me of Thomas. There were times I couldn't even stand to look at Grant, when the reality of everything he wasn't became too painful to face. I'd been a prisoner in Aurora, but Thomas had freed me. He'd fought for me. He'd *believed* in me, in what I was capable of and what I could become, something I hadn't even known I needed until I got it. And then he'd let me go.

But really, I lost him. I allowed him to slip away, because I was afraid to turn my back on the only life I'd ever known. I hadn't been home for more than ten minutes before I fully regretted the choices that had brought me there. I should have stayed in Aurora. My work there wasn't finished, and

I hadn't wanted to leave, not really. I'd never believed in fate before Thomas, before the series of events that changed my life forever, but I was starting to. I was as certain as I'd ever been about anything that my destiny was waiting for me on the other side of the tandem, the mysterious veil that separated our worlds. But I wasn't foolish enough to assume that it would wait forever.

The world in which I was born didn't feel like home anymore, and probably never would again. Everything was so familiar, yet so dizzyingly unreal, like a movie set, and Grant was just a paper copy of the boy I'd left behind. But I refused to fall apart. I was made of stronger stuff—my time in Aurora had taught me that—and crumbling to pieces was a waste of Thomas's sacrifice. So I did the only thing I could think of: I got a job. A job I was really sucking at.

Table twenty-three was in the back of the restaurant, and there was only one person sitting at it, hidden behind an open menu. I took a deep breath and pasted a smile onto my face. "Hi. My name is Sasha, and I'll be your server. What can I get you?"

The customer lowered the menu, and I realized with a start that it was Gina. My best friend, or she had been; we hadn't spoken since my return, though not for lack of trying on her part. My skin grew hot as her eyes met mine.

"Hi," she said. There was an edge to her voice.

"What are you doing here?" I should've known she'd keep trying. Gina wasn't the sort of person to take the hint and walk away. Part of me was glad she hadn't given up on me yet, but our relationship was a relic of a much simpler past, and there was nothing I could think of that could fix it.

"I called you," Gina said. "I call you all the time, but you never answer. What was I supposed to do?"

"Would you like something to drink?" I asked, trying to keep my tone light and impersonal. I stared at my notepad so hard I could've burned a hole right through it. *Just go away,* I thought. *Please, please, please just go* away.

Honestly, I was *desperate* to talk to Gina. All I wanted to do was tell her the truth about what had happened, to unburden myself to her, to *someone* I trusted, but she wouldn't believe me, and I couldn't bear to have her look at me like I was crazy.

"Let's just talk, okay? Like friends. We're still friends, right?"

I felt so guilty. I wanted to crawl under the nearest table, shut my eyes, and wait for closing time. Instead, I ignored her question and waited for her to answer mine.

"I'm not thirsty," Gina said. "Please sit down. You're making me nervous, hovering like that."

"I can't sit. I'm working."

"You're *working*?" Her voice rose, and heads started to turn. "Now you're working, but six weeks ago you decided to *elope* with Grant Davis without telling anyone, not even *me*?"

"Please stop," I begged. People were staring, and soon the whispers would start. It happened all the time. They knew who I was, what I looked like. When I disappeared, my yearbook picture was in the papers and on the nightly news. A well-meaning group of neighbors took it upon themselves to plaster the city with MISSING posters. At least once a day now, we got a table of gawkers who wanted to observe me in the wild; they nursed sodas, taking advantage of the free refills while they speculated about where I went and why.

The restaurant staff tried to protect me, but they couldn't shield me from the people who would approach me on the street or knock on my front door to ask insanely personal questions. Reporters went through our trash and interrogated my classmates. They chased my seventy-eight-year-old grandfather down the street with cameras and microphones. The elopement story had satisfied the idle gossips, but the truly curious hadn't given up yet, and I felt their eyes on me everywhere, all the time. That was why I was in therapy—not to talk about what I'd been through, because obviously I couldn't, but to find a way of coping with the scrutiny. Sometimes I thought I was making progress; other times—like now—I wondered why I even bothered.

"What happened to you?" Gina asked. "You seem so sad."

I twisted the fabric of my apron so tight around my fingers that they began to throb. "You just don't get it."

"No," she said. "I don't. But I want to. Talk to me, Sasha. I feel like I don't even know you anymore."

"Maybe you don't." I turned and ran to the kitchen, ripping my apron off as I slammed through the swinging door. Johnny glared when he saw me.

"What are you doing in here? We have customers!"

"I'm going home," I told him, dumping my apron on the counter. *Poor Gina,* I thought. Six weeks ago I would *never* have turned my back on her like that or pushed her away when she was trying to help me. Gina wasn't the only person who felt as if she didn't know me anymore. Sometimes I didn't even recognize myself.

"Your shift's not over."

"I don't care." I knew that if I stayed I'd end up telling Gina everything, just so I didn't have to carry around my secret any longer. The restaurant felt so small and threatening. I had to get out of there. "Nikki can cover for me. I have to go."

I left without waiting for Johnny's response. He could fire me the next day or not, I didn't care. The air outside was thick and humid, but there was a cool breeze coming off Lake Michigan. I took it into my lungs and tried to calm down.

"Everything is fine," I said, as if speaking the words out loud would make them true. My voice quavered, and I felt like I was going to pass out, but I forced myself to put one foot in front of the other.

"Everything is fine, everything is fine, everything is fine," I repeated, until the words were gibberish, strings of letters that meant less than nothing at all.

I trudged through the neighborhood, past brownstones and playgrounds and storefronts that were as familiar to me as my own name, but no matter how hard I tried to connect, to conjure up happy memories and imagine a brighter future, none of it felt right. It was like a story I was trying to tell myself, a lie I couldn't bring myself to believe. When I crossed Fifty-Third Street, my house came into view. The shabby Victorian, with its cheerful cornflower-blue shutters and wide wraparound porch, was the only place on Earth I felt safe now. It was home, or as close to it as I could manage in this world.

I passed the mailbox without stopping, figuring Granddad would've already gotten the mail, but then I remembered he'd gone to St. Louis for a conference and wouldn't be back for a couple of days. Something made me pause halfway up the porch steps and double back. I opened the mailbox with a mixture of dread and excitement, unsure of what I expected to find but certain that something was waiting for me.

On top of a neat stack of letters, circulars from the neighborhood grocery co-op, and catalogs full of things neither Granddad nor I would ever buy was a little white origami star.

I grabbed it and left the rest of the mail behind, running into the house and letting the door slam behind me. My hands shook as I pounded up the stairs, shedding my bag and shoes along the way. I barreled into my room and flung myself down on the bed, closing my eyes.

Let it be from him, I begged the universe. *Please, please,* please, *let it be from him.*

One of the last things I saw before I went flying through the tandem was Thomas being shot. A month had passed since that night. Grant kept telling me, in a tone of voice that was supposed to be somber but came out sounding hopeful, that Thomas was probably dead. I guess he thought if I kept hoping Thomas was alive, I'd never move on or find a way to be happy with the life I was born into. But I didn't have any intention of doing either.

I peeled the star open slowly and took a deep breath. The note read:

HE'S ALIVE

And that was all.

TWO

"Where'd you get this?" Grant asked, handing the note back to me. I could tell he hadn't slept more than a couple of hours and he'd been wearing the same clothes for days. There were dark half-moons under his eyes, and he was fidgeting with his watch, compulsively opening and closing the clasp. I covered his hand with mine to make him stop, then pulled away. Most of the time, I tried not to touch him. It just made things too unbearably weird.

"It was in my mailbox when I got home." I squinted into the distance, over the tops of the trees and buildings across the narrow strip of grass. When I'd finally returned his call, Grant had asked me to meet him in the park down the street from his house. We were sitting on the swing set in the playground. The late-evening sun glinted off car hoods; the streetlamps were starting to flicker on. If we were in Aurora, ribbons of swirling green light would already be visible in the sky, but this was just another normal night on Earth, and all I could see were clouds.

"Who's it from?" Grant looked at me, and I held my breath for a beat, forgetting again, for a moment, that he wasn't Thomas. I swallowed hard and shifted away from him.

"I don't know. But whoever it is must have a way of communicating with the other side." I stared at him.

"You think it was me? Yeah, right, Sasha." Grant ran his fingers through his hair; he was letting it grow long, which was decidedly un-Thomaslike. I'd been building a mental list of differences between the two of them, but every time I looked at Grant, my heart lurched. I kept hoping it would stop, but it never did. Maybe it never would. Thomas was a piece of glass buried deep beneath my skin—painful but impossible to remove.

"If I can see through my analog's eyes, it stands to reason that you can, too."

"Just because you want that to be true doesn't mean it is," Grant said. I sighed, because I knew he was right. For whatever reason, my ability to see through Juliana's eyes was unique. Dr. Moss, a physicist I met in Aurora, said I owed the strength of my bond with Juliana to the fact that my father was born in Aurora. That revelation had turned my whole life upside down—it was as if I had lost my parents all over again, and with them, the person I'd always believed myself to be. Thomas wasn't the only reason I felt out of place on Earth; I was half Auroran, and his world was my world, too, in a way. I wasn't done with it yet, and after getting that note, I knew it wasn't done with me.

"I have to find out who sent this," I told Grant. "I have to know if it's true."

"And then what?" He narrowed his eyes at me.

"What's that supposed to mean?"

"I'm not stupid, you know." Grant shoved his hands into his pockets and hung his head, deliberately not meeting my gaze. It reminded me of how he'd been in the Farnham prison cell: defeated, the high school god brought to his knees. The experience was written on his face in scars only I could see.

When he spoke, his voice shook, and it was obvious he felt that I'd betrayed him somehow. "You've been looking for a way back since the day we came home."

"So?"

"*So?*" He shook his head. "You're unbelievable. Don't you remember what happened over there? What they did to us? We were kidnapped. We were *held hostage.* Are you seriously going to waltz right back into that world because of some guy?"

"Hey!" I snapped. I'd put up with enough of his crap. No matter what lies we'd told, we weren't boyfriend and girl-friend—we weren't even *friends.* Aurora was the only thing knitting us together. I didn't owe him an explanation. "You don't know everything that happened to me over there. Don't pretend you do."

"I wish he had died," Grant said, clenching his fists so tight his knuckles turned white. "Maybe then I wouldn't have to constantly look over my shoulder, wondering when they're coming back for me."

"Screw you, Grant," I spat out. It made me so *angry,* looking at him, completely fine, whole and intact and doing *nothing,* while Thomas suffered on the other side of the tandem. Even if Thomas was alive, alive wasn't *okay;* it wasn't *free.* How could Grant say he wished Thomas were dead? Juliana tried to steal my life, but I would never want her to be hurt or killed. "It's your fault it happened in the first place!"

"I knew it," Grant said, gritting his teeth, as if he was holding himself back from saying something much worse. "You do blame me."

"He was going to send you back! If you hadn't lost your temper and hit him, we would've been on Earth by the time Lucas and Juliana got there, and Thomas wouldn't have got-ten hurt!" I'd never straight up accused him of that before. It always seemed like a waste of breath: making him feel guilty wouldn't change anything. But if he was going to start whipping blame around, I wasn't going to give him a free pass.

"How the hell was I supposed to know that?"

I kneaded my temples. He had a point. "You weren't."

"I'm sorry," he said, but it was hard to tell if he meant it.

"No, I'm sorry," I insisted. "I'm sorry you're afraid—"

"I'm not afraid," he lied.

"I'm sorry you had to go through what you went through. But you don't get to tell me what to do, or what to think, or what to want."

"What happened wasn't even a little bit your fault," Grant said. "Even I know that."

"I was the one they needed," I reminded him. "You were just the door into my life, and you suffered because of it, and I'm sorry. If I could go back and change it, I would."

"Would you really?"

I hesitated. "No."

"Then maybe you do owe me an apology." He sighed. "Look, I get that you think it's none of my business, and maybe it isn't. I'm not exactly an expert on being happy. I just don't think— There's nothing for you over there. You're from *Earth*. This is where you belong."

"It doesn't feel like I belong here," I confessed. "Not right now. There are a lot of things I don't have figured out, but I'm sure about that." We kept having the same fight over and over again, and I was exhausted. All Grant wanted was to forget, to pretend it had never happened. Knowing that made me want to hold on to the memories even tighter. "Come on, I'll walk you home." It made me nervous to think of Grant wandering around the neighborhood after dark. I always worried he'd do something reckless.

Grant looked around the deserted park. "This is where it happened, you know. He was waiting for me. He stepped out from behind that tree, and he looked exactly like me, right down to the clothes he was wearing. I thought I was hallucinating. You know what the funny part is?"

"What?"

"He looked as scared as I felt."

It wasn't funny at all. Meeting your analog is like an electric shock. It cuts right down to the core of you like a spear through your chest and awakens a part of you that you never knew existed, something deep and ancient and true. It's terrible and wonderful all at once, unnatural and so very right. That person is you, but also not you; it takes a while for our brains to comprehend the paradox, and even longer to believe it. By then, the damage might already be done.

"Grant," I said, suddenly remembering the reason we were there in the first place. "Why did you call me?"

Grant cleared his throat. "I'm moving."

"*Moving?* Moving where?"

"My dad offered to let me live with him," he said. "For the rest of the summer."

"And after that?"

He shrugged. "We'll see how it goes."

"But Los Angeles is so far away." Grant wouldn't stay in touch. When you're running from something, you're not supposed to look back. Cutting ties would be easy for him. He was dying to do it. He just hadn't been able to work up the nerve until now.

He paused, shuffling wood chips with the toe of his Chucks. "I can't breathe here. There's no way I'll be able to survive another year." Grant was supposed to start college in the fall, but he'd deferred, because he couldn't bear to think about school. Neither could I; every time I caught a glimpse of September on the calendar, I started to panic. In a classroom full of people, there would be nowhere to hide.

"What's that look?" he asked, searching my face.

"Nothing," I said, because the truth was embarrassing. As much as it hurt to look at Grant, the prospect of never seeing him again was a hundred times worse. He was the only connection to Thomas I had left, and the only person on Earth who understood even a fraction of what I'd experienced. Without him, I would truly be alone.

And then, all of a sudden, Grant's face wasn't his face, and it wasn't Thomas's, either. It was another boy's, nobody I recognized. I could see him only dimly, as if I were looking through a piece of fogged-up glass. His lips moved, but I couldn't hear him at first, and then his voice came at me in a rush of sound: *Are you sure you want to do this?* I didn't know how to answer him, or if I even could, but I heard myself say *Yes, I'm sure* before his face faded away.

"Sasha?" Grant shook my shoulder. I blinked, trying to erase the image of the unfamiliar boy's face from my mind. "Are you okay?"

"I'm fine." Maybe I should've told him, but I didn't know how to explain it, not even to myself. All I could be sure of was that the visions coming through the tether that bound me to Juliana were getting worse. They didn't happen only in dreams anymore. They could strike at any moment, shards of another life slicing through my own reality. Sometimes I couldn't tell whether something was happening to me or to my analog.

And sometimes I couldn't tell whether the visions were coming from Juliana or someone else. These new visions were not like the ones I'd had before. They felt different—

intentional, even. Like messages instead of dreams. I was afraid to think too hard about who might be sending them, but I knew she was there, and that neither she nor Juliana was going away. I would have done anything to make them stop, but I couldn't figure out what to do.

"Come on," Grant said, steering me toward the sidewalk. "How about you let *me* walk *you* home? It's getting dark."

The house was empty. Most of the time, I liked the quiet, but tonight it was oppressive. It was weird having Granddad gone; he hadn't wanted to leave me alone, but his hovering was getting on my nerves and I persuaded him to give me space. I needed time to finish my project. It would be a relief not to have to hide what I was doing. I could spread out across the whole house if I wanted.

The first thing I did when I got to my room was the first thing I did every time I woke up, or came home, and the last thing I did before bed every night. Two items had come with me through the tandem—just two, plus Juliana's clothes, which I'd been wearing. The clothes had lost their magic a long time ago, but I pulled a plastic bag out of my nightstand drawer, removed its contents, and laid them flat on the bed.

Item number one was the drawing Callum had given me in the Castle gardens. The edges were torn where he'd ripped it from his notebook. I'd folded it and unfolded it so often that the paper had lost its crispness and the charcoal was smudged. It was a simple sketch of a metal doorframe emitting a bright light, but I felt the same uneasiness I had the first time I saw it. It was a door into the unknown, and it forced me to ask myself where I was going even as it helped me remember where I'd already been.

Item number two was the Angel Eyes map I'd taken from

the king's study. It was a digital rendering of Aurora's North American continent, with Farnham and the United Commonwealth of Columbia clearly divided. The only unusual thing about it was the collection of dots in random locations within the two countries; I'd noticed they were more concentrated around bodies of water, but other than that, I had no idea why the map was so important.

"It was real," I said aloud. That was my other mantra, the one my therapist didn't know about. *It was real.* My mind flooded with things I couldn't keep safely hidden away in Ziploc bags: Thomas and I on Oak Street Beach, before I even knew who he was; the heady, charged moment when he told me that he saw me, the real me, beneath the Juliana disguise; our first kiss, at Asthall Cottage. Reuniting with him at Adastra Prison, when I thought I'd lost him for good. Those were all real, too; I just didn't have anything to prove it except my own memories.

Without warning, another vision slammed into me. I was standing on the shore of a wide river. The wet hem of my white dress clung to my ankles as I climbed up the bank. I looked up at the sky, and an enormous building swam into view. I was excited, but I was tired, too, shaking all over and sick to my stomach. I glanced down at my left wrist, which was tattooed with a symbol that filled me with power and purpose: two overlapping circles in silver ink.

Wrenching myself out of the vision, I sank to my knees, breathing hard. I pulled up my sleeve to check my wrist, but there was nothing there.

By the time I trekked up to the attic, the sun had sunk below the horizon. I switched on the light and surveyed the large, cluttered room. It smelled like sawdust and cardboard, the scent of a past best left forgotten. But I hadn't come to forget. I had come to learn, and to remember.

One half of the attic was full of furniture, carefully arranged like a Tetris puzzle and draped with old sheets. The other half contained what had once been an overwhelming number of boxes, but now that I'd made my way through most of them, it didn't seem like enough.

The furniture had belonged to my parents, and the boxes were theirs, too. For the last few weeks, I'd been sifting through what remained of their lives, excavating my family history in the hope of discovering something—anything— that could help me understand who they really were. I used to think I knew them. They died when I was seven, so I had some memories, but not many, and they were a child's memories, anyway, barely distinguishable from dreams. Now Mom and Dad were total enigmas.

When I came back from Aurora, I'd had to lie to a lot of people—police, reporters, the director of my school—but I couldn't bring myself to lie to Granddad. So I'd given him a version of the truth, and he told me a secret he'd been keeping for ten years, confirming what I already knew to be true. Dad was born in Aurora; he was a KES scientist who crossed through the tandem to frustrate the attempts of researchers on Earth to develop many-worlds technology. That was how he met Mom. She was one of the researchers whose work he was trying to sabotage, but he fell in love with her instead. He turned his back on his mission for her, and for me.

Every time I thought I'd gotten a handle on all this, it reared up and walloped me in the face. I always missed my parents, but I'd never needed them as much as I did now. I wished I could talk to Dad about Aurora or ask Mom for advice. Mom had known who Dad was, and she'd loved him anyway. She'd accepted him, stayed with him, started a family with him. I could only guess why, but I understood. If I'd never met Thomas, I would probably have thought she was foolish for following her heart instead of what logic must have been screaming at her: *He's not worth it.* I thought giving Thomas up for the safety of home was the brave choice, the *right* choice. But knowing what she'd done raised a question that kept me up nights: of the two of us, who was the brave one, and who was the fool?

Everything repeats indeed.

There were only two boxes left. Most of what I'd found was useless: tax returns, bank statements, receipts. I'd hoped my parents' research would help me find a way back to Aurora, but it was incomprehensible. I found a box full of old makeup and toiletries from their bathroom, and another with a huge plastic bag stuffed with dried-out pens. There were clothes and linens and carefully wrapped dishes, none of which had been touched in a decade. I wanted to feel a connection to these things, but I didn't, although I did find a tattered baby blanket with my name stitched into the corner. I couldn't bear to leave it, so I brought it down to my room and tucked it away in a drawer.

I'd been saving these two boxes for last. One was marked PHOTOS and the other MEMORIES. I tackled the photo box first and spent hours flipping through albums chronicling Mom's childhood and college years. There wasn't a single picture of Dad before age thirty, but then I came across their wedding album, and there he was, wearing a seersucker suit on a tropical beach, smiling at the camera with his arm around Mom's waist. The sight of them young and happy and alive made me so unbelievably sad. I couldn't even look at my baby pictures. I put the photo box away, figuring I could go back to it whenever I wanted.

Mom was a devoted keeper of scrapbooks, and the memory

box contained five stuffed binders full of ticket stubs and invitations, birth announcements and programs. I found a small jewelry box with their wedding rings, their marriage license, and my original birth certificate. Buried under everything else was a manila folder with several newspaper clippings. Most of them were irrelevant, random things Mom must have kept for reference. I almost didn't go through the whole pile, but something—a vague, unsettling feeling in my gut—told me to keep looking.

Hidden between a recipe for homemade potato salad and an old advice column, I found an article with the headline "Princeton University Researchers 'Closer Than Ever' to Discovering Secrets of Parallel Universes." The piece included a picture of three people: Dad on the left, Mom on the right, and in the middle, with an arm around each of them, someone else I recognized. The man in the photo looked exactly like Dr. Moss—from *Aurora*.

"What the hell?" I whispered. The caption read *Drs. George Lawson and Mary Quentin pose with lead researcher Dr. Anthony March.*

THREE

Dr. March was not an easy person to track down. A Google search told me he no longer worked at Princeton, but other than a brief stint at Northwestern, there was no sign of him in over five years. Then, on a popular science website, I came across an interview with him that was only a few months old. It said he was working on a book and listed him as a professor emeritus.

There was no doubt in my mind that Dr. March had been the one to leave the star in my mailbox—a message from Dr. Moss, I assumed. Thomas had said Dr. March didn't exist, but not only did he *exist*, he was exactly who I should've known all along he was: Dr. Moss's Earth analog. Dr. Moss had called Dr. March his research partner and claimed to have consulted with him about my connection to Juliana. I could think of no other explanation than that Dr. March and Dr. Moss were able to communicate over their own tether; when I'd asked Dr. Moss if he knew of anybody else who could do that, he'd said, "Not as such." He hadn't said *no*.

If Dr. Moss had the technology to cross the tandem, it stood to reason that Dr. March did, too. That meant there was a chance—a small one, but greater than there had been before—that I could find my way back to Aurora. Back to Thomas. Back to the self I was just beginning to discover.

The reporter who'd conducted the interview was named Magdalena Polovsky, and her email address was listed in the sidebar of the post. I wrote her a quick email, saying I'd read her piece and wanted to talk to Dr. March as part of a school project and asking if she could put us in touch.

It took two days for Magdalena Polovsky to get back to me, and by the time her email landed in my inbox, my insides were tied up in knots.

Hi, Sasha.

Thanks for letting me know how much you liked the interview! I think it's a bit of a snooze, myself—you'd think a guy who researches *parallel universes* would have something slightly more interesting to say, but I guess not. Maybe he's hiding all the good stuff? I bet the NSA has its claws in him good and deep. I originally tracked him down through his publisher, but he's pulled the book—maybe he's not writing it anymore? Not sure.

Anyway, my editor asked me to get him to comment on that new Will Base movie about parallel universes, *An Earth Away,* and this time I had to go through this weird virtual assistant he hired. She calls herself Carla, although I'm pretty sure that's not her real name, and in all likelihood she's a robot. Her email address is below if you want to give it a shot. She never did respond to me, but he's a former professor, so he probably looks more kindly on students than he does on reporters.

Good luck!
Lena

I spent a long time crafting my email to Dr. March. I decided to tell him I recently discovered he'd mentored my parents, and I was hoping to talk to him in the interest of finding out more about them. I added a short note to Carla at the top, asking her to pass the message along, and settled in for what I figured would be a pretty long wait.

Which was why I was surprised to get a response in just under two hours.

Dear Ms. Lawson,

I regret to inform you that Dr. March is very busy and unable to make any time to see you in the near future. This is what he has told me to tell you.

However, for the past few months I've been scanning and archiving his old correspondence, and there are many letters in which he makes reference to your parents, in a fond, respectful, even paternal way. I think he's avoiding not *you* but the pain of talking about two people whose loss he still feels very keenly, or for which he perhaps feels responsible. I try not to have opinions about his personal life, but in this case I'm making an exception, both because I believe that confronting one's wounds is the only way to heal them and also because Dr. March could use someone to talk to.

Dr. March keeps to a very precise schedule, so I can tell you with certainty that he will be at Helena's in Norwood Park at noon tomorrow. He eats lunch there every Wednesday.

Best,
Carla

I had to take two buses and the El to get to Helena's, a Polish restaurant on the far northwest side of the city. I'd just stepped out onto the platform at the Jefferson Park Blue Line station when another vision hit me. A hand flew at my face, but I couldn't protect myself as I was struck over and over again. My ears rang with the force of the blow; I tasted blood.

Who are you? a cold voice demanded. *Where do you come from?* I was afraid but determined not to show it. I glanced down at my wrist, at the tattoo that was both a reminder and a key to the door that would take me home again, and I said, in the steadiest, calmest voice I could muster, *Give me what I've asked for, and I'll tell you.*

"Miss! Miss! Are you okay?"

The vision skittered away, leaving behind an awful sense of doom. My heart had frozen into a lump of ice. I was on my knees at the edge of the platform, digging my fingernails into the concrete, and a young boy was bent over me, peering at my face.

"Are you okay?" he repeated.

"I—I think so," I said. He helped me to my feet. "What happened?"

"We were getting off the train and you shouted and fell," he explained, guiding me to the exit. "Do you need to go to the hospital or something?"

"No, I'll be fine." I managed a smile. "Sorry if I scared you."

"You were the one who looked scared," he said.

A bell tinkled as I opened the door to Helena's. The restaurant was dim and practically empty. I recognized Dr. March immediately. He was sitting in the back, hunched over a book, a pair of reading glasses perched on the end of his nose. A shiver rolled down my spine at the sight of him: coming face to face with your own analog is hard, but meeting other people's doubles is no picnic, either. It really makes you question your sanity.

"Can I help you?" A short, dark-haired older woman came out from behind the deli counter and stopped me at the hostess podium, wiping flour off her hands with the corner of her apron. She had a thick Eastern European accent and some sort of religious medal hanging around her neck. I wondered if this was Helena.

"Yes," I said, feigning courage I didn't quite feel. Now that I was there, I wasn't a hundred percent sure I wanted the answers I'd come for. I pointed at Dr. March. "I'm looking for that man."

"Looks like you found him," she said. I must've seemed nervous, because she smiled and put a hand on my shoulder. "Don't worry, sweetie. I just know the professor likes his privacy."

"I need to speak to him," I said. "It's important."

Helena shrugged. "Suit yourself. Want me to bring you something?"

I shook my head.

"You can't sit in my restaurant and not order anything," Helena said with a frown. "I tell you what, I'll bring you some pierogi, fresh from the pan. You like pierogi?"

"Uh, sure," I said. I wasn't hungry, but it felt rude to refuse.

"Coming right up." She nodded at Dr. March. "You go ahead and sit down. If he kicks you out, just move to another table, okay?"

"Okay." I walked over to Dr. March. Even when I was standing right in front of him, he didn't bother to glance up from the book he was reading. I kept reminding myself that he wasn't Dr. Moss, that they were different people, but it didn't cushion the blow of looking at someone I recognized and realizing he didn't know me at all. It was amazing he was even there, in my city, sitting in a restaurant a mere five miles from my house. Two months ago, I thought destiny was a crock; now I saw the hand of fate everywhere I looked. "Dr. March? I'm—"

"I know who you are," he said with a weary sigh, closing his book. "Carla forwarded me your email. I should've known she'd tell you where to find me. I thought a virtual assistant would be able to resist getting involved in my affairs, but apparently not."

I didn't know what to say.

"Well, are you just going to stand there like some kind of specter, or are you going to sit down and explain yourself?" Dr. March asked. I took my seat, afraid he'd tell me to go away if I hesitated.

"I was hoping you'd be able to tell me about my parents," I began. "George and Mary Lawson?"

"Yes, they worked for me for a time." His voice was emotionless, and I wondered if I'd made a mistake in coming. Maybe he didn't care about my parents at all. "What did you want to know?"

"I guess I'll start with . . . what were they like?"

Dr. March drummed his fingers on the table. "Your mother was a postdoc in my lab. Your father came in as a research fellow."

"And?"

"And what?"

"That's it?"

"It's been a long time," Dr. March said. "What makes you think I even remember them?"

I stared at him. "You must."

"Must I?"

"You've got to at least remember my dad. How many people could you possibly have worked with who were from another universe?"

"Keep your voice down," Dr. March hissed. "Do you want people to think you're crazy?"

"They already do," I told him. "But I'm not. I was there. You know I was. You helped Dr. Moss figure out why I could see through my analog's eyes. You left that note in my mailbox."

"I don't have any idea what you're talking about."

"Yes, you do. You folded it into a star," I said, placing the note on the table. "Dr. Moss is one of two people who knew that would mean something to me, and the other one's not your analog. You can talk to him through the tether. Why?"

"I thought you came here to find out more about your parents." Dr. March's mouth was a thin, grim line.

"I came here to find out about a lot of things. How can you talk to Dr. Moss? Are you a crosser, too?"

Dr. March laughed. "No. *Crosser* is a term Moss invented when we figured out why *you* could see through the tandem via the tether. He always did like to name things. *Tandem* was his, too, and *tether*. But you're the only crosser I know of."

"Then why—?"

"We have no idea," Dr. March said. "Moss says it's because we're so intelligent, our brains operate in a fifth dimension. I'm sixty percent sure he's kidding. But we can do it, just like you. Better, of course. We've had years of practice—at talking to each other and at shutting each other out."

I started to ask another question, but he interrupted me. "As for your mother, she was . . . brilliant." His expression morphed as he spoke of Mom, storm clouds dispersing to let the sun break through. "One of the most gifted students I've ever had the pleasure of teaching. Her mind was an open sky. To her, anything was possible, and she worked tirelessly to make our dreams a reality. It was no wonder your father fell so hard for her. He must have loved her very much to abandon his mission. Until Moss and I put the pieces together about you, I didn't know who he was. I should've, though. When I hired him, he seemed almost too qualified for the job." He shook his head. "There's no fool like an old fool, as they say."

"I wish I'd known them," I said. Granddad had been a wonderful parent, but he shouldn't have had to raise me all by himself. He shouldn't have had to lose his only daughter, either. Sometimes when he was talking to me—especially when he was telling me about his work—it seemed as if he were really talking to her.

"I wish you had, too. They were great people, great scientists, and their deaths were a colossal waste." Dr. March narrowed his eyes. "How are the visions? Getting worse, I presume."

"How did you know that?" Was it obvious how little I'd been sleeping, how jumpy and scared I was, worried that at any second a vision could overtake me?

"It's the natural progression. Once you open the door to your analog's mind, the connection intensifies exponentially. Soon it'll become difficult to sort out whose thoughts are whose—whose memories, whose life. It's why Moss and I had to stop communicating, except on rare occasions. Unless you can learn to shut the transmissions out, you'll never really be you again. Believe me, I know."

"I'm not going to live my whole life with someone else in my head," I said. The visions were already so bad, I couldn't imagine them getting worse, but I knew from Dr. March's grave expression that I had much to fear from the future if

I didn't do something about them soon. "How do I shut my analogs out?"

Dr. March raised his eyebrows. "Analogs? You mean you've got more than one up there?" He tapped his head.

"I think there are two," I said. His scrutiny was making me nervous. I would've bet money he was already thinking of experiments to run on me, but I was nobody's lab rat. "Juliana and someone else."

"Well, that's interesting. You have no idea who she is?" I shook my head. "Very curious. I wonder if she knows she's getting through."

"You think she's doing it on purpose?" I'd gotten that sense, too. But even if I wanted to speak to my analogs directly along the tether, I wouldn't have known how, so why did she? The thought that my analogs could peek inside my head whenever they wanted or send me messages through the tether made my stomach squirm.

"I have absolutely no idea," Dr. March said. Helena approached and set down a plate of pierogi in front of me.

"For you," she said, smiling at me. "On the house."

"Lucky you," Dr. March grumbled as Helena walked away. "I've been coming here for years and never got so much as a free refill."

"So what should I do?" I asked.

"To be honest, I'm not sure I can help you," Dr. March said. "The tether is peculiar, and there's very little, if any, true experimental evidence to support our theories."

"But you do have theories."

"I've always thought . . . but it doesn't seem very likely," Dr. March said.

"Tell me, please," I begged. "Whatever it is, I'll try it. Anything to stop this from getting worse." Before I went to

Aurora, the visions I'd experienced as dreams weren't that bad. But with the tether wide open and all kinds of things pouring through, the thought of going on like that forever was terrifying. How was I supposed to figure out who I was meant to be when the lines between my mind and theirs grew blurrier by the day?

And how was I supposed to be with Thomas if I didn't know who I was?

"Do you know what the tether is made of?"

"Energy," I said. "Dark energy."

"Right," he said, smiling in a proud way that reminded me he'd once been a teacher. "I think of the tether as a circuit, an endless loop of power. So I've always wondered: what happens if you overload the circuit? Can you break it, in the same way you blow a fuse? For what it's worth, I think you can."

"How would that work? It's not like it's got an outlet you can plug a hair dryer into."

"I don't know," Dr. March said. "The tether's always been more of Moss's pet project. But in all the years we collaborated, one thing he wouldn't let go of was the idea that, under the right circumstances, the energy in the tether could be released. We never got it to work. There was one time it felt as though we were close, but something was missing."

"What?"

He gave me a rueful smile. "According to Moss's calculations, we needed a third analog."

"No way."

"Three is an important number," Dr. March said. "From Christianity to music to the Pythagorean theorem. Three is balance. Unity. Harmony. We know far less about how the worlds behave than I wish we did, but from what information we do have, it's clear: the multiverse adores a triad."

"So you're suggesting I . . . what? Track down my analogs and try to unleash the tether's energy so we can snap it apart?"

"It's as good a plan as any," Dr. March said. "I don't see you coming up with a better one. Of course, you could always try heavy drinking. It's working for me. Sort of."

"I'm seventeen," I said. He shrugged. "Let's say I find a way to break the tether—what happens then? Will it hurt? Could it . . . damage my brain or something?"

"I have no idea," he said sharply. He seemed to be tiring of my questions. "Probably not, but anything is possible. You of all people should know that."

"Juliana is in Aurora. If I'm going to try this, I'll need to go back there." I had no idea where to even start looking for my other analog, but Thomas would help me; I knew he would. There was nothing we couldn't figure out together.

"You want my advice? Stay in your own damn universe. Cut your losses, fight the tether's influence as best you can for as long as you can, and try to live a normal life. No good comes of crossing into other worlds. Your parents learned that the hard way."

"With all due respect, I don't think so," I said. "I think they learned that safety is an illusion, and if you're going to have a life worth living, you have to take risks. You have to fight to hold on to the important things."

"Like what?"

"Family. Love. Destiny," I said.

"Destiny?" Dr. March scoffed. "You don't really believe in that."

"How can you communicate with your analog using only your mind and *not* believe in destiny?" One of the things I learned in Aurora was that there are connections deep

49

beneath the surface of reality. The more you look for them, the more you find. My bond with Juliana had existed since I was a child, and in Aurora it had helped me—I had a hard time convincing myself that was a coincidence.

"Just because something seems inexplicable doesn't mean there's no explanation for it," Dr. March said. "And since you brought it up, what *about* family? I know your grandfather, Sasha, and I can only imagine how much he cares for you. You'd really leave him behind, after all he's done for you?"

I swallowed hard. Granddad had been a wreck the day I came home, and he barely let me out of the house for weeks, afraid of what might happen to me if I stepped past the threshold of our doorway. It would kill him if I left. But it would kill me to stay put and lose myself to the tether, especially if there was even the smallest chance of being free of it.

"I can come back," I whispered. "Someday."

"What makes you so sure? Aurora is dangerous, and who knows what sort of a world your second analog comes from, or what kind of person she is. Once you pass through the tandem, you might not have the option of returning. Are you willing to risk your whole life—your good, safe life here on Earth—for death at the hands of some so-called destiny?"

"I don't know," I admitted. Only a few minutes ago, I'd been certain, but Dr. March was right about Granddad. And there were *so* many risks.

"Well, that's a better answer than 'yes.'" Dr. March wiped his mouth and tossed his crumpled napkin across his plate. "Your mother knew what she wanted, and she did what she liked. I have a feeling you may have picked up that habit. I might not have agreed with some of her choices, but I certainly believed in her right to make them." He stood and took out his wallet, tossing several bills on the table. Then he handed me a business card. "Sleep on it, and if you still want to go back to Aurora, come to my office."

"Thank you," I said. I scribbled something on the back of his card. "Do you know what that symbol means?"

"Yes," he said. I glanced at the image of two overlapping circles and felt that all-too-familiar sensation of exhilaration mixed with apprehension. "It's a dyad. An ancient Greek symbol for, well, many things: the number two, 'otherness,' the metaphysical force by which unseen things become seen."

"Metaphysical force? You mean fate?"

"By all means, Sasha, believe in fate," Dr. March said. "Believe in elves that come out at night to cobble shoes if you like. But before you let some idealistic notion that the universes give a damn what happens to any of us guide your choices, consider this: Just because you have a destiny doesn't mean it's something good. Look at the characters in every single Greek tragedy. Each one of them suffered at the hands of fate the sort of things you wouldn't wish on your worst enemy."

SELENE SAT WIDE-AWAKE

in the darkness, waiting. The overhead fluorescents flashed on, and guards filed into the room. She could see in their faces how badly they wanted to harm her and how little they were expected—or encouraged—to control that desire.

But it was all part of the plan. Three days earlier, she'd walked right into the Labyrinth, their precious Academy, with its bright lights and metal walls and refrigerated air, and announced her intention to see the General. She wasn't the first of her kind to pass through the veil into this world, and those who had gone before her had brought back information. She didn't know how long her people had been aware of Aurora, but she was certain they hadn't discovered how to pass through the veil until after the cataclysm that ruined their planet a century ago.

She closed her eyes and pictured Taiga before Typhos, the pitiless asteroid that had killed so many. She didn't have to imagine it; she had the memories of those who had come before her. There were plenty from when Taiga was lush and verdant, when the air was fresh and clean. When Home was a compound instead of a fortress, the last bastion of life in the landscape of death and destruction that was Typhos's horrible legacy.

"Hey!" a guard shouted in her ear. She opened her eyes and gave him a bold, unflustered look. "What are you doing?"

"Listening," she said. It was an ancient art practiced only by the most disciplined minds, a sort of meditation in which all the troubles and worries of the physical world melted away. She did her divining in this between space, bringing forth from the strange and cryptic calculus of Kairos a truth so pure it could transform the world.

Through years of training, she had learned that interpreting prophecy was not all that listening was good for. It had many uses, one of which was conquering pain and fear.

"Well, you better start talking." The guard raised his hand, and Selene braced herself for another strike.

"Stop." Another man entered the room. He was of average height and much older than the first; his dark hair was shot through with gray, and he was dressed in an expensive-looking suit, every inch pressed to perfection. Behind him, a young man about Selene's age stepped through the door. The older man didn't introduce him, but she knew exactly who he was. "I'll take it from here."

The man dismissed the guards, and they shuffled out of the room. They respected him, even feared him. So this was the mysterious General. But for the moment, Selene was far more interested in his son.

Thomas had reacted so strangely when he first set eyes on Selene, his detached expression melting into one of both shock and relief. Then he realized she wasn't who he thought she was, and a mask of indifference descended, but his brief loss of control was enough to tell her what she needed to know. He might have looked like all the other soldiers she'd encountered, but underneath the façade was the real boy she'd met only in someone else's memories and dreams. Selene was glad to know he had not disappeared. They might have need of him someday.

She turned her attention back to the General.

He gazed down at her as if she were a curious specimen of fauna, newly discovered in some previously unexplored territory. She sat in the center of the room, her wrists and ankles bound by metal chains to

53

a hook in the floor. They'd refused to give her food or drink or let her sleep for any reasonable period of time. She was tired and hungry, but her fascination with this powerful man renewed her energy.

"Who are you?" he demanded. "What is your name?"

"I'm not going to tell you that," she said. "Not until you give me what I came here for."

He let out a short bark of laughter. "Yes, they informed me of your demands. It shouldn't surprise you to hear I won't be indulging them."

"Then I'll tell you nothing." She fixed him with a cold smile. "I'm not the sort of person to give in to intimidation."

He made a show of contemplating her words. "Intimidation? Perhaps not. But torture . . ." In spite of all her defenses, her natural confidence and calm, the expression on his face chilled her. He could hurt her if he wanted to, and he would enjoy it. "Torture might serve me much better."

She forced herself not to look away as the back of his hand connected with her jaw. Sparks exploded before her eyes; her skull felt as though it might split open. A tear leaked from the corner of one eye, and she tasted blood in her mouth. She tried to hide her contempt. It would only make him angrier and more determined to harm her. She refused to be afraid, but she couldn't allow herself to die at his hands or be injured so far beyond repair that she couldn't fulfill her destiny. There were limits, lines she couldn't cross.

"Bring me what I've asked for," she said slowly, patiently, "and I'll tell you who I am and where I come from. Then I'll go back there. I give you my word." Her mere presence in his world bothered him. He wanted her gone, and she would go—once she had what she wanted.

"And what value do you suppose your word has to me?"

"If you knew who I was, you wouldn't ask that question."

He stared at her. "Who are you?" There was awe in his voice. She smiled. She could have that effect on people.

"Give me what I want," she said, "and you'll find out."

The General left without another word. His son followed, but she called out his name, and he turned to face her in surprise. Their eyes met, and she saw straight to the core of him, through layers of pain and insecurity and desperation and fear. And love. No matter how hard he struggled to conceal it, he couldn't help looking at her and wishing she were somebody else.

"You should know she's alive," Selene said. His eyes widened. "And she's on her way."

FOUR

I slipped off my shoes and stepped onto the sand. Oak Street Beach was crammed with people looking to escape the heat. The last time I was there, it was empty, the water as black as ink in the distance. It seemed endless then. Endless enough to imagine it was all there was and that Thomas and I were the only people who had ever been there, the only people who even existed. I sat down and closed my eyes, digging my fingers and toes into the sand, as if I could hold on to the memories by anchoring myself to the earth.

Sometimes I forget how big everything is, he'd said. It seemed like such a long time ago. Thomas had been lying to me then, about so many things, but in a way it was the most honest moment we'd ever spent together. He wasn't Grant that night, or the Thomas he pretended to be in Aurora. He was the Thomas who might have been, if things were different; the Thomas he really *was* behind the badge and the bravado. Sometimes I wondered if I was the only one who'd ever seen that Thomas. But I *had* seen him, and I couldn't forget him. I missed him, I needed him, and I believed he felt the same about me. Thomas had freed me, but I was starting to see how I might have freed him, too.

I didn't have the guts to say goodbye to Grant. I knew he'd just try to stop me. And Gina—there was no explaining it to her, even though I wished I could. Granddad would be back from St. Louis in a couple of hours, and I knew I wouldn't have the courage to leave if I had to look him in the eye and tell him where I was going. On my way home from seeing Dr. March, I'd purchased a copy of *The Odyssey* and left it on the kitchen table with a note scribbled inside. I could've written a novel trying to explain how I felt and why I was doing what I was doing, but instead I wrote *Even the longest journey ends with a homecoming.—Sasha*

I didn't know if that was true. I didn't even know if I believed it. But I wanted to. I didn't intend to be gone forever. If I was lucky, I'd be back before school started. I would see him again, and soon. I knew Granddad wouldn't understand. I just hoped he would forgive me, and that one day I could apologize to him face to face.

I stopped in front of a small brick building, double-checked the address on Dr. March's card, and pressed the buzzer. A few seconds passed; cars sped down the street behind me, making a soft whooshing sound, and a sudden breeze kicked up, shaking the limbs of the trees. I buzzed again as a terrible feeling settled in my chest—what if Dr. March wasn't there? It had taken all my nerve to come in the first place, and if he didn't answer the door, I wasn't sure what I was going to do next.

The door to the building unlocked with a loud click, and I stepped inside. I followed a long hallway to a door at the end, which swung open before I could knock. Dr. March did not look pleased to see me.

"So you've made your choice, then," he said. "Very well. Come in."

The place was a pigsty. A long desk stood in one corner of the room, littered with what looked like fast-food wrappers and cups of takeout coffee. The rest of the room was packed full of boxes, not unlike Granddad's attic, except these were all crushed and falling apart, spilling papers everywhere, completely disorganized. "What happened here?"

He gestured grandly at the mess. "This is what's left of my life's work. Would you believe I was once at the top of my field?"

"Um . . ."

Dr. March sank into a battered leather desk chair and rocked back on its wheels. "After your parents died, I didn't have the heart to continue our research. So many of our projects depended on your mother's insights and your father's tenacity. Without them, everything felt impossible."

"I know what you mean." Just going on after that kind of loss was hard enough.

"They were very important to me, your parents. Together we made great leaps." Dr. March stood suddenly. "But this . . . this I built long before I met them, just me and Moss. It was supposed to be the future of interuniversal travel."

He walked to a dark back corner of the room and tore down a dusty drop cloth I'd assumed was hiding another enormous stack of boxes. When I saw what was under it, I was so surprised that for a second I forgot to breathe.

"Do you know what this is?" Dr. March asked, surprised by my expression.

"No," I said, drawing closer. "But I recognize it."

The object was a freestanding metal doorframe, just like Callum's door to nowhere. I took the drawing out of my pocket and held it up for comparison. Dr. March's door had a control panel affixed to the right side, and there was no light shining out of it, but other than that, it was a perfect match. I looked through the door, for some reason expecting to see Aurora on the other side, but all I saw was more of Dr. March's junk.

"We call it a portal," Dr. March explained. "There's one on Earth and one in Aurora. If they're both activated, you can use them to pass through the tandem. You walk through one, and you come out the other. Once we figured out that going through the tandem makes you sick, we modified it with a buffer."

I touched the portal tentatively. "So where do I end up? Where's Dr. Moss's portal?"

Dr. March's face darkened, as if a cloud had passed over it. "I don't know. They can be broken down and reassembled, so it could be anywhere. It might not even be in his possession anymore. You said you were willing to take risks. Here's your chance."

I nodded. "How does it work?"

Dr. March paused, then said, "Are you absolutely *sure* you want to do this?"

"Yes," I said firmly. I'd spent the whole night and all morning weighing the options, and in the end I'd decided: I was going back to Aurora. Everything was waiting for me there: Thomas, my analogs, and something else I couldn't put into words. I didn't know where my path would lead, but I was determined to find out, determined enough to accept the fact that I might not come home again. I hoped to, but I understood that there were no guarantees, and I was resigned to that truth. "I'm absolutely sure."

He sighed, then began flipping switches and punching in codes on the portal's console until it shuddered to life. Light filled the room. It was like a message from the universe itself, saying *Welcome*. Aurora was calling me home.

SHE WAS ASLEEP IN HER

cell when she felt it: a tug on the bond so hard and urgent that it woke her. The sensation was so real, so physical, that it nearly knocked her out of the cot they'd brought in after releasing her from her shackles. She sat up, breathing hard. An otherworldly energy coursed through her veins, stronger and more potent than adrenaline, and she knew Sasha was getting close. The power surged, and in the darkness of that dark, dark room, her hands began to glow.

She closed her eyes and listened for Sasha. It wouldn't be long now.

AVRORA

FIVE

At first the room was as dark as a cave except for the glow of the portal; then lights flickered on, illuminating a large brass seal in the floor. *King's Elite Service,* read the banner across the top, and at the bottom, the motto *Surpass to outlast.* Well, crap.

I took a step forward, and alarms began to shriek. The noise was so shrill it was like a needle to the brain, so loud I couldn't even think. A door slid open and guards stormed in, training their guns on me. Terror trilled up my spine, and I turned back to the portal in panicked reflex, but then I noticed a familiar face in the sea of armed strangers. I moved toward him instinctively, as though the floor had tipped and propelled me forward, but the expression on his face was grim, and the look in his eyes was a warning: *Stay away.* The alarms died, and silence blanketed the room.

"Put your hands up," Thomas commanded. The tone of his voice was like a slap to the face, so impersonal and empty, it almost didn't belong to him at all. If anything, he sounded like Grant in one of his darkest moods, impenetrable and distant. I was relieved to see him standing there, alive and in one piece, but I couldn't get over the way he was looking at me, like I was a stranger. What had they done to him?

"Stay right where you are," he said. He jerked his chin at the portal. "Meyers, shut that thing down. Farrow, Krueger—grab her."

They twisted my hands behind my back, and no amount of struggling was going to free me. The portal shivered as it shut down; I'd lost my only escape route, and Thomas, whom I'd crossed the multiverse to find, was looking through me like I was made of glass. The boy from the beach suddenly seemed very far away.

Sasha. I closed my eyes. The voice in my head sounded like my own, but it didn't belong to me, and it didn't belong to Juliana. Another vision tugged at me, and I slipped into it as easily as diving into water. I was lying on my back in a hard bed, staring up at a concrete ceiling, and then I was back again. The sound of her saying my name echoed along the tether. Her presence was more than just a feeling now; it was a bright green light at the back of my brain, one I had never seen before. I had to know who she was. At the moment, it felt like the most important thing in the world, even more important than Thomas. I opened my eyes and found him staring at me. He was standing so close, I could hear him breathing.

"I'm taking you to the General," Thomas said. If he'd noticed me blink out for a moment, he didn't acknowledge it. "He'll want to question you himself."

I stared at Thomas's back as he and the other agents led me down a series of curved corridors. *He's alive,* I kept thinking. *He's alive, he's alive, he's alive.* It felt more like my mantra than *Everything is fine* and *It was real* ever had. I wished I could figure out what he was thinking. The General wasn't capable of making Thomas forget me, no matter how all-powerful he sometimes seemed, which meant one of two things: either what Thomas felt for me before hadn't lasted through whatever he'd been through since we parted, or else this display of indifference was an act. For the moment, I was choosing to believe the latter, but it didn't change the facts of our circumstances. Back on Earth, I kept hoping he'd escaped, gotten as far away from the General and the KES as he could. But here he was, and here I was, captor and captive once again.

We stopped in front of a door marked PRIVATE: AUTHORIZED ACCESS ONLY. The guards held me in the hall while Thomas entered.

"You asked me to tell you if anything came through the portal," I heard him say. Any*thing*. Not even any*one*. *He's faking*, I reminded myself sternly. It didn't make me feel any better, though.

"Bring her in," the General replied. I tensed. It was impossible to take the General by surprise, and I had the terrible feeling I'd just walked into another of his traps.

The guards dragged me inside. The General sat behind a long glass desk, reading some kind of report. We all stood silent and unmoving, waiting for him to speak.

"Hello, Miss Lawson," he said finally, glancing up. "I thought we might be seeing you again. It's useful to know that the portals still work." He paused for my response, but I stayed quiet. I'd learned from experience that when it came to the General, it was best not to say anything at all if I could help it. "Do you want to tell me *why* you're here?"

"Not really." I resisted the urge to look over at Thomas.

"Well, it doesn't matter," the General said. "You're here, and you'll do what I tell you. Much has changed since you were last here, but one thing has not: this is my world. I command it and control it. Don't make an enemy of me, Miss Lawson, I warn you. I declared war on Farnham to find you, and I'm willing to do much more than that to keep this country safe."

"Safe from what?" Farnham and the UCC had been at war for two hundred years, but from what I understood of their history, it had been a long time since Farnham had posed a real threat to the military might of the UCC.

The General slid a large, dark piece of paper across the desk. At first I thought it was a photograph, but when I looked closer, my throat tightened. It was a copy of the map Callum and I had found in the king's study, the same one I had in my back pocket. "I believe you've seen this before. Do you know what it is?"

I shook my head.

"I suspected not. Operation Angel Eyes is a satellite we launched about fifteen years ago, around the time that Dr. Moss's many-worlds project was starting to yield results. I wanted a way to keep track of movement through the tandem."

"Disruptions." I'd been staring at the map multiple times a day for the last month, and the thought had never even crossed my mind, but now it seemed obvious. "That's what these are."

"Yes, disruptions caused by travel through the tandem. As you can imagine, crossings are strictly regulated: I have to sign off on every single one, and for more than a decade Angel Eyes showed no unauthorized passage. Until, one day, it did."

"When?" I wondered which of the disruptions belonged to Thomas, and which of them belonged to me. I still had no idea why the king would have wanted me to have the map so badly. And Juliana had used it to barter with the rebel group Libertas for her freedom, but what possible value could it have to them? The more answers I got, the more confused I was.

"About two years ago," the General said. "It started with a few anomalies, which we assumed were glitches. But over the following months, there were more and more disruption events we could not account for, and we had to conclude that what we were seeing was a calculated penetration of our universe by another."

"Which universe?" I demanded. "Earth?"

"No. It's been years since any Earth governments or corporations have done productive work on many-worlds technology, and we knew Dr. March's portal wasn't being used because its twin was here."

"You're saying Aurora is being invaded by a *third* universe?"

"Exactly."

"But how?" There were an infinite number of universes. Some were similar to each other, and others were extremely different, but travel between them was nearly impossible. I was starting to understand just how important the connection between Dr. March and Dr. Moss was, because it had established a route from Earth to Aurora.

I'll tell you everything. Her voice was like a whisper in my ear, and the green light of her mind pulsed along the tether. I closed my eyes, trying to shut her out, but it was useless—she was always there, and she would not go away. But if I could sense her mind, why couldn't I sense Juliana's?

"I believe we're very close to finding out," the General said. I blinked and tried to clear my head. I couldn't pay attention to both of them at the same time. "We've caught one of them. She's in a holding cell just down the hall."

"She?"

"Yes. She refuses to tell us anything, naturally. She won't divulge the name of her home universe, and she's silent on the subject of her reason for being here." The General paused. "She does have one demand. She wants to see her Aurora-analog. She wants to see Juliana."

"She's my analog, too," I said softly. This wasn't a coincidence. Someone—or some*thing*—was pulling the strings, but it definitely wasn't the General.

"Precisely," the General said with a frown. Maybe he was thinking the same thing. He looked older to me, weaker. For a man who claimed to control the world, he seemed strangely uncertain.

"Where is Juliana?"

"Still with Libertas. The situation in the Tattered City has deteriorated further, due to the war. They've completely overrun it, and they're hiding her well."

It was just about the worst thing he could've told me. I had to find Juliana, but I'd gone up against Libertas before and escaped only with Thomas's help. I had no idea what his loyalties were now, and even if he still cared about me, he might not have a choice. What if I couldn't count on him this time? What if I had to do it alone?

You have me, the girl said. *We can find her together.*

Who are you? I demanded. It made me feel crazy, yelling at someone else *in my own head,* thinking that she could hear me, but I knew she could. The green light intensified, and for some reason, I knew that meant she was pleased. That was the strangest thing about the tether: there was an internal logic to the way it worked, and I understood instinctively, which was comforting in a way, but frightening, too.

Come and find me, she said. *And I'll tell you.*

"Sasha," Thomas said. I met his eyes, hoping to see a spark of feeling, but there was still nothing. The way he was acting, he could have been any KES agent and I could've been any prisoner. I noticed he was wearing the KES ring he'd left behind when he followed me into Farnham; it caught the light as he took a step toward me. "We need you to talk to her. Find out why she's here and how she passed through the tandem."

I turned to the General. I couldn't stand to look at Thomas anymore; the longer things went on like this, the harder it was going to be to convince myself he was only playing a part. "And then what will you do with me? You're not going to make me pretend to be Juliana again, are you?"

"No, Miss Lawson. I won't be making the same mistake twice. What I do with you depends entirely on how successful you are at getting your analog to talk," the General said. I highly doubted that letting me go was on the table. The General didn't give second chances.

I have a plan, my analog said. *Neither of us will be here for long, but you have to trust me, Sasha. You have to help me.*

"She asked for Juliana. What makes you think she'll talk to me?"

"You're her analog just as much as Juliana is, and as far as I'm concerned, one of you is just as good as another."

"All right," I said. The anticipation of seeing this new analog made my chest feel uncomfortably tight, but the green light throbbed like a heartbeat and a strange sensation, something like calm, flooded my body. "Take me to her."

SIX

Guards escorted me down wide, curving hallways, but Thomas did not come along. He had been the General's most trusted agent once, as well as his favorite son. I couldn't imagine the General forgiving Thomas's betrayal and welcoming him back into his confidence without punishment, but that seemed to be what had happened. And it was hard for me to imagine Thomas *wanting* to come back to the KES and serve his father again. I wished I could talk to him, but he was so far out of my reach, and I was starting to worry I wouldn't get the chance.

Still, there was a glimmer of hope. The General had insisted I wear an anchor in case my analog tried to make physical contact with me—he didn't want me going through the tandem accidentally. It was only a slim piece of silver, but it felt as if it weighed a hundred pounds. As Thomas had fastened the anchor around my wrist, his fingers had brushed my wrist, sending a shock spiraling through me; it hadn't occurred to me to prepare myself to be touched by him, and I was caught off guard. I glanced at him tentatively, and he swallowed hard as he met my eyes, his expression softening for a brief, charged moment. He hadn't forgotten me. I was sure of that now. It made everything seem possible again, including the mind-bending reality I was about to face.

With every step I took, my analog's presence on the tether grew stronger. I could feel myself getting closer, just as I had when Juliana approached the Farnham prison cell. It was a sort of knowing that was both physical and transcendent—a buzz in my bones, a tidal shift that sent surges of adrenaline crashing through my veins. I didn't want to think about what the General would do if he discovered I had a direct connection to my analogs, but sometimes it felt so hard to contain, like the truth of it could be read in my eyes.

When we reached her, I knew it. I felt it down to an atomic level.

The guards unlocked the door. I entered alone, and it closed behind me. My palms were slick with sweat, and there was a lump in my throat I couldn't get rid of. She sat on the edge of the bed with her back to me. Her hair—my hair—our hair—cascaded over her shoulders in a straight chestnut waterfall. The air fizzed with electricity, and I felt I was going to be sick.

Then she stood and turned. I drew a sharp breath at the sight of her face—my face—our face. You never do get used to seeing your analog. It's always a surprise, always difficult, always painful, and yet so, so right, like two pieces of a puzzle fitting together. I missed Juliana suddenly, as if she were a part of my body that had been cut away. My analog smiled.

"You found me," she said.

"*You* found *me*," I replied. It wasn't a coincidence, but maybe it wasn't fate, either. *She* was the one who had made it happen. I felt the urge to run away, the familiar repulsion that always sprang up in the presence of my analog, like the universe was warning me just how dangerous it was for us to get close. "How did you know I'd come here?"

"I saw you planning it all, through the bond," she said, tapping her temple.

"So you know who I am." Maybe I should've been surprised, but I wasn't, not after everything I'd seen through the tether. I hated the thought of this girl rooting around inside my head, but it was a relief not to have to explain.

"Of course I do, Sasha," she said. "I've been with you for weeks, showing you my memories. Don't you remember?"

"I remember some things." A long room with ten people sitting at a triangular table. A boy's face, the white dress she was wearing, and digging my fingers into the dirt as I climbed up a muddy riverbank. But there was so much I'd already forgotten. "Sometimes they slip away."

"I think that will change." She stepped forward. I backed away instinctively. I was too wary of her to let her get near me. "My name is Selene. The more time we spend together and the closer we are to each other, the more control we'll have over the bond. Haven't you noticed how much stronger it's already become?"

The only thing more bizarre than coming face to face with my analog was hearing my own voice come out of her mouth. It was like standing in front of a mirror and seeing my reflection move on its own—the stuff of nightmares. But at the same time, strange as it sounds, it was like meeting a twin sister I never knew I had: comforting, like coming home after a long time away.

"How can you do that?"

"Do what?"

"Send me your memories. And talk to me in my head. Can you read my mind?" That would be a whole new level of weird, exactly the sort of thing I needed to break the tether to avoid. I didn't *want* to control it—I wanted to *destroy* it. If she'd been spying on me all these weeks, she had to know that.

"Not exactly."

"That's not a no."

"I can sense some of your feelings and intentions," Selene explained. "I'm sure you can sense mine, or you'll be able to very soon. Sometimes I can tell what you're thinking, but only when you're projecting. As for the memories . . . since I was young, I've been cultivating an ability that, among other things, gives me greater control over the bond than I would otherwise have. We call it listening, but it has very little to do with what you can hear with your ears."

" 'We'?"

"The others in my world. Those of us who are left. I'm so glad we found each other, Sasha. We have important work to do together."

"What work?" I demanded. I had my own work to do, and it occurred to me for the first time that I didn't just have to *find* my analogs—I had to convince them to do what needed to be done, and I wasn't even sure what that was yet.

"We have to locate Juliana," Selene said. "That's why you came here, isn't it? But first, we have to get out of this place. We can't do anything locked up here."

I bit my lip. I'd been thinking the same thing, but I couldn't just follow her blindly—I didn't even *know* her. It made me nervous, the way she kept saying "we," as if we hadn't just met, and that she already had a plan. And I still had no idea why she was in Aurora in the first place. "How are we going to do that? It's not like the General's going to let us walk out the front door."

"Of course not. I have something else in mind. I couldn't do it without you, but now that you're here . . ." She grabbed my hand and I jumped, but she didn't disappear. I glanced down at my wrist, expecting the anchor to have vanished, but it was still there, too, glinting in the light. On her wrist, I saw a silver tattoo of two overlapping circles.

"We're not supposed to touch," I said in bewilderment.

"You and Juliana can't touch," she said, holding on tighter. "And neither can Juliana and I. But you and I are not from Aurora. We cancel each other out here. In my world, we'll have to be much more careful."

"Your world?" I was intensely curious about where Selene had come from, but I had no plans to leave Aurora. I'd just arrived. My mind turned back to Thomas. I wasn't going anywhere until I knew where we stood with each other. I didn't think my heart could take any more wondering.

You asked why I was here. Selene's voice ricocheted through my head. I tensed up. It was hard to get used to hearing thoughts that weren't mine. *My world—my planet—is dying, and I need your help to save it. Yours and Juliana's. To do that, you both have to come with me to Taiga. Not forever. Just for a little while.*

She gripped my hand so hard it felt as if my bones were being crushed. *I would tell you more, but it would take too much time, and we're out of that now. The guards are coming to get you.*

"How do you know that?"

She smiled. "Listening."

The door slid open. "Time's up," one of the guards said.

I have to tell them something, I thought to Selene in a panic.

My name. You can tell them my name, the name of my world, and that I mean them no harm.

The General won't believe that.

It doesn't matter what he believes. We're leaving this place tonight, and then he won't have any power over us.

A guard grabbed my arm, and Selene reluctantly let go.

*　　*　　*

It's almost nightfall, she said. *Stay awake while everyone sleeps, and I'll come for you. Trust me, Sasha. It's the only way you're going to get out of here. You're not alone anymore. Together we're going to do incredible things.*

"So?" the General said. His gaze fell on me like a spotlight.

"Her name is Selene," I told him. I was really not in the mood to be interrogated. I wanted out of there as fast as possible. "Her world is called Taiga, but I couldn't get her to tell me how she managed to pass through the tandem. All she would say was that she means Aurora no harm."

"Do you believe her?"

"Excuse me?"

"I asked, do you believe her?"

"Why does that matter?"

"Call it curiosity," he said, narrowing his eyes. No wonder Thomas was always so restless—I could barely handle five minutes under the General's scrutiny, and Thomas had lived most of his life that way.

"Yes. I do."

"Then you're just as big a fool as you always were," the General said. "I thought your experiences here would have taught you that to trust other people is to surrender yourself to their will.

"That's all for now. The guards will take you to your cell."

I did my best to get my bearings as the guards led me through the building, thinking it would be useful, if Selene really was going to get us both out, to know where I was going. But I kept getting distracted by what the General had said. What did he know about trust? And yet . . . Thomas had gotten me to trust him so that I'd perform my Juliana pantomime as instructed. I'd almost poisoned Callum, who had trusted *me,* in order to get back home. Maybe the General was right. But I really hoped he wasn't.

"Here," a guard said. He opened a door and shoved me into a room. It was exactly the same as Selene's—identical cells for identical girls. The door slid shut, and then I was alone.

Or at least I thought I was. I hadn't taken two steps into the room before a hand shot out and pulled me into a darkened corner.

SEVEN

Thomas crushed me against his chest, knocking the breath right out of my lungs. He took my face in his hands and pressed his mouth to mine. I closed my eyes and sank into the kiss, letting it tell me, in a way that was impossible with words, exactly how he felt. It was all there—how happy he was to see me, how much he'd missed me, and how deeply he cared. I wrapped my arms around his waist and held on as tight as I could, afraid that if I didn't, he would slip away. His mouth was warm, and he tasted like sugar. I almost laughed, remembering the toggles, that candy he liked. My heart was pounding—it had been an act after all. He hadn't forgotten me. He ran his hand down my spine and let it rest at the small of my back as his lips met mine once again.

"Hi," he murmured, smiling. He let out a shaky breath.

"Hi," I whispered, taking his hand. It was trembling.

"I'm sorry about before," he said, gently tracing my jaw with his fingertips. "The General hasn't asked how I feel about you, but I doubt he's forgotten what happened. Acting like I still . . . it would only make things harder for you. I have to be careful how much I let it show, to everyone."

"I understand. You scared me for a minute, though. I was afraid I'd made it all up." I choked out a laugh, though it wasn't even close to funny, the idea that I'd invented us. *It was real.*

"No," he said, kissing me as if to prove it. "Never." He stared at me as if he was afraid I might disappear, as if he could keep me there if he didn't look away.

"What are you doing here?" he asked in disbelief.

"I came for you, dummy." As if it weren't totally obvious. After that kiss, it was hard to focus on anything but his lips, the feeling of his skin against mine, and the way he smelled, like warm cotton and juniper berry soap. His breath was soft on my cheek. It felt so familiar, so right, the way nothing else had since before we separated. Destiny or no destiny, I was home.

"How did you know I wasn't . . . ?"

"Dr. Moss sent me a message," I told him. "Through Dr. March."

"Dr. March isn't—"

"He's real," I said. "He's Dr. Moss's Earth analog, Thomas. They can talk to each other through their tether. He put this in my mailbox." I took the star out of my pocket and pressed it into his palm. "I tracked him down and persuaded him to help me get back here through the portal."

"I feel so stupid," he said, wincing in embarrassment.

"Why?"

"I should've known Dr. Moss and Dr. March were analogs. If I'd figured it out on my own, you wouldn't have had to go for weeks thinking I was dead." He had to force the last word out. His saying it made me imagine it, and my heart crumpled at the thought of what could have been.

"I never did," I lied, laying my head on his chest. His heart was beating so fast. It killed me to remember how close it had come to not beating at all. "I knew you'd find a way out of there."

"I almost didn't. They were going to execute me."

I looked at him more closely and started to see what happiness had managed to hide: bruises and cuts all over his face, in various stages of healing. My stomach clenched in horror. I was afraid to ask what else they had done to him. All I kept thinking was that maybe if he hadn't sent me back, I could've helped him.

"Don't," he said, reading my face. "It's not your fault." But it *was*, at least partially. I was the reason he had been in Adastra Prison in the first place. He'd gotten shot protecting *me*. No matter what he said, I couldn't forget that.

"What happened?" If he needed to talk, I was going to listen, even though it scared me. I owed him that. He'd always listened to me.

"They wanted information." He stroked my hair, wrapping a small piece of it around his finger as his mind traveled miles away and days into the past. "About Juliana. I didn't tell them anything—I would never—but they were . . . persistent."

"They tortured you, didn't they?" I put a hand to his jaw and drew my thumb across his cheekbone. I didn't understand how anyone could want to hurt him. The thought of Thomas suffering broke my heart, but I swallowed the impulse to cry, wanting to be brave.

He looked past me, over my shoulder into the empty room, and retreated further as I stood there, watching. I waited for him to surface from his thoughts.

"It doesn't matter," he said, clearing his throat and giving me a reassuring smile. "It's over. I'm here. You're here. We're both alive. I think that means we won."

It was nice of him to try, but he didn't fool me. "How did you get away?"

"The General sent a squad to extract me." He kept his voice calm and steady, as if he were talking about someone else. He was a trained soldier who faced death every day; he could compartmentalize with the best of them. But beneath it all, he was rattled and confused. I could sense it. Something terrible had happened to him, and for the first time since I'd met him, he seemed truly lost. "They brought me back here."

"Where *is* 'here'?" We were in a KES facility of some kind, but I was pretty sure it wasn't the Tower in Columbia City.

"The Labyrinth," he explained. "A fortress that houses the KES Academy. The General moved his headquarters here after he invaded Farnham."

"Why?"

"I'm not sure, but it's completely remote," he said. "Not in the middle of a major city, like the Citadel. From what I can tell from the rumors I hear and the news reports on the box, Columbia City is scary right now. There have been violent protests against the war with Farnham. It's not as bad as the Tattered City, but it's getting there. The royal family fled to Bethlehem House, and the General came up here."

"So the queen is safe? And Simon and Lillian?" The queen hadn't always been kind to me, but I didn't want anything to happen to her. And Juliana's brother and sister—they were little children. They needed to be protected.

"Yes," Thomas said. "They left the king at the Citadel. He's too fragile to be moved."

"But he's—?"

"He's still alive." Thomas kissed my forehead. "It's nice of you to care."

"Of course I care." I frowned. "So you're KES again? After everything that happened?"

"In a way," he said evasively. "To tell you the truth, I'm not really sure where I stand. The General acts like nothing has changed, like I never disobeyed orders, but we both know I did."

"Why would he trust you again?" *To trust other people is to surrender yourself to their will.* Why was Thomas the exception?

"I keep asking myself that same question," Thomas admitted. "Dr. Moss once told me that the General needed me, because he knew the day would come when there would be war with other worlds. I didn't think much of it at the time, but then I found out about the unauthorized disruptions, and your analog, and it all started to make some kind of sense."

"What do you think he plans to do about it?"

"I don't know, but invading Farnham was only the first step," Thomas said. "He claims he did it because we needed to be a united front against our new enemies, but the General never has only one motive for doing something. He's been waiting a long time for this."

I ran my thumb over his KES ring. "What about this?" It was a symbol of belonging, the closest the KES could get to branding him. Was he wearing it for show, or was he really one of them again?

"It was in my room when I got here. Sitting on the dresser, like some kind of test. So I put it on." It wasn't exactly the answer I was looking for, not an answer at all. I wished I could read his mind as Selene could read mine. Thomas was quiet for a moment. "I didn't have anywhere else to go."

He sounded so despondent; I couldn't bear it. I wanted to erase the bad feelings and replace them with good. I pulled him in for a kiss. For a few seconds, all that had gone before, and all that was sure to come, vanished, and we sank into that bright, safe universe that only existed when we were together. Then reality rushed back in.

"You're in so much danger, Sasha," Thomas murmured.

The sound of him saying my name warmed me to my core, as it always had, since the very beginning. "I'm afraid for you."

"Don't be afraid."

"Aren't you?"

"We're together," I reminded him. I was scared, of course I was, more for him than for myself. But I didn't want him to know that. I wanted him to believe that I could withstand anything, that I was his equal in courage. I wanted to deserve him. "What's there to be afraid of?"

"Lots of things." His hand drifted down my neck. I leaned in and closed my eyes. I was trapped, but when he held me I felt free. "The General, for one. He's not going to cut you a deal this time. In his mind, you're his indefinitely. You and your analog."

"Selene. Her name is Selene."

"Selene," Thomas repeated. "I don't trust her, Sasha. She knew you were coming. She told me you were on your way. How could she possibly have known that?"

"The tether," I told him. "She's been using it to contact me. She says she needs my help."

"With what?"

"To save her world. Whatever that means." I grabbed him by the fabric of his shirt and drew him to me, so close that our noses were touching. "I don't want to talk right now. I just want to do this." I brushed his lips with mine. He caught my mouth and pressed his palm against the nape of my neck, burying his fingers in my hair.

"We have to get you out of here." He took a deep, steadying breath and sagged against the wall. I traced the arc of a long, angry scar across his temple with my fingertips. I'd known he was strong, but to survive torture without breaking took a different kind of strength, one most people didn't have. What had it been like for him, alone in that cell, waiting for death? What had it done to him?

"I'm not going back to Earth," I insisted. "I came here to find you, and I'm not leaving without you."

He rubbed the back of his neck. "I don't think Earth is even an option right now. If you run, that's the first place they'll look."

"I know." Guilt over leaving Granddad behind again—this time on purpose—gnawed at me constantly. The least I could do was not draw danger to his doorstep. "Selene's got a plan. She wants me to escape with her tonight."

Thomas laughed. "This is a high-security military compound. There's only one person I know of who managed to escape the Labyrinth since it was built. How does she think she's going to get out of that cell, let alone the building?"

"I have no idea. But I believe she can do it. She seems capable of pretty much anything."

"Yeah, that's what worries me."

"Come with us," I implored. "We can leave together. I know you don't want to stay here."

Thomas raised his eyes to meet mine, and I realized I didn't know that at all. But I wanted so badly to believe it. "I have to. For a little while, at least. To distract them and give you time to get away."

"So you think I should go with her?"

"I think you already know what you need to do," Thomas said. "But first things first." I was wearing a bobby pin to keep my bangs out of my eyes, and he plucked it out. My hair fell in my face, and I gave him a curious look—what the hell was he doing? Then he took my wrist and did something to the anchor; it fell open on its hinges and dropped into his palm.

"How did you do that?"

"There's an emergency latch release on the inside of the band," he explained, shoving the anchor into his pocket. "You just need something thin and strong enough to trip it. It de-activates when you remove it."

I rubbed my wrist, happy to be rid of that thing. "Now you tell me."

He gave a low chuckle, sliding his hands up my arms. I shivered in spite of the heat that hung in the air between us. "Now when you run, they won't be able to track you."

"I'm afraid to go," I confessed. All the time I'd spent in Aurora, I'd been in the care of someone else. Even when I'd escaped from the Castle, I'd been with Callum. "I don't know this world. I don't even know where Juliana is."

"Juliana?"

"I need to find her. I have to break the tether before it breaks me." I told him about the visions, how they were be-coming more and more frequent, blurring the edges of my reality. The fact that Selene could read my mind and push her own thoughts and memories into my head was further proof that the tether was dangerous. But for the first time since Dr. March planted the idea in my head, I felt that breaking the bond connecting me to my analogs was possible. I only wished that I knew how to actually do it.

Thomas cupped my face in his hands. "You're brave, Sasha Lawson. And you're smart as hell. If you want some advice, here it is: trust your gut, and don't let fear get the best of you."

"Is that in the KES training manual?" I joked.

"You bet it is." He smiled. "Lesson one."

"And Selene? You said yourself you don't trust her. I'm not sure I do, either." Reason told me I shouldn't, but everything I felt through the tether insisted I could. It was difficult to de-cide which part of myself to listen to.

"She clearly has powers neither of us understands. And she's the only person I've ever seen who's capable of unnerving the General. That makes her an ally worth having, at least for now."

"What about you?"

"I'll find you. I promise. I'll always find you if you want to be found. But first we have to make sure you get as big of a head start on the KES as possible." He lowered his voice. "I don't know how Selene plans to break you out of the Labyrinth, but when you've gotten past the fence, you need to head to the river."

"The river. Got it."

"Keep off the roads as much as possible and out of sight of the Hudson. It's a heavily wooded area, so stay under cover of the trees, but make sure you can always hear the water on your left-hand side. About ten miles downriver there's a town called Almond," Thomas said. "It has a train station, but there's only one train a day, so you have to make sure to get there by ten-fifty-one a.m. I'll meet you there, and we'll figure out how we're going to track Juliana down. Together."

I smiled. "Feels kind of like old times, us doing things together."

"We make a pretty good team, you and I." He bent to kiss me. I felt like a house with all its lights on, bright and safe in the warm glow of home.

EIGHT

Staying awake that night wasn't a problem—I was so wired from being with Thomas and so nervous about what would happen when Selene came for me, I couldn't have slept if I'd wanted to. Every time I heard the slightest noise, I thought it was Selene, and my heart leapt into my throat. But when minutes had become hours and it seemed impossible that it was still night, all the lights in my room suddenly turned off, and I knew that it was time.

I waited in darkness, and the faint sound of people shouting from far away was the only thing I could hear. I thought of what Selene had said about listening, how it was a form of meditation. I sat down on the bed, closed my eyes, and attempted to do something I hadn't done since the last time I was in Aurora: tune in to one of my analogs and see through her eyes.

Where are you? I asked. I wasn't even sure she would be able to hear me.

I'm on my way. Selene's presence burned bright green along the tether, and I slipped into her mind. Her pulse raced as she ran along the empty pitch-black corridors, navigating as if she had a map of the entire compound in her brain. But she wasn't solving the Labyrinth; she was following the string, the path along the tether that would lead her to me. Voices echoed off the metal walls, but she never hesitated, never looked back, and then she was at my door. She pressed her hand against the LCD panel, and it exploded with light like a Fourth of July sparkler. The door slid open, and she saw me on the bed, my face illuminated by the glow of my hands.

My eyes flew open.

"What the—" I cried as Selene hauled me to my feet.

"It's the power, Sasha," Selene said. "Look!"

"What are you talking about?"

"Your hands," she said. The light was fading, but I could *feel* it surging through me, crackling in my fingertips like electricity. "I can do it, too. That's how I took down all the lights in this part of the Labyrinth, but it won't last forever. Their backup generator will kick in any moment. We have to go *now*."

She dragged me into the hallway, pausing to get her bearings before choosing the hallway to our left. As we hurried down the curving corridor, Selene trailed her fingers along the wall, running them over the rivets as if she were reading Braille.

"What are you doing?" I whispered.

This place really is a labyrinth, Selene explained. *The rivets guide you to the center. They get closer to each other the farther inward you go.* She stopped in front of a blank wall.

"There's nothing here," I said.

"Yes, there is." She stepped forward, and the wall slid open to reveal a staircase. "There are doors everywhere. You just have to know how to find them."

"How do you know all this?" I asked as we ran down four flights of stairs.

"My people have been coming to this world for years, doing reconnaissance. Several of them managed to infiltrate this compound and report back on its secrets."

So that was the source of the undocumented disruptions on the Angel Eyes map. Maybe the General was right: maybe the people from Selene's world *were* trying to invade. I paused on the landing.

"You lied to me," I said. She froze and looked up at me from the landing below. "You said you meant Aurora no harm, but if that's true, why have your people been coming here for *years* and bringing back information?"

Selene hesitated. "I don't know. They found the doors between Taiga and Aurora decades ago by accident. I can only assume they were curious. Wouldn't you be?"

"You're hiding something." But how could she be, when we could see into each other's minds? I searched the tether for a sign she was being untruthful, but I couldn't find one.

"Whether or not that's true, which it isn't, you can't stay here," Selene insisted. "This is your chance to escape. You won't get another, I promise you. I'll explain when there's more time. I'll tell you everything you want to know, but if you don't come with me now, you'll be trapped here, and you'll have no answers. All you'll be left with is regrets."

"Is that a threat?"

"It's an absolute certainty. Now, are you coming or not?"

I heard the sound of doors slamming and heavy footsteps on the stairs. "Please, Sasha," Selene begged. "Just trust me."

The part of my brain that was too rational for things like destiny or gut feelings screamed at me to run away, that Selene was suspect and dangerous. But something about the way the tether trembled told me she was being sincere. Finally, my self-preservation instincts kicked in, and I followed Selene down the last dark flight of stairs.

"It's this way." Selene pointed down a narrow hallway. We were on the basement level of the Labyrinth; the floors and walls were concrete, and the ceilings were low. Pipes hung above our head, so close I could touch them. We made our way through a series of twists and turns, guided only by Selene's intuition. I could still feel the power—whatever the hell it was—crashing through me in waves.

"Where are we going?" It seemed like the last thing we'd want to do was journey deeper into the Labyrinth.

"There's an access to a secret tunnel down here somewhere." Selene peered around an enormous cage. "It leads to a guardhouse on the opposite side of the fence that surrounds this place."

"A guardhouse? I thought we were trying not to get caught."

"It was decommissioned a long time ago, when they moved the front entrance to the opposite side of the building," Selene said. I stared at her. "Our scouts were very thorough."

"And here I thought I couldn't trust you less."

"You trust me more than you've ever trusted anybody," Selene said. "Except maybe that boy you came here to find. Thomas. That's his name, right?"

"Stay out of my head!"

"Don't you understand?" Selene asked. "The bond that connects us is what's going to keep us alive. We can see into each other's minds for a reason. We can read each other's thoughts, communicate with each other across infinite space, and unleash a kind of power that has never been seen before, all because we have a *destiny*, Sasha. You might not like it, but today, and for many days to come, we're going to need it."

"What destiny?" Was she saying that because she knew it was what I wanted to hear or because she believed it?

"I said I would explain everything when we had more time, and I will. But right now we have to keep going." Selene's head snapped up. "They're coming. They're very, very close. Quick, over here."

Selene pulled me into a niche on the other side of the wire cage. We crammed together in the narrow space, clutching each other. A group of KES agents thundered by, toting flashlights and assault rifles. The group's leader, a petite Asian girl about Thomas's age, swung her flashlight in a circle. I held my breath as the beam of light swept my face. The girl stared at us, eyes wide, frozen in her tracks.

"You find something?" a voice called from down the passageway.

"Nothing," she said, after a long pause. I thought I was going to pass out. The girl lifted a finger to her lips and looked me straight in the eye before turning and heading in the opposite direction. "This way." The group moved on, and I sighed in relief.

Who was that? But Selene shook her head.

I have no idea, she said. *There's still someone here. Don't make a sound.*

A second later, the beam of a second flashlight blinded me. I covered my face, and a hand closed around my wrist, yanking me out into the open. Thomas let out a long, deep breath. "That was really close. Adele almost saw you."

"She did see us," I told him. "But she didn't say anything. Who is she, Thomas?"

"A friend of mine," he said, but he couldn't explain why this friend of his let us go any more than we could. An illtimed, ridiculous lightning bolt of jealousy shot through me. What kind of friend? "What are you two still doing here?"

"We're looking for the tunnel to the empty guardhouse," Selene told him. "Do you know where it is?"

"Just around that corner," Thomas said, pointing left at the intersection of two perpendicular hallways. She started off in that direction, but he grabbed her. "Not so fast. That's the way the rest of the agents went. You need a distraction." He surveyed Selene. "And a change of clothes."

"Why?" she asked, genuinely befuddled. It was stupid—crazy—but I wondered if Thomas felt anything when he looked at her. *Of course not,* I scolded myself. Thomas knew better than anyone else how different two analogs could be. After all, he hadn't fallen for Juliana. He'd fallen for me.

"You're going to stick out in that dress," I explained. "But where are we going to get her something different to wear?"

"I have an idea. Stay here. Don't move." He disappeared into the darkness. Selene and I huddled together in the shadows as best we could, trying to stay out of sight. Just when I feared that Thomas wasn't coming back, he reappeared with a stack of black fabric in his arms.

"I took these from the laundry. We all wear the same thing here—black on black on black." His gaze slid over to me. "I got some for you, too. If you look like KES recruits, people might not notice you." He didn't seem convinced, but it was worth a shot.

"Good call," I said, reaching for the clothes. He turned around to give us some privacy. This wasn't the moment to get all shy about stripping three feet away from him, but I felt a blush rise up in my cheeks anyway.

"Now? We don't have time for this!" Selene protested as I shucked off my jeans and T-shirt and pulled on a pair of tight black pants and a long-sleeved shirt from the pile.

"You'll thank me when you don't get caught off an anonymous tip from someone who saw the princess of the UCC on a train platform wearing a dress that belongs in a museum," Thomas pointed out. I put a hand on his arm and felt his muscles relax. He gave me a weak smile, and I returned it, but I was worried: reconnaissance or not, Selene couldn't know anywhere near as much as she needed to about Aurora, and I was starting to wonder just how different her world was, from Aurora and from my own.

Selene changed, then handed her dress and my old clothes to Thomas. "Burn these," she said. Thomas tossed them into the darkness.

"Later. When you're good and gone." He pulled me in by my waist and his lips collided with mine, but the kiss was over too quickly. I stumbled a bit when he released me, and he caught my elbow with a gentle hand.

"Be careful. I'll see you soon." He gestured for us to hide, and we slunk back into the shadows as he pressed his finger to his ear and said, "Subjects spotted going north in the southeast corridor of the basement level, headed toward the back exit." He took off running in the direction opposite the one the other agents had gone in, and a minute later they all ran after him. When everything was quiet and the hallway seemed clear, we made our way to the secret tunnel and found it behind an unmarked door ten feet away.

"Come on," Selene said. "Let's go."

The tunnel was so small we had to crouch. We walked until we spotted a metal ladder leading up to a hatch. I climbed up first, but when I tried to unlock the hatch and push it open, I couldn't get it to budge.

"It's too heavy," I said. "There's no way one of us by ourselves can lift it." And there wasn't space for two people to stand side by side on the ladder. The edge of the hatch was puckered, as if someone had taken to it with a blowtorch.

"I think they sealed it off." I landed on the dirt floor with a muffled thump.

Selene frowned; frustration rolled along the tether in big, choppy waves. She hadn't planned for this.

"What do we do now?" I looked around, as if I expected the answer to be written on the walls of the tunnel like ancient hieroglyphics. In a brief moment of lunacy, I became convinced we were going to have to dig ourselves out.

"There's another way," Selene said, but a shudder of uncertainty along the tether told me she wasn't excited to try it. "You're going to have to be very brave, Sasha. There's no turning back now."

"I know." I couldn't think of a single thing I was more afraid of than what the General would do to us if he caught us trying to escape.

"Come on," she said, starting back down the tunnel. She stood in front of the door and closed her eyes, dropping her head and breathing deeply. The tether tightened and swayed as she listened. I closed my own eyes, trying to figure out how she did it, how she read the inaudible vibrations of the universe like a text. I began to see, through her eyes, white lines of light bursting past me like threads on a loom. They spun and looped and crossed over each other, fusing and separating, and as I watched, patterns started to emerge. I couldn't make sense of them, not as Selene could, but I knew they were there.

"All clear." Selene yanked the door open and we spilled out into the Labyrinth's basement, right back where we started. She pointed down a hall that shot off to the right. "That way."

"It's really cool that you can do that," I said as we hurried down one corridor after another. Selene's confidence was a relief; after all the switchbacks and reversals, I was so turned around I didn't think I could find anything, let alone another exit.

"I could teach you," she said, charging through another door. We were standing at the foot of a winding spiral staircase. I craned my neck to see how far it went. "If you want to learn."

"We're going up?" That didn't seem right, unless there was somebody coming to rescue us with a helicopter, which I doubted. "Is jumping out of a window your plan B?"

"Something like that." She started up the staircase. It creaked and groaned beneath her weight—like much of the basement, it seemed far older than the rest of the Labyrinth.

What? I shouted over the tether. *I was joking!*

We don't have time for this, Sasha, Selene said, pausing on a step and glaring down at me. *Come on!*

I absolutely did not want to climb that rickety, endless staircase, but I had zero other options. I concentrated on putting one foot in front of the other; my hands shook harder with every step I took, and my face felt as if it were on fire. By the third turn, my breathing was so shallow I thought I wouldn't be able to keep going; black sparks wiggled on the outskirts of my vision. I was going to pass out. I knew the signs. I used to have a reasonable fear of heights, but since my first trip to Aurora, it had blossomed into full-blown acrophobia.

I balled up my fists and forced myself to keep moving, even as my vision blurred and a heavy darkness began to pull at my mind.

"No." Selene grabbed my hand and yanked me up so we were standing face to face. I could barely see her in the blackness, but the tether was wide open and beating like a heart. "Look at me, Sasha. I know you're afraid of high places, but you have to control your fear." Strength and serenity poured through the tether like a balm. I took a deep breath.

"Better?" I nodded. She gave me a tight smile, and we

continued on. I still felt as if I were going to throw up, but at least I managed not to faint.

At the top of the staircase there was a concrete landing and yet another door. I almost didn't want to know what it was going to lead to. There was no stopping Selene, but even she took a sharp breath when she saw what was behind that door.

It was a town. A normal, average suburban town . . . at the top of a staircase. Which made absolutely no sense. About twenty feet to our left there was an elevator, and I realized we had to be on the roof of the Labyrinth. But if that was true, then why did it seem as if I'd just stepped onto the set of a classic TV show?

The town was deserted. Once my eyes adjusted to the darkness, I was able to make out shapes, then actual buildings. A road stretched out in front of us. There were no lights, though I could see streetlamps towering in the distance like overgrown shepherd's crooks. The night thinned further, and I noticed trees swaying in the distance. Fences swam into view, white slats set slightly apart like rows of teeth. From where I was standing, everything seemed eerily perfect. The aurora universalis bent and twirled in the sky above, and in spite of the circumstances, I felt a gust of calm blow through me. It was good to see it again.

The generator must've kicked in, because lights popped on as we passed them, as if by some spell, which was a nice touch. I almost believed the fake village capable of magic; it looked and felt like a place straight out of a fairy tale in which a wicked sorceress had condemned everyone to eternal slumber.

"Is this place real?"

"It's a façade," Selene said. "Part of the KES Academy. They use it to run training simulations."

"Did you learn that from another of your scouts' reports?"

Selene didn't bother to respond, and I let the matter rest. I was too far in it with her now.

We made our way down the main street, which was lined by full-grown, picturesque oaks. I glanced at the storefronts as we strolled past them. There was a butcher, a baker, and a grocery store; a shoe store and a boutique; a few restaurants; an Irish pub; a hardware store; an antiques shop. There were houses that would never be lived in, cars—or motos, as they called them here—in the driveways, never to be driven. Somewhere in the distance I heard the sound of rushing water.

I was awestruck by how detailed the town was. We passed the office for the *King's Town Gazette;* there was a bicycle leaning against the tree out front, and its basket held stacks of folded bundles tied with string, waiting patiently for the town's invisible paperboy.

Eventually, the Stepfordesque landscape gave way to something much grittier and more industrial. All around us, warehouses and office buildings loomed; some were brand-new, and others looked like the kind of places where you might find squatters huddled over trash-can bonfires—broken windows, cracked sidewalks, walls covered with graffiti. I tried to imagine Thomas in this strange, not-quite-real place. I kept forgetting he had been a student at the Labyrinth; for a while, at least, this compound had been his home.

"There it is," Selene said.

"There what is?"

"The edge of the roof." She pointed straight ahead, and sure enough, the path we were on dead-ended at a concrete parapet.

"Crap," I said. "Now what?"

"Now we jump."

"You cannot be serious," I said in a low voice. It was too quiet up there on the roof, and there were so many places someone could hide. At any moment I expected a group of KES agents to swoop down on us like a flock of crows. "We'll be killed!"

"No, we won't." She climbed up onto the parapet; it made me so crazy nervous, I had to turn away. "Come and look."

"No thanks." I hid my face in my hands. "There has to be another option."

"Look," Selene commanded. I gritted my teeth and inched forward to glance over the edge. Directly below us, a river flowed. "We'll hit the water, not the ground. We'll be fine."

"It's like fifty feet!" I protested. "At this height, it could be water or Jell-O—it's still going to hurt."

"What's Jell-O?"

"Forget it," I said. "And forget jumping."

"Then forget everything else," Selene said. "This is your path out of the Labyrinth; this is your opportunity to do what you came here to do."

"You don't care what I came here to do," I replied hotly. "You care what *you* came here to do."

"I promise you, Sasha, they're the same thing," Selene said. "You know I'm not lying to you. The tether would tell you if I was."

"How can I be sure of that?" Selene was much better at controlling the tether than I was. She could've been using it to trick me.

"You can't be," she said. "But you are. The sooner you admit it to yourself, the sooner we can both get what we want." I thought of Juliana—what did she want now? Whatever it was, it was probably the opposite of what either Selene or I was hoping to achieve. We would have to force her to help us, which made me a little sick to my stomach. But when the time came, I wasn't sure that I'd care.

Selene held out her hand. "Do you trust me?"

I hesitated. *To trust other people is to surrender yourself to their will.*

"I guess so." I put my hand in hers. What other option did I have?

"Okay." She helped me up onto the wall. My stomach swooped as I stared down at the black water.

"We'll be all right if we do it correctly. The water is very deep here. We need to go in feet first, with our bodies as straight as possible. Can you remember that?"

"Yes," I said in a small voice. What the hell was I doing? I felt the darkness closing in again, but Selene fed me calm and confidence through the tether. I clutched her hand, squeezing it gratefully. At least if I had to do this, I wasn't alone.

"Ready?"

"Not at all."

"Too bad. It's time."

Before I could react, before I could pull back or rip my hand out of hers, we were in free fall. My entire body was paralyzed with fear. I closed my eyes as the water rushed up to greet me; just as I crashed into the river and got swallowed up by the waves, a thought fluttered through my brain, but it wasn't my own.

I'm dying.

PART II : THE SPARROW

GO THEN; THERE ARE OTHER WORLDS THAN THESE.

—STEPHEN KING, **THE GUNSLINGER**

I'M DYING, JULIANA THOUGHT.

The room was cold and damp. It smelled like dirt and mold and something fried, because it wasn't very far away from the place where they did all the cooking—if you could call it that. She had sampled plenty of Libertas cuisine over the past sixty days, and there was nothing she ached for more from her old life than the wonders of the Castle kitchen and its army of exemplary chefs. She kept wishing someone might come with a bit of soup for her aching throat, but it had been hours since anyone had last checked on her, and she doubted that they cared very much how she was faring.

So she wasn't actually dying. It just felt as if she were. This flu had been caught in her lungs for days, wracking her body with core-shaking coughs, fever, chills, and even a bit of vomiting, which, unfortunately, had happened when nobody was around to witness the splendor of her malady and consider that perhaps she might need some medical attention.

Maybe this was her cosmic punishment for all the wrong she'd done. Even her analogs had no interest in her welfare; from what she'd learned by carefully spying on them, all Selene and Sasha seemed to care about was using her to get what they wanted. Sasha, at least, she understood; if the roles were reversed, she doubted she'd have much compassion, either. But Juliana didn't know what to make of Selene. Part of her found comfort in knowing they were looking for her, but another part of her wanted nothing to do with them. At least Thomas was alive. Discovering that had been worth the exhaustion of living with three minds in her head.

It was a few days after the horrible incident in the Farnham prison when Juliana first found out about the third girl. Her nights had been mostly sleepless; she awoke multiple times from the same dream, one in which Thomas was shot and killed and she could do nothing to stop it. Her eyes would open, streaming with silent tears, and she would choke back a few guilty sobs before sinking back under and watching it all over again.

And then one night she had a different dream. Not a nightmare this time but instead like a film playing, a little scene that seemed like a blessing. It wasn't until she'd had several of these dreams in a row that she understood, and even then she didn't. But she knew they were coming from someplace other than her tired brain. She pushed them away as hard as she could, slamming her soul against them as if she were throwing her whole weight against a locked door. They stopped coming. But the door remained locked only if she wanted it to—she could control what she saw, and sometimes she chose to watch.

"I'm worried about that cough," Peter said. Juliana peered at him through the small opening between their cells, but there wasn't much to see, just one blue eye covered by dark curls.

A few weeks earlier, Juliana had awakened to the sound of scratching in the brick wall next to her cot. It kept happening, sometimes several times a day, for hours, and it made her skin crawl. She'd tried to move the cot, but it was bolted to the floor. She kept imagining rats scurrying inside the walls.

But then the wall began to move. Just one brick, rocking back and forth as if something were pushing it, trying to knock it free. Juliana tumbled out of bed and fled across the cell, getting as far away from the wall as possible. What kind of horrible, oversized vermin lived in this godforsaken hellhole? As if being a prisoner of Libertas weren't bad enough.

The brick slid out of the wall and fell onto her cot. "Is anyone there?" called a voice from the other side. "Can anyone hear me?"

His name was Peter, and she could tell from his faint accent that he was well educated, wealthy, and from Farnham. That wasn't surprising; Libertas operated in both countries, and Juliana wasn't even sure which one she was in. After what happened at Adastra Prison they'd taken her somewhere, but she'd been blindfolded the whole time. Peter claimed not to know why Libertas had taken him, but she guessed they were holding him for ransom. Every day she woke up thinking he would be gone, that someone would've paid Libertas for his safe return. But every day he remained, and soon she found herself dreading the morning when all that lay on the opposite side of the wall was an empty cell.

"They should bring you to a doctor," Peter fumed. "How long are you supposed to suffer like that?"

"Until I shuffle off this mortal coil, I guess," she said with a sigh, falling back against her pillow.

"At least you're well enough to quote Shakespeare," he teased. Juliana smiled.

"I used to hate Shakespeare, you know."

"What changed?"

"I'm not sure. I guess I'm starting to relate to his tragedies."

Peter laughed. "Me too. My brothers and I used to act out Hamlet *in the garden when we were little. We had this one tutor who forced us to memorize it."*

"What part did you play?" she asked. So he'd grown up with a tutor. That was interesting. Even she had gone to school until her father pulled her out that last year.

"Yorick's skull," Peter replied, in perfect deadpan.

She giggled. "I'm sure you were amazing."

"Sasha," Peter said after a long stretch of silence. It was strange to hear him call her that, but it was the name she'd given him. Her recent experiences had taught her to be cautious, knowing how big a bargaining chip her own identity had become, and Sasha's name was the first that sprang to mind. "If you could go anywhere right now, where would it be?"

It took her a long time to come up with an answer, and she wasn't even sure that the one she gave was true. "To my mother's house, I guess. It's the only place I think I would feel safe. What about you?"

"I'd go as far away from my mother as possible. Maybe somewhere with a beach. I like the ocean."

She didn't know what to say, so she just slipped her fingers through the small rectangular opening, reaching for Peter's in the darkness. It was a new sensation for her, this aching want in her chest, a desire to be close to someone. She'd spent her whole life pushing people away, even those who wanted to help her—even Thomas. There was a brief period when she thought she might be able to fall in love with him, but that was only because he was so obviously besotted with her, and spending time with him made her feel a tiny bit less lonely. It was different with Peter. Maybe their circumstances had created a false intimacy, but maybe what was developing between them was real.

Not that it mattered. She had no idea what was going to happen to her, but he would get out soon, go back to the fiancée he'd mentioned once, though she noticed he hadn't brought the girl up since their first conversation. And Juliana—well, she still hadn't given up hope that someday she would be free. But for the moment, what they had was enough.

She heard footsteps in the hallway outside her cell and the jangling of keys. "They're coming," she whispered, pushing the brick back into the wall and turning over in her cot, feigning sleep. She was terrified Libertas would find out that the two of them were communicating and take Peter away from her. She wasn't sure she would be able to put up with this much longer without his company.

The door to her cell slid open, and a dark figure stepped into the room. Light bathed the whole room in a sick white glow, but she kept her eyes shut.

"Wake up," a stern voice commanded. When she didn't move, the guard shook her. "Wake up. The Shepherd wants to see you. Now."

"What?" She sat up, yawning.

"Come on," the guard said, grabbing her arm and tugging her so hard she tumbled out of bed onto the cold concrete floor.

"Don't you dare touch me," she growled, ripping her arm out of his grip.

"I don't take orders from you," he spat, hauling her to her feet.

"I said don't touch me!" she shouted, planting her palms on his chest and giving him a hard shove. A great burst of light shot out of her hands, and the guard went flying across the room. He slammed into the wall and slumped to the ground; his head flopped over like a flower with a broken stem, and he fell still.

"Oh my God," Juliana whispered. She hurried over and felt for a pulse; he was still alive, for now. She stared at her hands in shock; they were glowing. What was happening to her?

A thought cut through the panic in her head: This is my chance. She rifled through the guard's pockets and found his keys; there was a gun tucked into the waistband of his pants, and she took that, too. She knew how to use a gun—Thomas had taught her. He was the only bodyguard who was willing to show her how to defend herself in case she got into the kind of trouble the KES couldn't get her out of. It was one of the reasons she'd decided to trust him; he didn't think he was a god, incapable of failure, despite the fact that he made her feel safer than all the rest of them put together.

She fumbled with the keys, testing them on the lock to find the one that opened the door. When one turned, she slid the door open as *quietly as she could; someone had probably heard the commotion, and it was only chance that no one had come yet. Once she was out, she went to Peter's cell. If she was getting out of this place, she was taking him with her.*

He was near the door when she yanked it open, but all she could make out at first was the shape of him: medium height, lean build, and long, elegant fingers, the only part of him she'd ever touched. She glanced at her own hands; they weren't glowing anymore, and she wondered if she'd imagined it. But the unconscious Libertas guard in her cell—him she had not imagined.

"Peter, come on, we have to—" The words died in her throat when she got her first real look at him.

"Juli?"

"Prince Callum." She managed to get his name out, but that was it. Let it never be said that the universe didn't have a sense of humor. The boy she'd spent the last few weeks getting to know, the one she'd foolishly believed she was falling for against all her better instincts—he wasn't just some wealthy kid from Farnham who'd had the bad luck to be caught up in Libertas's web. He was a prince of Farnham, her own fiancé.

Or he had been. Who knew what they were to each other now?

"God, Juli!" He drew her in for a tight hug. She stiffened, but he did not let her go, and she relaxed in his arms, wrapping her own around his waist and burying her face in his shoulder. It felt so good to be held. Even in her long-ago life it hadn't happened very often. Don't let go, she thought, but she was too proud to say the words out loud.

"I'm so sorry," he murmured into her hair, her ugly hair with its bad dye job and grown-out roots. "I should have known it was you. I should've recognized your voice, but I—"

"It's okay," she said. Tears pricked the back of her eyes. It wasn't her he thought he was reuniting with; it was Sasha. She felt an

overwhelming desire to tell him everything. It was the right thing to do. But she couldn't even begin to formulate an explanation.

And then he kissed her. A real, true, slow, deep kiss that at first only served as a painful reminder that he'd done this before, with a girl who looked just like her but wasn't. But she sank into it, letting everything she'd felt for him as Peter guide her forward. It wasn't as though she'd never been kissed before. She'd even kissed Thomas once, just to see how it would feel. But nothing compared to this. Peter or Callum, it didn't matter. She was kissing the boy who made her happy. Thinking about anything else seemed like a waste of time.

Callum smiled. "Since when are you a blonde?"

"Uh, they dyed it when I got here," Juliana said. "I don't know why." It might not matter to her what his name was, but it would certainly matter to him that she wasn't the same girl he'd met at the Castle. She wasn't going to let the General's games be the reason she lost him. She was going to have to pretend to be Sasha pretending to be her.

"What happened?" Callum asked. "How did you escape your cell?"

"I'll tell you later. First we have to find a way out of here." She took the gun out of her waistband.

"Where'd you get that?"

"Same guard I took the keys from. Come on." She took his hand and tugged him forward. She didn't want to waste another second in this hopeless, haunted place.

They crept down the dim, cold stone hallway, trying to make as little noise as possible. She heard footsteps and shoved Callum back against the wall. An unfamiliar young guard strolled by, whistling as he made his rounds. Juliana pressed the muzzle of the gun against his temple before he could react. Callum tensed beside her, but she knew what she was doing. Thomas had trained her well.

"Put your hands up," Juliana commanded. She could see his fin-

gers inching their way toward the radio at his belt. "You're going to show us the way out of here."

"Be careful with the gun, princess," the guard said. There was a tremor in his voice that told her he was new and unhardened. It was her lucky day.

"I won't hurt you," she told him. "If you help us."

The guard pointed straight ahead. "This way."

He led them down a series of empty passageways; it was still the middle of the night, and nobody was around. It wasn't the patrols that worried her; it was whomever the Shepherd would send when she didn't show up as he'd commanded. But they met no one. Finally, the guard stopped in front of a metal door that boasted the ten stars of the Libertas insignia. He pressed the stars in a specific order, and the door swung open, revealing a dark hall.

"Great," Juliana said. "Thanks." Then she swung the handle of the gun at his head, hitting him just hard enough to knock him unconscious. He dropped to the floor. She looked down at him and sighed.

"Juli," Callum said in disbelief. "You just coldcocked that guy."

"Yeah," she said, stepping over the man's limp body. "I think that's what my deportment instructor would call 'behavior unbecoming of a lady.'"

He let out a strangled laugh. "No doubt."

"What was I supposed to do? We skipped the 'What to Do If You're Being Held Against Your Will and Get the Chance to Escape' chapter of the princess manual." She hazarded a smile. "Do you think I'm terrible?"

"No," he said, running his fingers through his hair and staring down at the unconscious guard. "I'm impressed. And a little embarrassed."

"Why?"

He shrugged sheepishly. "I should be the one protecting you."

"Oh, don't be stupid," she said. A proud flush colored her cheeks. She liked how he was looking at her, as if she were strong and fearless. She'd been waiting forever for someone to look at her like that. "I promise, you can have the next one. Come on. Let's get out of here before someone realizes we're gone."

THOMAS AT THE LABYRINTH

"They what?" the General roared.

"They escaped," Adele said. Thomas admired the way she kept her fear of the General out of her voice. It had taken him years to learn how to do that. He struggled to keep a smile off his face—*they'd escaped*. Sasha had escaped. Maybe his suspicion of Selene had been wrong; she clearly knew what she was doing.

"You," the General snapped, turning his attention to Thomas. "Was this your doing?"

"No," Thomas said. "I haven't spoken to either of them outside your presence since they arrived here." And nobody could prove that he had. As far as the General knew, his feelings for Sasha were gone, replaced by a renewed sense of loyalty to the KES.

The General's jaw tightened. It was rare to see him so worked up. Things really were changing in Aurora. The General was starting to worry.

"We've deployed the search teams," Thomas continued. The General glanced at Adele, and she nodded.

"They can't have gotten far on foot, and the one from Earth

is wearing an anchor with a GPS tag. We'll catch up to them in no time."

"No. Call off the search."

"Sir?" Thomas wasn't sure what was happening. The General wasn't going to let Sasha and Selene escape—not now, and not ever. He considered them property—*his* property—and the General relinquished nothing without a fight. So what was he playing at?

"You want us to stop looking?" Adele narrowed her eyes. "But they'll get away."

"I know that," the General barked. "You don't catch the fox by scouring the countryside, hoping for a glimpse of its tail. You give the hounds the scent and follow their lead. I would bet my life that those girls are looking for Juliana, and so are we. They obviously think they know what they're doing. Let them take us to the princess. Then we'll have all three of them."

Thomas took a deep breath. He needed the KES out of the hunt altogether. He already had a plan for how to send them off course. When he was in the Labyrinth basement, he'd reactivated the anchor and tossed it in the trash compactor. The refuse truck kept a precise schedule, and it had left the compound just before lockdown. If the KES followed the anchor, it would take them straight to the dump.

"Sir, I'm concerned that you're underestimating them, especially the one called Selene," Adele said. "She brought down the power in three quadrants of the Labyrinth, and we still haven't figured out how. She knew how to navigate the compound, and she found a way out. She's smarter than she seems."

"I'm perfectly aware of that," the General said. He looked pointedly at Thomas. "The one called Sasha trusts Agent Mayhew. She thinks she's in *love* with him. So let's see what she's willing to do for him. Mayhew, put together a team—take whoever you think can get the job done—then find those girls and convince them you're on their side. Nguyen will be your second. Use all the resources of this agency to help find Juliana, then bring all three of them to me."

Thomas knew how it would look if he protested, but this was just about the worst situation he could be in. He'd hoped to slip out of the Labyrinth to meet up with one of the search teams, then find Sasha at the Almond train station and take it from there. He'd spent the whole night coming up with a strategy. Having a team along was going to completely mess that up. Choosing the right people would be crucial. The only variable was Adele. Why had she let Selene and Sasha get away when her orders were to seize them on sight? He and Adele had been close friends once, but he was starting to wonder how well he really knew her. If Adele had her own agenda, it would only make things that much harder.

"As of this moment, this is a shadow mission," the General said. "Prepare to leave immediately, tell no one but your team the particulars of your assignment, and do not fail."

"Yes, sir."

"I'm warning you, Thomas," the General said, staring him down with rage in his eyes. "If you so much as think about letting those girls go, I will deploy an exterminator to hunt Miss Lawson down and get rid of her once and for all. Do you understand me?"

"Yes, sir." His voice was as taut as a steel cable. There was no doubt in his mind that the General was telling the truth. Exterminators were assassins on the KES payroll; if the General sent one after Sasha, Thomas wouldn't be able to protect her for long. Anger boiled up inside him, and he had to clench his jaw to keep from saying something he would regret, dig his nails into the flesh of his palms to keep from lashing out at the General with his fists.

When Thomas had been brought back to the Labyrinth and all seemed forgiven, he'd thought that maybe, just *maybe*, he could stay with the KES. That maybe he still had the opportunity to do some good within the organization that had once been his home. But now he saw that it was impossible. The father he'd feared but always respected was gone, replaced by this cruel tyrant he barely recognized. If the UCC was going to survive, the General had to go.

NINE

The water was freezing cold and impossibly dark. When we landed, Selene's hand was ripped from mine and I couldn't see her anywhere. I couldn't even tell which way was up—everything looked the same, unending blackness in all directions. My lungs were pinching, desperate for air, but I kept my mouth shut and willed myself not to panic.

Selene? A burst of green rippled through the tether as her head broke the surface and she took a huge gulp of air. My body relaxed, as if it had been me, and when she said, *Use the bond,* I knew what she meant. I imagined it as a glistening towrope stretching from my mind to hers. I followed it upward, trusting it, and after what felt like decades of swimming I felt a hand grab the collar of my shirt and yank me up the last few feet.

I gasped, sucking in air as fast as I could. Selene bobbed next to me. "Don't overdo it. You'll make yourself sick."

"What do we do now?" The water was carrying us swiftly downstream. I looked back in the direction we'd come from, but I couldn't even see the Labyrinth in the distance.

"We need to swim against the current and get to the shore. Can you do that?"

I'd fallen almost fifty feet into a river and hadn't died—I could do anything, or at least I felt as if I could. We hauled ourselves out of the river and collapsed, soaked and sputtering, onto the muddy bank. I wrapped my arms around my body for warmth; my teeth rattled together like dice in a cup. Selene shivered next to me.

"Juliana," Selene said after a few minutes of silence. "She found the power."

"I know." I'd seen and felt everything about her escape through the tether, including Callum. The guilt was sharp; it ate away at me—guilt for lying to him, guilt for getting him involved in all of this madness. I'd abandoned him in Farnham, or maybe he'd abandoned me. It was all so messy. I was afraid for him—and not just for his life. Callum was the last person in the world who deserved to have his heart broken, and I worried that, between the two of us, Juliana and I would shatter it to pieces. "She's running."

"That's good. It will make her easier to find." Selene stood up and wiped her hands on her pants. "Have you noticed that our clothes are almost dry?"

"Water-resistant fabric, I guess." I let her help me to my feet. Leave it to the KES to think of pretty much everything.

We followed Thomas's instructions, fleeing to the forest and following the river south. The sun rose, and the light streamed through the trees, casting everything in a verdant glow that reminded me of Selene's presence on the tether. We picked our way through the underbrush, careful to stay beneath the thickest parts of the canopy. I could hear the sound of helicopters overhead; it almost drowned out the rush of the river.

"Do you sense her, Sasha?" Selene asked. "Juliana, I mean."

"Sort of." Juliana's mind was a faint red glow at the horizon of our shared mind space. "Can she hear us?" I called her name over the tether, but there was no response.

"It's no use," Selene said, staring off into the distance. The forest seemed endless. It was hard to believe we would ever reach Almond, or the train station, or Thomas. "She's not listening."

"You mean we have a choice?"

"Of course you have a choice. You always have a choice."

Not in my experience. "So what was that thing you said about destiny?"

"You always have a destiny, too," Selene said. "You can either accept it or turn away from it, but it's going to be there whether you like it or not. Fate is an arrow that flies straight and true. It pierces every obstacle it encounters and hits its mark every time." She sat down on a fallen tree stump and rubbed her ankle. Thomas hadn't given us shoes, so while I was in my Converse, she was wearing a pair of delicate silver sandals with thin straps. They must've been hell to walk in.

I sat down beside her. "I didn't used to believe in fate."

"But you do now," Selene said, with as much certainty as I felt. She plucked Callum's wet, limp drawing out of my pocket and spread it across her lap. I tried to take it back, but she fended me off. "The prince drew this before he met you, and he gave it to you as a symbol of the future. And then, in another world entirely, you come across the same door, which led you back to where you started. To me. To her. To the boy you love. Of all of us, you have the most to gain from believing in fate." Selene handed the drawing back. I couldn't explain it, but I knew it was a piece of a much larger puzzle, just waiting for me to put it together. Sort of like the tether itself. Whether I liked it or not, the tether was proving to be very useful, and we'd barely even started our search for Juliana. Maybe Selene was right: maybe we needed it more than I thought. "And what about you? What do you have to gain from believing in fate?"

"A new world for me and my people. A bright and beautiful future . . . I hope." She rose to her feet.

I followed her deeper into the woods, making sure to keep one ear out for the sound of the river. The sun was climbing higher into the sky, and I was starting to fear we wouldn't make it to the train in time. The KES were good at tracking things down; it was only a matter of time before they found us. "You hope?"

"Taiga looked just like this once," Selene said, looking up at the thick canopy. "Miles of forest, as far as the eye could see. The planet was covered with trees. We took care of them, and they took care of us; we lived in them. We built our cities in their branches. Or maybe I should say *they* did. It was a long time ago, way before I was even born. If you want, I can show you."

"How?"

"Close your eyes." I did as she said and tried to make my mind blank, to create some space for Selene's show-and-tell. I felt a slight tingle at the back of my brain, a warning that someone else's psyche was bleeding through, and I resisted the urge to push her away.

The darkness behind my eyes disappeared, and I was thrust into a lush, green landscape, a beautiful wooded glade in the middle of an expansive forest. Sunshine dribbled through the emerald canopy and sprinkled my skin with light spots like confetti. Except I wasn't me. I could tell immediately, though I couldn't explain why. I glanced around the glade as if looking for something, or someone, and then began moving toward a small set of stairs that led up to a wide wooden boardwalk. Everything had a strange, translucent quality to it.

I'm sorry, Selene said. *These aren't my memories. They've been passed down to me from previous generations. They're very old and worn out.*

What do you mean, these memories are old?

Wait, she instructed. *There's more to see.*

I strolled along the boardwalk; a soft, cool breeze tickled my throat. The wooden road wove through the forest, and after a while I began to see shops on either side, peddling shoes and pots for cooking. We passed a doctor's office and a seamstress, a jeweler and butcher shop and bakery. All the structures were rustic looking, as if they'd been constructed out of the trunks of the very trees that surrounded them—or grown organically out of the soil themselves. The farther we went, the more I saw, except now I was looking at houses not just at the edges of the boardwalk but built up high into the trees, with bridges made of wood and rope strung between platforms that rested inside cradled branches.

What is this place?

My planet, Selene told me. *Taiga. Or, rather, a city on Taiga called New Athens. It corresponds exactly with the Chicago of your world and the Tattered City of this one.*

It's beautiful, I told her. *You must love living there.*

It was very beautiful, yes.

Was? I'd emerged from the thicker parts of the forest to an even wider boardwalk, which, according to a sign, was called Center Walk. It was crowded, and everyone seemed to be carrying some kind of basket or canvas satchel filled to the brim with fruit and fabric and other things. It was market day, and all along Center Walk temporary stalls were set up, shopkeepers selling their wares to the passersby.

There's a reason why these memories are so faded, Selene said. *They're from a hundred years ago, when Taiga was like this all over—healthy and green, covered in woods and rain forests. It was a very wet planet, but these memories are from summer.*

I caught a sliver of the sun just barely hidden by the canopy. Honey-colored rays of light slid over the faces of the people on Center Walk. *What happened?*

An asteroid called Typhos, Selene said. I blinked in surprise, catching a glimpse of her face before my eyes closed again. *When it struck, the planet became unlivable overnight.*

I glanced around at the memory, which was rippling and receding. *If this was what Taiga looked like a hundred years ago, then what does it look like now?*

Like this. She pushed another memory into my head. This one was sharper, and I knew it belonged to Selene. I was standing in front of a window, hand pressed against the glass—I recognized the shape of the fingers as my own.

On the other side of the glass, which appeared to be several inches thick, was a vast wasteland of gray nothingness. The ground was covered in mounds of ash, and the few trees still left standing had withered into cracked and broken sticks pointed straight up at the sky. I could see the round ball of the sun high above me, glowing like a dying ember behind a scrim of dust. Nothing seemed to be alive or moving out there. It was just as horrifying as every postapocalyptic novel and movie I'd ever seen had said it would be.

"Now there's almost nothing left," Selene told me. Her sadness coated the tether like oil. I opened my eyes, and her memories fluttered away. "The sky was blackened with soot. Everything died. Everything except my people. We're the only living things that remain."

"Why were they spared?" I tried to imagine Earth as desolate as Taiga—no life, no sun, no flowers or animals. The thought of it opened up a black hole inside me. I understood what it was Selene was searching for, what she would sacrifice anything to obtain: a safe, true home. Just like me. Maybe we weren't so different after all.

"At the time of the impact, my society—Apeiron—lived separately from other people on Taiga, in a glass-and-steel compound at the edge of New Athens. We call it Home. When Typhos came, we hid within its walls and waited."

"For what?" It didn't seem like there was any coming back from that kind of destruction.

"For the prophecy that would tell us how to bring Taiga back to life," Selene said. "We have a sacred text called Kairos. It looks like an indecipherable jumble of numbers, but it's really a mathematical code. If you solve the code, you find the truth. Prophecies, all of which have come to pass in one form or another. Kairos told us about Typhos. That's how we knew to gather supplies and build Home. It kept us alive for a century, but our resources are dwindling, and Home won't be able to support us for much longer. If we don't rescue Taiga, my people . . . they'll die, Sasha. Every last one of them."

"How do you know all this?" I asked.

"It's my job to translate Kairos's prophecies." There was a touch of pride in her voice. "They call me Korydallos. It's the title that we give our oracle. I have a mathematician, Leonid, who solves the code. Then I read the text and draw conclusions. That's where listening comes in. The universe helps guide me to the proper interpretation."

"And you've been doing this for how long?" She seemed too young to be a prophet. Juliana was too young to rule a country. And I was too young to be trekking through a parallel world. Perhaps it wasn't age but what you were capable of, the lengths to which you were willing to go to get what you wanted, that mattered most. Still, it sounded like the beginning of a very bad joke: a princess, an oracle, and a completely normal teenager walk into a bar. . . .

"When I was twelve, I was taken from the crèche and apprenticed to the previous Korydallos. Her name was Corinna, and she taught me everything I know. When she died, I became the new Korydallos. That's how the position is passed down, generation to generation."

Selene held aside a tree branch for me. The ground was padded with moss and moist dirt, and the air smelled like fresh, growing things. The forest was so calm and peaceful this early in the morning. Birds chirped at each other from their nests, and every once in a while we'd hear a little woodland creature rustling in some nearby bushes. If this was what Taiga had been like before the asteroid hit, no wonder Selene was so desperate to get it back.

"What's the crèche?"

"I know I said I would answer all of your questions, but you have a *lot* of questions."

I shrugged. She sighed. "We don't have families in the traditional sense. Not like here or in your world. Women are inseminated, and children are raised in a nursery—the crèche—by people whose job it is to take care of them. Apeiron is mother, father, partner to us all, and we are brothers and sisters to each other. When you turn twelve, you are sorted into one of two Pillars of Apeiron: the Learners or the Listeners. The Listeners are people of spirit; they serve as nurses, cooks, artists, cloth makers, and priests, among other things. The Learners are people of knowledge: engineers, mathematicians, lawmakers, teachers, and so on. You belong to your Pillar and to Apeiron as a whole. That is what family means to us."

"Let me guess," I said. "You're a Listener."

"You could say I'm the leader of the Listeners," she said. "The Learners have leaders as well. We work together to ensure the safety and well-being of our people."

"Does your position have anything to do with why you know how to do the . . . the thing? With your hands?" I didn't know how to describe it. Selene nodded. Whatever that light was, that *power,* she could wield it, and so could I. I just needed her to teach me how.

"It comes from the bond," Selene said. "Or—what did your scientist friend call it?"

"The tether."

"The tether. It's made of energy, as you know. When you opened that door to Juliana's mind back on the roof of that tower, you activated our ability to release it, to use it as a tool."

"Or wield it as a weapon."

"All tools are weapons in the hands of the wrong people," Selene said. "I suspected we had the ability before I came here, but it wasn't until we were in the same universe that it became possible to actually use it. It's part of our destiny, Sasha. The power is going to help us save Taiga. And it's going to give you what you came here for."

Dr. March said we had to release the energy from the tether in such a volume that the tether itself couldn't handle it. As unsettling as this new, strange power was, knowing it existed, that we could control it, came as a relief. I was getting closer to my goal with every step. Now it was time to tackle the next problem: finding Juliana. But we were going to need the tether to do that. The irony wasn't lost on me.

"Okay, one last question." Selene raised her eyebrows. "One more, and I swear I'm done."

"All right," she said. "One last question."

"What did the prophecy say?"

A broad smile spread across Selene's face. She'd been waiting for me to ask. "It said, 'And on that day, when the sparrow, the starling, and the lark fly together, it shall bring about
the new world, and all that was once will be again.'"

"The sparrow, the starling, and the lark?"

"Now do you see?"

The sparrow was Juliana: it was her KES code name. I was
the starling, from Operation Starling, the name of Thomas's
mission to fetch me from Earth. "I see how Juliana and I are
the sparrow and the starling, but what makes you the lark?"

"*Korydallos* means 'lark' in Greek," Selene said. She pointed
to a break in the trees straight ahead of us. "What's that?"

"It's a road." It was a narrow country highway, and on the
opposite side a small clapboard building stood watch over
a set of train tracks. My heart started to beat faster. We approached the road, careful to stay in the shadow of the trees.
According to the clock on the station building, it was later
than I thought: ten-thirty. There was no real platform, just a
long slab of concrete. The building was unattended and locked
up tight. The place looked almost haunted to me, a relic from
a bygone era. There was an enormous bronze plaque affixed
to the building's left side, facing the tracks, but I was too far
away to read what it said. There was nothing else around, and
there were definitely no people. Was this all that remained
of Almond, or all that had ever been there in the first place?

"Thomas is meeting us here. We're getting the ten-fifty-
one train to . . ." I'd never asked Thomas where the train was
heading. I didn't even know if it would take us in the right
direction, and I realized we had no money to pay for tickets.
If Thomas wasn't there when the train arrived as planned, we
were pretty much screwed.

"Money?" Selene asked. When we finally tracked Juli-

124

ana down, I was going to have to get her to teach me how to keep Selene's mind at a distance. It was frustrating how much better my analogs were at controlling the tether than I was. Juliana had even managed to use the power without any help—by accident, but still. And she was doing an incredible job of shutting us both out, which never ceased to frustrate me. This would all be so much easier if she would just let us in.

"Pieces of paper and little bits of metal that you use to pay for stuff."

"Oh," she said. "You mean currency."

"Sure. You don't have that in Taiga?"

"No, we don't need it. At Home we all contribute and take whatever we need. But I've read about currency," Selene said. "I understand how it works."

Maybe Selene understood the principle, but she didn't know anything about the UCC's money, and neither did I. I had no idea what it looked like or was called or was worth, and I could only guess where we could get some, other than stealing from people, which wasn't really an option, not least because there *were* no people in Almond.

"Well, we don't have any, so I figure we'll get about one station, maybe two, before the conductor asks us for tickets and we have to tell him we don't have them," I said.

"What happens then?"

"Best-case scenario, they kick us off the train at the next station. Worst case, they hand us over to the KES, who will probably have caught up with us by then." I sighed and sank down onto the grass. "I really hope Thomas shows up."

More than anything, I just wanted to see his face again. We'd had so little time together since I came through the tandem, and I was always half-afraid, no matter how many times I told myself *it was real,* that everything that had happened to me in the past month and a half had been a dream.

"He will," Selene said, patting my shoulder.

"You know that for a fact?" She shook her head. "I thought you could see the future."

"I'm an oracle," she said, "not a psychic. There's a difference. *But* I've seen the way he looks at you, and I have a feeling he would do whatever it takes to keep his promise. You have to have faith in him, Sasha. Just as you have to have faith in me."

Ten minutes passed, and there was still no sign of Thomas. I was afraid the train would come and go without us or bypass the station altogether if there was no one on the platform.

"Maybe he's waiting for us," I said, standing up and brushing the dirt off the back of my thighs. "We should go over there."

"It's very open," Selene said. "What if someone sees?"

"I think we'll just have to risk it."

Selene grabbed my arm. "This is the part where I trust you."

I nodded. "Let's go."

We ventured down to the road and started to cross. It wasn't until I reached the other side and began picking my way over the train tracks that I noticed Selene wasn't beside me. I turned around to see her standing stock-still in the middle of the road as an enormous truck bore down on her. There was terror etched across her face; she'd never seen a moving vehicle before. Fear lanced through me—*Selene's* fear. I shouted at her to run, but she remained frozen on the asphalt. She shut her eyes and braced herself for impact as the truck driver blew his horn in a desperate, earsplitting staccato. I rushed into the road and seized her hand, yanking her into my arms and shoving her off the road onto the grass.

"What are you doing?" I demanded. Selene's face was a blank mask of shock. "You could've been killed!"

"What *was* that thing?" she asked, her voice trembling. The tether shook and swayed.

"You don't have trucks on Taiga?"

"We don't even have *roads*."

I sighed. "You have to be careful. You're lucky he didn't hit you."

I pulled her to her feet. The clock read ten-forty-seven: we had only four minutes until the train arrived, and there was no sign at all of Thomas.

"Come on," I said. "Let's get over to the platform. The train is almost here."

TEN

The train was exactly on time. I shielded my eyes, glancing down the tracks, and caught the glimmer of its headlights in the distance. Bells sounded, signaling its arrival. I couldn't shake the certainty that Thomas wasn't coming. It was hard, knowing what had happened to him in Farnham, not to worry. I kept hoping to see his familiar shape emerging from the shadows of the surrounding forest, and when it didn't, my mind went to a dark place. If Selene noticed, she didn't say anything; she seemed miles away. Listening. The fear had drained out of her, and she was as placid and determined as ever. The tether swung as if pushed along by a light breeze.

"What's this?" Selene was standing in front of the bronze plaque, which carried the Seal of the Commonwealth—I recognized it from my time in the Castle.

"Some kind of commemoration?" I ran my fingers over the raised words. *Here in the city of Almond, King's Dominion of New York, the fathers of the Commonwealth met for the first time to discuss the possibilities of a Second Revolution against the British Empire.* I looked around, half expecting an entire town to have sprung up around us like Brigadoon, but it was just Selene and I and the lonely station shack. If this town was such an important historical landmark, where had the rest of it gone?

"Revolution," Selene said, as if trying the word out for the very first time. *There are barbarians who wage war with each other, who kill each other over nothing,* she thought.

"What?" But she hadn't been talking to me—I'd been *overhearing* her. She shot me a look of surprise, then turned away. I refocused my attention on the approaching train.

I almost didn't notice the big black utility vehicles speeding toward us from the opposite direction. At first I thought it was Thomas coming to meet us, but then another car emerged: if it was him, he wasn't alone. They came to a stop in the middle of the highway just as the train pulled into the station. I saw KES agents pouring onto the asphalt through the gaps between train cars, and I grabbed Selene's arm.

"They're here," I told her. The tether pitched like a boat in a storm, and I felt I was going to be sick.

The train doors opened, and we clambered up the steps. I fell into one of the seats and pressed my face to the tinted window. The agents swarmed the road below us, but there was no way they were going to get around the train to the other side before it pulled out of the station. I squinted, trying to make out Thomas's face, but I didn't see him. I did, however, spy the girl who'd pretended not to see us in the Labyrinth: Adele. She gave a group of agents some furious commands, and they fanned out, running in all directions. She'd protected us once, but that didn't mean she was going to do it again. She certainly *looked* as if she was trying to find us. Panic rose in my throat, but then the train's breaks released with a huff and we began to move.

"We made it," Selene whispered, taking the seat next to me. "What now?"

I caught my reflection in the window and was reminded, in a way that came as a shock, exactly what—and *who*—I looked like. Who *we* looked like. Forget money or tickets; our appearance was our biggest problem. We couldn't let the conductor or any other passengers see our faces. One girl with a resemblance to the crown princess might be able to get away with it by hiding behind her hair or something, but two? That Selene and I looked exactly alike already made us conspicuous, never mind the fact that we were dead ringers for Juliana.

Luckily, the few passengers in the car we'd boarded were so busy watching the KES agents recede into the distance and murmuring to each other about what was going on that they hadn't noticed us yet, but I didn't expect things would stay that way. Through the glass door that separated the car we were in from the one behind it, I could see the conductor threading his way through the aisle, picking up tickets, passing them through a scanner, and counting out change.

We have to hide, I told Selene.

Where?

There was a bathroom right below the stairs that led to the train's upper level. It looked big enough to fit us both. *There.* She slipped out of the seat. *Be careful,* I warned her. *Don't make it too obvious or people will notice.*

But nobody seemed to be paying any attention. After the commotion at Almond, they'd all turned back to what they were doing: reading or dozing or playing with handheld gadgets.

Selene slipped into the lavatory first, and I followed, sliding the door closed and taking care not to lock it in case that triggered something that labeled it occupied. Besides, a lock wasn't going to do us much good anyway if someone was trying to get at us. We were cornered. I held my breath, hoping there was something—the universe, maybe, or destiny, or just plain old dumb luck—that would keep us from being discovered.

They're gone, Selene said after minutes had passed. I inched the door open a crack to check if the coast was clear.

Okay, I said. *Let's get out of here before someone actually wants to use this thing.*

The train continued to fill with more passengers. Selene was too busy marveling at the train to worry—she kept asking me questions over the tether about how it worked, as if I had any idea. I was freaked out. Eventually the conductors were going to come around again to collect tickets from the people who'd gotten on at the last couple of stations, and we couldn't hide in the bathroom every single time they walked through the cabins. The sun climbed in the sky, and with each passing minute I felt more and more exposed.

I tried to focus my mind, to listen the way Selene did, but I couldn't hear anything besides the pounding of my own heart and the rumble of the train tracks beneath our feet. The man sitting in front of us was reading a newspaper, the *Columbia City Eagle,* and I glimpsed the main headline over his shoulder: "Conflict Escalates in Farnham-UCC Borderlands."

The photograph accompanying the article was of a bombed-out neighborhood, structures that had once been houses reduced to cinders and bones. In the corner of the picture I could see the tattered remains of a Farnham flag: a black phoenix rising on a crimson background. I swallowed back bile. This was the General's great war, the culmination of decades of planning, but it wasn't his only war. Another would be fought on a cosmic battlefield, and Selene and I were directly in the line of fire. Or were we warriors?

The train lurched, and a woman passing through the aisle slammed into me, dropping her purse and scattering the contents. "Sorry!" she said, stooping to pick everything up. I tried to help her, hiding behind my long hair so that she wouldn't recognize me—I just wanted her *gone*, as quickly as possible—but when I sat up to hand her a few of the fallen items, I glanced toward the car door and noticed a figure dressed in black barreling through the forward compartment. It was Adele, with two other agents, both guys: a stocky Native American boy whose dark eyes darted around like search-and-destroy missiles, and a tall, Eastern European–looking dude wearing a black knit cap and sunglasses. If they saw us, we were toast.

I yanked Selene out of the seat, slipping past the woman and knocking her purse to the ground again. "Sorry!" I called as I dragged Selene past the bathroom and through the car doors. The ground sped past below us. The wind was loud in my ears.

"What's wrong?" Selene asked. The tether shivered. We'd been on the run only a few hours, and already we'd almost been caught more than once. I wasn't sure how long I could keep this up, but the only thing that made sense to me was to keep moving. It was a coping mechanism my therapist had taught me: to deal with crippling anxiety, don't try to imagine too far into the future, just make one decision at a time. It wasn't advanced game theory or anything, but it kind of helped. Once I chose to do something, I felt much more calm.

The KES. They're on the train, and they're coming. We have to move.

The train is slowing down, Selene said in alarm. We were approaching another station. Its name flashed up on the digital display in the car in front of us: WARREN'S RUN. I yanked open the door, and we tumbled through it. I was afraid the commotion would make people look up, and I imagined their eyes locking on us, minds scrolling through a gallery of familiar faces until they realized who we were. But even though people did glance up, their eyes sort of slid over us—they were looking to look, not to find. After all, there was almost nothing more unlikely than the princess of their country riding public transportation.

Okay, I thought. *New plan. We get off here and find a place to hide. We don't really know where we're going anyway. We need to figure out where Juliana is. Maybe we can work on that while we come up with a new plan.*

It was too much pressure, the way Selene was blindly following my lead, as if I had any clue as to what I was doing or what a new plan even looked like.

Let's keep moving, I said. The closer we got to the station and the more we slowed, the better I felt, but just barely. We hurried through the next car and then the next, Adele and her two agents one step behind us. I wondered why they didn't give chase—they would catch us if they did.

The train screeched to a stop in the station. We hopped off as soon as the doors opened; I was relieved to find this station quite a bit more packed, though it didn't seem any larger or better kept than the one at Almond. I knew from experience that it was easier to get away when you used a crowd as cover. I thought we'd nearly made it, but then I heard someone shout "Stop!"

I took off down the platform at a dead sprint, with Selene at my heels. In the maelstrom of people boarding and getting off the train, we were able to get a good head start. I pushed through the throng, threading through the thicket of bodies like a needle. Selene kept pace with me; she was so close I could hear her breaths coming hard and fast. I threw a glance behind me to see if we'd lost the KES agents, but they were gaining on us. I focused on the steps that led down to the street, thinking if we could just make it that far, we could get away clean, lose ourselves in Warren's Run.

I was so busy staring at the ground, at the place where the platform gave way to stairs, that I didn't notice the person standing directly in front of me until I barreled into him. He threw his arms around me, pinning mine to my sides, and shoved me into the shadows beneath the eaves of the station building. I fought back, thrashing and clawing at him as best I could with my hands restrained. I didn't even think to look at his face.

"Sasha," Thomas panted in frustration. "*Stop*. It's me."

THOMAS AT WARREN'S RUN

I have to find her. The refrain kept repeating through Thomas's head. He'd lost her once; he wouldn't lose her again. Not after she'd come back, whole and unharmed—come back for *him*. He knew it was rash—foolish, even—to believe that what was between them could withstand the brutal machinations of the multiverse, but he was committed to his folly, and he would find her.

It had been a shock to find her in the portal room, and he remembered the way his throat ached to say her name, the way his heart beat at his chest like a trapped bird when he saw her face. He felt the same way now, but just as before, he couldn't show her or say a word. Adele and the others—Tim and Sergei, Cora and Navin—they were his friends, but they were KES first, and they would expect him to be, too.

And then there was the one who was *not* his friend. Hector Rockaway—Rocko, as they'd called him at the Academy—had been brought along on this shadow mission, too, and Thomas was pretty sure he knew why. *He probably wet himself when they told him,* Thomas thought. Rocko had hated him ever since they were new recruits, resented him for being the General's son, and he wouldn't hesitate to turn Thomas in for any misstep whatsoever. Rocko was the only KES agent on the mission who hadn't been part of Thomas's extraction. *If they'd brought him along, I'd have had a bullet in my brain weeks ago.*

"Sasha, stop. It's me." Sasha relaxed at the sound of his voice, and she looked up at him, close to tears with relief. He set his mouth in a grim, straight line and gave a small shake of his head; her expression sobered, but he could still see her lips curling a fraction at the ends.

He held her a second or two longer than he should have, relishing her nearness, her solidity; the rise and fall of her chest against his told him that she was real, something he still hadn't quite wrapped his head around. He shut his eyes against the vision of her crawling on the floor in pain, begging for his help, the terrible, untrue, but visceral things he had experienced in prison. He couldn't ignore the gut-twisting feeling that it wasn't a hallucination but a premonition, that the time would come when it would be as real as she was now and that even then he wouldn't be able to save her.

Behind him, Adele cleared her throat. He turned to see her, Tim, Sergei, and Selene all staring at them. He released Sasha and stepped away; Selene went to Sasha's side, as if drawn to her by a magnetic force, and took her hand. A moment ago, it had been him and Sasha against the rest of the world. Now, again, it was the two of them on different sides of the line that always seemed to be there, waiting to push them apart.

"Please, for the love of all that is good and decent, somebody say something!" Tim joked. "The tension is killing me."

"We're not going with you," Selene said. "We'll die before we let you take us back in." Sasha cut her eyes at Selene so sharply that Thomas almost laughed, but Selene was serious. She was bold; he had to give her that.

"That won't be necessary," Adele said dryly, glancing at Thomas in exasperation. Selene was quite the topic among the KES agents; they didn't know what to make of her. She'd done a good job of cultivating her own mystery in her time at the Labyrinth, and she was the subject of every conversation, although from what Thomas had heard, it was all more rumor than fact. "We're here to help you."

"Why?" Sasha asked. Thomas had asked Adele the same question as soon as he got her alone after the General gave them their assignment. Why had she covered for Selene and Sasha in the Labyrinth basement when she'd been ordered to bring them in?

"I owe you," Adele had said. "You helped me once; now I'm returning the favor. You care about her, I can tell. If the General's right that she thinks she loves you, then I'm pretty sure you love her back. I thought letting her go would help lessen my debt to you a little."

"You don't owe me anything." He knew what she was talking about, but it had been a long time ago, and he'd never expected her to repay him. But if by doing so Adele was going to help Sasha, then he wasn't going to complain.

"Sure I do."

"And I'm not in love with her." Denying his feelings felt like a betrayal, but he had to lie to protect Sasha. "She's probably not in love with me, either. She had a crush on me, that's all. I'm sure she's over it. It was a long time ago."

Adele had shrugged. "Whatever. Let's just find her, okay?"

Back at the Warren's Run train station, Sergei started to speak, but Adele cut him off. "We'll explain later. We need to get off this platform right now. It's way too exposed."

"Who are you?" Selene stood beneath the eaves of the station house, and the slant of the sunlight threw dark shadows across her face, hiding the look in her eyes and obscuring her expression.

"Agent Nguyen of the King's Elite Service," Adele said, not bothering to disguise how insulting she found the question. Lesser agents would shrink beneath Selene's inscrutable, knowing gaze—even Thomas found it unnerving sometimes—but Adele's belief in her own superiority was stronger than her fear of pretty much anything. "Who the hell are *you*?"

"I'm—" Selene began.

Adele cut her off. "Yeah, I know your name. Let's move." She and Sergei flanked the stairs while the rest of them trooped past her. Thomas felt her eyes on his back as they walked down the quiet streets of Warren's Run, past Dutch colonial stone houses and old wooden shop fronts. Like Almond, it was one of those small, quaint Second Revolution–era river towns that had been hit hard by the last economic crash and never recovered. Locals called the train they'd been on the *Desperation Express*, because people took it only when they had no other choice.

It was a sorry state of affairs for Warren's Run, the site of the first real battle between British forces and the colonial insurgents during the Second Revolution. In spite of the name, Warren hadn't run; he'd advanced on the larger, better-funded imperial army with a boldness that Thomas had always admired, and eventually he'd won, giving the UCC the chance to spread its wings, like the eagle on its seal, and fly.

But Thomas was grateful the town was practically deserted; it would make it easier to slip away unseen. "I guess I should probably make some introductions," Thomas said. As they'd made their way through town, Navin had come in over the comm to inform them that he and Cora—who'd driven to

Warren's Run in one of the KES motos—had found an abandoned garage a few streets over from the main road. It was an old carriage house, retrofitted for a new century and then left behind. The plaque outside the door declared that this had been General Warren's command center during the nearby battle, and everything—from the toolboxes to the oil canisters to the motos on blocks all around them—was covered with a layer of dust so thick one could almost believe the place had been sitting empty since the Second Revolution. There were historical curiosities just like this in all the towns that lined the banks of the Hudson, because this was where the war had started. And if the General was right, this was where a new war was about to begin, with Selene as its flag bearer. Or its architect, though Thomas seriously doubted that.

"Yeah," Navin said, peering at Sasha and Selene. "Which one of you is which, and how do I tell the difference?"

Thomas had no trouble telling them apart; he was certain that even in a room full of a thousand copies, he could pick Sasha out every time. There was something about the way she looked at him, even casually, that set his insides humming like a tuning fork. It had nothing to do with her appearance, which made it easier not to be fooled by imposters.

"We're identical." Selene sniffed. "Like twins. I suppose you'll just have to guess."

"Selene's the one who always looks like she thinks she's smarter than you," Adele remarked. Selene's face darkened, and Cora and Sergei reached for their sidearms, as if they thought she might attack Adele. But Thomas had a feeling Selene was above petty violence—and besides, how much damage could she possibly do?

Sasha put her hand on Selene's shoulder and shook her head. "I'm Sasha," she said. "This is Selene." She slipped her necklace out from underneath the collar of her T-shirt. It was a small charm, a crescent moon and a star, hanging from a thin silver chain. "If you need to tell us apart, I'm the one wearing this. *Or* you could just ask," she added.

Thomas ran through the roster—Tim McComber, Sergei Azarov, Navin Patel, Cora Gunner, and Hector Rockaway. He forced himself to say Rocko's name without betraying how he really felt about him.

"And you've already met Adele," he finished. "They're all KES agents, like me."

"Yes, we can see that," Selene replied. The proprietary way she said *we*, as if she and Sasha were a team, when everything inside him shouted that *he* and Sasha were a team, bothered him. He wondered what Sasha thought.

"Why are they here? You can't possibly expect us to trust them. We might not be as smart as you," she said, with a glance in Adele's direction, "but we aren't stupid."

"Thomas," Sasha said, looking squarely at him. He'd told her once that it wasn't in his nature to lie, and she deserved the truth from him, but there was no way to give it to her. He didn't turn away—it would've been too obvious—but he could feel the blood rushing to his face, and when she lowered her gaze, he knew she had at least an inkling that he was keeping something from her. "What's going on?"

"We were all recruits at the Academy together," Thomas said. This was treacherous territory; it was like crossing a canyon on a tightrope. "We're going to help you find Juliana."

"And why would you do that?" Selene demanded. Thomas looked to Sasha to back him up, but she was just as unconvinced as her analog.

"This is ridiculous," Navin griped with a roll of his eyes. "If we were going to drag you back to the General, we would've done it already."

"And if we wanted to kill you, we would've shot you when you tried to run," Rocko said. Cora punched him hard in the shoulder, and he glared at her.

"Don't scare them," she said. Cora had the big blue eyes of a cartoon character, made even brighter by the deep auburn of her thick, wavy hair. They were hypnotic, those eyes, and when you looked into them, you believed what she was saying. Thomas didn't know Cora as well as he did the others— she'd trialed out of the Academy within his first month—but he'd been on the receiving end of a few of those penetrating gazes, and he would do anything to avoid one, especially now. "We're on your side. Not everyone in the KES believes in what the General's doing, and at the end of the day, we don't serve *him;* we serve the royal family. It's our job to protect the princess."

"You don't want to protect her," Selene said. "You want to cage her, and she knows that. She won't let us get anywhere near her while we're with you!"

Sasha glanced at Selene, surprised at the outburst. After days of interrogation, a daring escape, and a night on the run, the girl was reaching her breaking point. Thomas sort of admired her for not having broken yet. Selene was stronger than he would ever have expected her to be—stronger than most people, in his experience—and in some ways it made her even more terrifying.

"What makes you so sure?" Tim asked, reclining against a seemingly stable stack of paint cans and sending them crashing to the ground. Tim fell right along with them, toppling head over feet onto the garage's oil-stained concrete floor.

"Graceful," Navin said as Sergei helped Tim to his feet. Tim shrugged and grinned.

"They can communicate telepathically," Adele said. Selene stiffened, and Sasha drew in a sharp breath. "What? You think it's some big secret? I've seen the surveillance footage from your cell, Selene. There's no way you plotted an escape from the Labyrinth without saying a word about it. Not so smart now, are you?"

Selene's expression hardened; she seemed more determined than ever—but determined to do *what*?

"Look," Adele said. "I had the chance to expose you in the Labyrinth, but I let you go. Why would I do that if I wanted to screw up your plans?" The girls didn't reply, but Thomas could see that Sasha was softening, and even Selene seemed stymied by Adele's question.

"Okay, that's enough," Thomas said. "We need to get out of this ghost town. Do you know where we're headed?"

Sasha and Selene shook their heads.

"We can feel her there, on the tether, lurking," Selene explained. "But we can't hear her, and we don't think she's listening to us."

"Can't you scream at her or something?" Navin suggested.

"That's not how it works," Selene sniffed.

"It is sort of how it works," Sasha said. "You forced your thoughts and memories through to me, didn't you?"

"Yes, but your mind is open, and Juliana's is closed. I have a better command of the tether than you do, but Juliana . . . her force of will is so strong. She's well practiced at shutting people out. The only reason we saw what we did was because her emotions were running so high, she didn't think to hide from us."

"I'm sorry—you saw something?" Thomas asked. Selene shot Sasha a conspiratorial glance, which wasn't at all reassuring.

"She was with Callum," Sasha volunteered. "Libertas was holding them both, and they escaped. But the vision cut out before we could see where they were being held or where they ended up."

"Okay," Thomas said. He was still a little rusty at leading missions, but his instincts had kicked in, the ones that told him to focus and strategize. "If we don't know where she is, we'll head to Farnham. That's the last place any of us saw her, and if Callum is with her, it makes sense she'd be there."

"What part?" Sergei asked. "It's kind of big."

"Adastra City," Thomas said. He glanced at Selene and Sasha. "You two keep working on her. Maybe she'll slip up and show you something, or maybe she'll stop being so stubborn and just tell you where she is. Come on, we've got to move. Navin, where'd you hide the moto?"

"Uh, so, about that," Navin said, wincing. "The moto died out on us a couple blocks away. We thought we might be able to find something here to jump it with, but none of these rust buckets have any juice."

"Way to go, Patel," Rocko said sarcastically. "A massive disappointment, as always."

"Hey, there's nothing I could've done— " Navin protested, but Thomas stopped him.

"Shut up, both of you," he commanded. "Use your brains instead of your mouths, and let's come up with a strategy."

"This town's not completely empty," Sergei said. "I bet we could find someone with a working moto we could use to jump the engine."

"It could come to that," Thomas said, although he wasn't too keen on walking the streets of Warren's Run flashing badges and asking for help. The people in these river towns had small lives, long memories, and a hunger for conspiracy theories that came from growing up not too far from a top-secret military complex. He didn't want anyone finding out there was a group of stranded KES agents in their midst and wondering what the hell they were doing there. "Let's call that Plan Z."

"We might be able to help," Sasha said, exchanging a cautious glance with Selene.

"How?" Cora asked.

"Oh," Selene said, smiling. "You'll see."

ELEVEN

"So this thing moves? On its own? Like the train?" Selene asked. She just couldn't get over the fact that something so heavy could glide forward without being pushed. It wasn't as if they were living in the Stone Age back there on Taiga—from the way she described it, Home seemed equipped with all sorts of technological marvels—but they didn't have moving vehicles and never had had them, not even before the asteroid hit. When I'd explained to her about fossil fuels on the train, she'd gotten angry. *But that would be so bad for the environment,* she'd said in bewilderment. I wasn't looking forward to dragging her into Adastra; she was reasonably at home in the wilderness surrounding the Labyrinth, but a city, with its pollution and its noise, would break her heart.

But there was something besides wonder lurking on her end of the tether. Her memory of almost getting run over by the truck flashed through my brain, carried along by a current of panic. Selene put up a good front, but she was discovering by degrees just how little she understood about this world that was so unlike her own, and how much of a disadvantage it put her at. It reminded me of how I'd felt when I first came here, how I still felt most of the time.

"Yes, just like the train. It's got an engine inside of it that makes the wheels turn," I told her. That was pretty much the extent of what I knew about cars. "But it needs fuel. And electricity."

"Which it doesn't have," Thomas said. He popped the hood of the car and bent forward to examine its guts. "Everything looks in order, but we definitely need a boost."

"A boost?" Selene repeated. "What's that?"

"A jolt to bring the battery back to life," Thomas explained. "Usually you siphon energy off someone else's battery, but . . ." He glanced around. "Not much in the way of that here."

"So what exactly do you two plan to do about that?" Adele asked.

"You said it needs energy." Everyone swiveled in Selene's direction, but she hardly seemed to notice. She ran her hand over the car's innards, sliding her fingertips across cords and cables, lingering on the dead battery.

"Well, she said electricity," Navin pointed out. "But yeah."

"We can do that. Give it the boost, I mean."

"Huh?" Thomas scrubbed his fingers through his hair and stared at Selene. He reminded me so much of Grant in that moment I had to look away. It was too confusing, still, to look at one and see the other. Grant would have made it to California by now. He was already living an entirely different life.

"Sasha and I have a gift," Selene said. "We can use it to . . . resuscitate this . . . vehicle."

"You can?" Thomas glanced at me.

"Maybe," I said. It was so hard to explain, what it felt like, what it *was*. "How much juice does it need? We don't want to short it out. That can happen, right?"

"Yeah," Thomas said. I wasn't sure he believed us about the power, but he humored us. "Well, let's give it a shot."

146

I stepped aside to make room for Selene, but she shook her head. "It should be you," she said. *You need the practice. The better you are, the more powerful we'll both be, and we'll need to be at full strength for what's coming.*

What is *coming?* I asked, but she ignored the question and backed away from me. So did everyone else—it was just the car and me in a face-off. The power crackled in my fingertips, begging to be released, but I didn't know what made Selene think I could do it. Accidentally making my hands glow wasn't even in the ballpark of jump-starting a car.

"No way," Thomas said. "Not a chance, Sasha. She thinks she can start this moto with—with—with her mind or whatever, that's fine, but let *her* try it."

"She's right," I told him. I was scared of the power, of what it could do and what it *was* doing to me. I felt as if I were sharing my body with a living creature, a dragon coiled up in my chest that raised its head every so often and roared, spitting sparks and fire that raced beneath my skin. But fear wasn't going to get us anywhere, and it certainly wasn't going to help us find Juliana. "I need to be able to control it. It's important."

"*Why* is it so important?" Thomas asked, lowering his voice.

"I don't know. It just is." I went back to the car, turning to Thomas for instructions. "Tell me where to put my hands."

Thomas pointed. "That's the battery, but honestly, I don't know what you should do with your hands. You don't have positive and negative charges." He gazed at me with dark, troubled eyes. "This is a terrible idea. You could burn yourself—or worse, stop your own heart."

"That won't happen," Selene assured him, although I couldn't fathom how she was so certain. "Faith, Sasha. *Listen.*"

Adele scoffed. "Faith? Look, I don't know who you think you are, but if you don't cut this little act out right now—"

"It's not an act," Selene told her. "Sasha trusts me. That's all that matters."

"Both of you be quiet," Thomas commanded. "If Sasha's going to do this, then you shouldn't distract her." He gave me an encouraging smile, which was big of him, since he really did not want me to do this. "Take your time. And be careful, all right?"

I swallowed hard and leaned forward. *You don't need to touch it,* Selene said, and I lowered my hands so that they hovered over the battery.

Let the power pour through you, she instructed. *Don't let it last too long; you don't want to overdo it. A little bit will suffice.*

I closed my eyes and focused on the power, the way it felt as it unfurled and snaked its way down my arms and into my palms. The dragon spread its wings and strained against its cage with so much force I thought the power might burst right through my skin. My whole body seemed to light up, but it was dark behind my eyelids, my vision blotted out by a blackness that roiled like storm clouds as my heartbeat sped up. Power coursed through my hands, and my head spun. I knew I was going to pass out, but right before I lost consciousness, a bright red flare went off at the back of my brain, exploding like a firework. I heard the car's engine turn over and someone call my name, but then I tumbled into a wide, infinite nothing. Lights-out.

IT HAD BEEN DARK WHEN

she and Callum escaped, but now it was full daylight, approaching noon. They'd been walking for what seemed like days. She hadn't realized how much her time in that cell had weakened her. Every step felt like a stumble, every breath like a gasp. She didn't remember how long it had been since Libertus last fed her, but she'd reached the point where she wasn't even hungry anymore—just desperately, achingly tired.

As soon as they'd emerged from the tunnel and onto the street, she'd known exactly where they were, because towering over them like a sentinel was Thirteen Bells. It was the defining landmark of the Tattered City. An enormous campanile built by a long-ago mayor as a symbol of wealth and power, it was an expensive project that served precisely zero real purpose, so Thirteen Bells was widely regarded as a folly. But it was certainly one of a kind.

The flu was working its way through her body; she began to cough hard, and Callum put a hand on her waist, steadying her.

"Juli, stop," he said. "You have to rest."

"No," she said once the fit had passed. "We have to get to Sophie. She'll help us."

Sophie Halliday was the daughter of the congressman who represented the Illinois Dominion, and thus the Tattered City. She and Sophie had attended Lofton together, but the girls hadn't spoken much *since Juliana left school. It had been a strange year, and she'd been busy with other things—specifically, planning a wedding to the boy who was now holding her upright. Guilt stung her heart; if she'd just stayed at the Castle, none of this would have happened. She would've married Callum and started building a life with him. They'd both be safe, and they wouldn't be here in the Tattered City, fleeing in terror from people who wanted to use them.*

But she knew that wasn't true. As grateful as she was for Callum now, and as deeply as she'd grown to care for him these past few weeks, she'd been a different person two months ago. She would've loathed him on sight—in a way, she'd loathed him all her life, or at least the idea of him. She would've made him miserable, and vice versa. So perhaps this was the tiny sliver of hope she kept searching for. Everything she'd suffered—everything she'd done—had led her to him.

She wanted to talk to him about it. She wanted to confess, to stop pretending and be real with him, but she couldn't bring herself to do it. She didn't want to see the look of pain and disgust in his eyes when he found out he'd been betrayed by her and duped by Sasha. She couldn't stand to watch him walk away. Callum was the only good thing in her life at the moment—him and the possibility of sanctuary Sophie provided.

*First, though, Juliana had to remember where Sophie lived. She hadn't been to the Tattered City in years; the KES had deemed it not safe enough for official state visits. But now that she was there, Juliana was starting to see how bad the damage was. Everything was dilapidated and crumbling, even in the North End, once a wealthy and thriving sector. Buildings were plastered with pro-Libertas propaganda, doors and windows tagged with antiloyalist graffiti. She'd lost count of how many times she'd seen the Libertas rallying cry—*We Serve No Government—*on handmade signs displayed in windows. In their ragged state, she thought she and Callum might stand out, but everyone they passed seemed as fatigued and hopeless* as she felt. Their lives had been stripped bare by revolution and war and their leaders' indifference, and it wasn't as though it had happened overnight.

Thankfully, the congressional mansion in the Tattered City was a local landmark. Juliana and Callum followed the signs meant for tourists—back when people came to the Tattered City on purpose—to Sophie's doorstep.

Juliana had been to so many of these official residences, they all started to blend together. Artificially aged to lend an air of historical gravitas and overstuffed with antiques for a whiff of old money, the houses themselves had always seemed like imposters. They were nothing like the Castle, with its refined elegance and tech upgrades, and she was almost embarrassed by them. But when they turned the corner onto Sophie's block, she stopped in surprise. The house was barely visible behind a ten-foot-tall metal wall, and the private security guards stationed outside the gate had submachine guns propped on their shoulders. She'd never seen a civilian house this well defended. If things in the Tattered City were this bad, Sophie might not even be there.

"Are you sure this is the right place?" Callum put his arm around her shoulders, perhaps as much for his own comfort as for hers. Being in the Tattered City made Callum understandably nervous. He'd been raised to hate and fear the UCC, and there was a reason for that. The last thing he wanted to do was step willingly into the house of an enemy.

"I'm sure," she said, taking his hand and squeezing it. "Sophie and her parents will help us. They're loyal to the crown, not the General. And Sophie's one of my closest friends."

Not that Juliana ever really had any close friends. She'd been popular in school because of who she was, but she would not have said she was well liked. Sophie was one of the nicest girls she'd hung around with at Lofton, and Juliana did believe she would help, but after only a few weeks spent on the opposite side of a wall from Callum, he was *her best and most trusted friend. Ironically, it had been the lies they'd told each other that had helped form their connection. Without the assumptions and the expectations that came with their real identities, they had been able to get to know each other as themselves instead of their titles. That had made all the difference.*

"I don't like the look of this place," Callum said. "But if you're sure."

"I am." Truthfully, she didn't like the look of the place, either. But Juliana wasn't going to be put off by a little security. Before Callum could protest, she marched up to the guards, who immediately pointed their weapons at her head.

"State your name and purpose here," one of the guards commanded.

Juliana pushed the hair out of her face and stared at him in the imperious way her mother had taught her. "My name is Princess Juliana Rowan, but you can call me Your Highness. I'm here to see Sophie Halliday."

"Oh my God, Juli!" Sophie cried, throwing her arms around Juliana's neck. Juliana had never been good with physical displays of affection, but she let herself relax in the embrace of her old friend. "Where have you been? The reports on the box have all been saying you were kidnapped by . . ."

She stopped and Juliana turned to follow her line of sight— straight to Callum. "Him," Sophie finished with venom. "What's he doing here?"

"Sophie, listen to me," Juliana said. She grabbed Callum's hand. She wasn't going to let anyone talk about him like that, not to her. "Callum didn't kidnap me—we were both being held captive by Libertas."

"Libertas?" Sophie's expression morphed into one of horror. "But—"

"Can we stay here?" Juliana asked. "Just for a little while, until I can . . . I don't know. I'll think of something." She closed her eyes

152

and took a deep breath, doing the mental calculations on who was left in her life she could trust. Once she would've said Thomas, but after what she'd done, there was no way he would ever help her.

"Of course," Sophie said. "My dad's not here. He was called away to Columbia City this morning. And Mother's at our house outside Jamestown. You know how she hates the Tattered City."

Juliana nodded. "What are you doing here? It doesn't seem safe."

Sophie straightened her shoulders and smiled unconvincingly. "Daddy says we should live among the people we serve."

As long as you're separated from them by a three-foot-thick wall, *Juliana thought. What had Congressman Halliday been doing all these years if it wasn't helping the people who'd elected him? How could anyone who claimed to serve the people have allowed things to get so bad?*

"Can I use your telecom?" She was starving and tired—all she wanted to do was sleep—but there was a call she had to make first.

Sophie led them down the hall to a sitting room, where there was an old-fashioned-looking telecom sitting on a table in the corner. She hovered as Juliana picked up the receiver.

"Would you mind giving me some privacy?" Juliana asked. Callum shot her a questioning look, but Juliana shook her head. She wanted him to stay.

When Sophie was gone, Callum asked, "Are you going to call Thomas?"

For a second, Juliana panicked, thinking he suspected something, but that was crazy. He knew Thomas was her bodyguard from the time he'd spent in the Castle with Sasha.

"No," she said. He seemed relieved. She dialed a number she knew by heart. It rang twice, and then came the telltale click of connection.

"Gloria Beach."

Juliana sighed in relief. All the tension bled from her muscles, and she sank into a nearby chair. "Oh, Gloria, thank God."

"Who is this?" Gloria demanded.

"It's—it's Juliana." How could Gloria not recognize her voice? They had known each other since she was twelve. Then she realized— Gloria thought she might be Sasha.

"Juli! Where are you? Are you okay?" Juliana couldn't hold it in any longer. She burst into tears. Callum appeared at her side; he put a hand on her shoulder and kissed her head softly. She leaned into his side. She never cried, hardly ever, especially since she'd stopped being a child. It had never occurred to her to wonder why, but now she knew: it felt so good to let go, she was afraid she'd never stop.

"I'm in the Tattered City, at Sophie Halliday's house." Juliana told Gloria the basics, leaving out any mention of the part she'd played in her own kidnapping, or of Sasha. "Please," she begged. "Come and get me."

"I will," Gloria said. "Can you stay at Sophie's for now? I'm not sure I can get out of the Castle unnoticed until tomorrow or the day after. The KES has the entire Citadel on lockdown, but I promise you, Juli, I will come for you."

Juliana swallowed hard. "Why is the Citadel on lockdown?"

"Oh, Juli," Gloria said. She sounded near tears herself. "Your father is dying."

TWELVE

The first thing I heard when I woke up was a buzzing noise, like a bee hovering somewhere nearby. I thought about it vaguely as I checked to make sure all my limbs were still attached, that I wasn't burned over ninety percent of my body, or in pain. It took me a few seconds to figure out that it wasn't an insect; it was music. Somebody was humming.

I only had to listen to a couple bars to realize it was Thomas. Nobody else in this universe would know that song. It was one Thomas and I had danced to at prom.

"Cut it out," Rocko griped. "You're giving me a headache."

I was lying down, my head in Selene's lap and my legs draped over Cora's knees. We were in the car I'd jump-started with my new power. To say I was freaked out would be a massive understatement, but Selene put her hand on my forehead as if feeling for a fever and poured reassurance through the tether.

"Look who's awake!" Tim crowed, leaning over the seat in front of me to peer at my face. "I thought Mayhew was going to have an aneurysm when you collapsed back there."

Selene helped me sit up. Cora smiled and offered me a

plastic canteen of water. I gulped it down, draining the entire canteen. "Thanks," I said gratefully.

"No problem," she said. "How are you feeling?"

I caught Thomas appraising me in the rearview mirror. He looked relieved, and to be honest, so was I. The power was such a scary thing; it could very well have gone another way. "Okay," I said. "A little sore."

"Good," Sergei said. "We were pretty worried about you."

"What happened?"

"Well," Navin said, "you started to shake, and then your eyes rolled all the way back in your head like this"—his face transformed from normal to ghoulish—"then you just dropped like someone had cut your strings." He smacked his hands together for emphasis.

"If you haven't noticed, Patel has a flair for dramatic story-telling," Thomas said with a soft laugh. I fought the urge to climb over the seats and put my arms around him, for no other reason than that we were finally together and I wanted to be near him. The temptation was even stronger because I knew I couldn't, that it would raise questions and suspicions. From the way he was looking at me, I could tell he felt the same way. That was comforting, at least.

"Yikes," I said, trying to play it off as if it weren't a big deal. No wonder Thomas had been worried. If I'd seen that happen to him, I would've gone into a complete panic. Watching him almost die once was quite enough, thank you very much.

"You didn't use a lot of power," Selene said, patting my shoulder. "I told them you would be all right. You just needed to rest."

"Yeah, all you did was turn yourself into a human battery," Navin said with a sarcastic shrug. "I'm asleep. Wake me when something weird happens." He closed his eyes and fell against Tim, who shoved him.

"I completely forgot," I said, gripping the seat in front of me so hard my nails dug half-moon shapes into the fabric. "Juliana and Callum—they're in the Tattered City."

Thomas's eyes widened. "Really? How do you know that?"

"I saw it, too," Selene explained. "But I couldn't tell where they were."

"The last time I was there, I saw this giant campanile in the distance," I began.

"Thirteen Bells," Adele said, perking up in the front seat. "City Center."

"It was in the vision, too," I continued. "They're at the house of some girl named Sophie."

"Sophie Halliday," Thomas said. "She's a friend of Juliana's from school."

"Congressman Halliday's kid?" Rocko asked. It was the first time he'd acted interested in our search for Juliana.

"Yeah," Thomas said. "I don't know where she lives, but it shouldn't be too hard to find out. Is Juliana hurt at all? How does she seem?"

A cold stream of jealousy trickled down my back at the sound of real concern in his voice. After how she'd betrayed him, did he seriously still care what happened to her?

Of course he does, I reminded myself. *Protecting her used to be his job.* If I were a better person, I would care what happened to Juliana, too, and to be honest, I had to admit that I did, deep down. It was impossible not to worry about her or not to want her to be all right. She was my analog; it was that simple. But I still resented her for everything she'd done. Part of me kind of thought she deserved what she was getting.

"She's scared. And tired. But she's safe, for now. She called

Gloria, though. We have to get to Juliana before she does, or we'll lose her."

"How long do we have?" Adele asked.

"A day or two, maybe. Gloria said the Citadel's on lockdown." I hesitated. "The king is dying."

The KES agents nodded somberly. "There was an announcement on the radio," Cora said. "It's so sad. He was a good king."

"Are you on drugs?" Navin snapped. "The positions the king took on health care, foreign policy, and immigration alone are enough to earn him the title of the *worst* king in the history of the UCC!"

"That's ridiculous," Rocko scoffed. "Just because you're a crazy socialist doesn't mean the man deserves to die."

"I didn't say he deserved to die," Navin seethed. He and Rocko launched into a full-on argument, one that I couldn't have followed even if I'd wanted to.

"Whoa," I said, exchanging a look with Selene. Navin and Rocko could debate whether or not Juliana's father had been an effective king until the end of the world, but I had a soft spot for him. I'd read to him and followed the clues he'd tried so desperately to communicate to me; the thought of him losing what was left of his life was heartbreaking.

"That's enough," Thomas said, interrupting them before they came to actual blows.

Adele glared at Navin and Rocko. "Yeah, cool it, both of you. It's going to be a long drive if you're constantly at each other's throats."

"Where are we?" I asked.

"Just about to pass over the border into Pennsylvania Dominion," Thomas said. "We're headed to a place called Gorman's Gate."

"Gorman's Gate?" Rocko narrowed his eyes. "Why are we going there?"

"What's Gorman's Gate?" I whispered to Cora.

She shrugged. "Just some old battlefield, I think."

"There's someone there I think can help us," Thomas said. "The only question is whether she will."

By the time we reached Gorman's Gate, the sun was close to setting. Darkness spread across the sky like ink, and everyone in the car was growing restless, even Selene, so you could feel the collective relief when Thomas pulled off a lonely country highway onto an even lonelier private dirt road.

"Okay," Thomas said, parking. "You all wait here. I'm going to go talk to her."

"Who's her?" Tim asked.

"Philomena Dryden," Thomas told us. "Or, well, that was her name when she was an active KES agent. I don't know what she goes by now. But this is where she lives. She's friendly."

"To whom?" Cora asked.

"To our cause," he said. Cora and Navin exchanged a look, and I could imagine what they were thinking: Thomas didn't seem to know very much about this woman at all. "Sasha, come with me?"

"Why?" Selene demanded. She was reluctant to be separated from me, even for a second; she was a stranger in a strange land, and I was the only person in Aurora she trusted. Thomas made a frustrated noise.

"I think it will go a long way toward getting Agent Dryden to hear us out," Thomas said, but he didn't explain further. As I climbed out of the car, Selene's mind poked at mine inquisitively, but there wasn't anything I could tell her. Maybe

Thomas didn't really need me. Maybe he just wanted me close.

Thomas and I walked in silence down the dirt road—actually, *road* was a bit generous. It was more of an overgrown path. As soon as we were out of sight of the car, I grabbed him by the hand and pushed him up against a nearby tree. He started to laugh, but I silenced him with a long, hard kiss. He wrapped his arms around me and lifted me onto the tips of my toes.

"I've been wanting to do that since Almond," I whispered when we came up for air.

"*I've* been wanting to do that since the Labyrinth," he whispered back. "Where have you been?"

I laughed. "Distracted."

He kissed me again. "What about now?"

"Now I'm perfectly focused." I snaked my arms around his neck and trailed a line of kisses down the length of his jaw.

He leaned his head back against the tree trunk and sighed. "I think we'd better keep moving." I groaned. "I know. But they're going to wonder if we're not back soon."

"Let's just run," I suggested. I was only half-joking. I would've given anything in that moment to take off with him and never look back. Forget the tether. Forget Selene and Juliana and the KES. Let them fight their own wars. Let the tether remain, no matter what it might do to me. If it meant being with him, alone and safe, then screw everything else. "They can't see us. By the time they notice we're gone, it'll be too late."

"Good idea," he said, playing along. "Where should we go?"

And just like that, my whole escape fantasy crumbled. There was nowhere to go. "I don't know," I said, feeling deflated. I disentangled myself and started up the road. "You're right. We should get moving."

"Sasha," Thomas said, pulling me back. "I wish we could do that, too. I'm sorry."

"Don't apologize; it's not your fault."

"It kind of is—"

I cut him off. "Thomas, forget it. I don't want to talk about blame. I just want to figure this out so we can move on with our lives."

"Okay," he said, but the look he was giving me made me sad. We held hands as we walked up the path, but there was a distance between us in the shape of a whole universe. I never would've admitted this to him, but I was afraid that we would never get to have what we wanted. Every time we got close, something was always going to be standing in our way.

"It's nice to be alone," Thomas said with a sigh. He seemed tired all of a sudden, and nervous, too. He was doing a good job keeping up appearances in front of the other KES agents, but now that we were alone, he let everything show. "Are you in any pain? They were just teasing me back there, but that was scary, Sasha. You looked so . . . lifeless, lying there after you fell."

"I'm okay," I assured him. Even the soreness in my muscles was starting to abate. Pretty soon it would be like nothing had happened—until the next time I had to use the power. "Selene wouldn't have let me do it if she thought it would hurt me."

"I know." He ran his fingers through his hair. It had been cut recently, probably when he arrived at the Labyrinth. He kneaded the back of his neck. I wished I could say something to make him feel better, assure him everything would be fine in a way that made some kind of difference. Thomas worried about me, and he worried about Juliana, and he worried about the world and everyone in it. I wanted to be a source of comfort, not concern. I wanted him to know I could take care of myself and him, too.

"You do?"

"I trust your instincts," Thomas said. "Sometimes I think I trust them more than my own."

"So what's the deal with this woman?" I asked. "Philomena Dryden."

"Like I said, she was a KES agent. She retired a couple of years ago. When my communication permissions were reinstated, the first person I contacted was Dr. Moss," Thomas explained. "He told me to go to her if I needed any help, gave me a code phrase that would prove to her we were on the same side. She lives here at Gorman's Gate."

"You keep saying 'Gorman's Gate' like I'm supposed to know what that means."

"Oh." He laughed. "Sorry. Sometimes I forget you're not from here. Gorman's Gate is the site of the last battle of the Second Revolution. It's mostly just a field, but the property is privately owned, and Agent Dryden is in hiding here. That's why I have to go alone. She won't talk to us if she sees a whole bunch of agents pile out of a KES vehicle onto her front lawn."

"Got it. How far is it?"

"Just up ahead, I think."

"Why did you need me to come along?"

"What, that back there wasn't a good enough reason?" He grinned. I touched my lips. I could still feel the imprint of his mouth on mine.

"You didn't know I was going to do that."

"Hey, if you hadn't, I was going to. Besides, I always need you," he said, smiling shyly. I gave him an affectionate shove.

"I think Agent Dryden had something to do with the many-worlds project. I figure she's more likely to help us if I bring an analog straight to her front door."

"So I'm the bait?"

"Well . . . sort of. Do you mind?"

"I guess not," I said. I'd been used for worse things. At least this earned me some one-on-one time with Thomas.

"All we need is food and shelter for the night." He seemed far away, suddenly, lost deep in thought. "We have to be at full strength when we go after Juliana."

"And then what?" I still wasn't clear about his goals in all this.

"And then you choose," Thomas said, so quietly I almost asked him to repeat himself. "Whatever you want, Sasha, that's what I want."

"I thought you said you'd never lie to me." He wasn't giving me the whole truth. I knew him well enough to figure that out.

"I'm not lying."

"Those people back there," I said. "Your buddies. They're not here to help me. They want to put Juliana back on the throne. But she can't take back the crown and go to Taiga with me and Selene, not at the same time." Not to mention the fact that from what I knew of Juliana, she wouldn't want to do either of those things.

"Honestly, Sasha, I don't care what they want. They're my friends and my colleagues. I like them, and I respect them, but I'm on your side. Yours. No one else's. I'm here to protect you. I'm here to help *you*. Because I *love* you."

Love. *Love*. Thomas just said that he loved me. I knew I should say it back—I felt it, didn't I? But for some reason I couldn't make my mouth form the words.

"Why?" It was just one word, but it was so hard to get out. Saying it made me feel small and vulnerable. I needed to know what made me different from Selene or Juliana—or Adele or Cora or any other girl in any other world. It was embarrassing, but I did wonder. *Love* was a scary word, too. A big word, big feeling. I wasn't sure what I'd done to deserve it.

Thomas laughed. "Why what? Why you? I could tell you, but I don't think we have that kind of time. It would take me— There are so many reasons. You're brave and you're smart and you're fragile and you're strong and you're resilient and you're so . . . beautiful. Sometimes I can't even look at you, because when I do, my heart does this thing where it swells up and pushes against my lungs and I can't breathe."

"You know two other people who look exactly like me." It was hard to keep my voice from trembling. I hated myself for feeling insecure about Juliana, *still*, after everything that had happened. But I couldn't shake this horrible feeling that he thought he was in love with me because I looked like her.

"I wasn't talking about looks." He placed his hand over my heart. "I was talking about this."

He bent to kiss me; the heat of our connection traveled through my body, warming me as the last of the evening light vanished. It was pitch black out there in the country, and the aurora waved like an old friend, stretching and gliding across the dark sky. We pulled apart, breathless, then fell together again. It all felt so urgent. Moments like this were few and far between, and even this one would end too soon.

"You're my true north, Sasha," Thomas said, kissing one cheek, and then the other. I closed my eyes. I knew what he meant about his heart swelling up so much he couldn't breathe. It was happening to me right then. "You're the only person who's never let me down. *That* is why I love you." He didn't seem upset that I wasn't ready to say it back. He didn't question me or try to coax the words out of me. He just kissed me. And kissed me. And—

And then a shot rang out, echoing like an explosion through the dark, dark night.

165

THIRTEEN

"You have five seconds to tell me who you are and what you're doing on my property before I blow your pretty little heads off."

Thomas and I put our hands up in surrender.

"My name is Thomas Mayhew," Thomas said. "Dr. Moss sent me."

There was a tense pause, and then a middle-aged woman stepped out of the shadows, brandishing a rifle. The bright, round moon made her blond pixie-cut hair glow almost silver. "Moss gave you my location?"

"He said to tell you he'd seen the face of God," Thomas said.

What the hell did that mean? Thomas spoke the code phrase in a strange, uncertain way that made me think Dr. Moss hadn't explained. Dr. Moss didn't strike me as the type of person who believed in God—like Granddad, science was his one true religion—but the words meant something to Dryden. Her expression softened into something like relief, and she let out a stream of air through her nostrils.

"Mayhew? Any relation to—"

"I'm his son," Thomas said. "But I'm not loyal to him. I'm

loyal to this country and to the people I pledged to serve. I think, unless I've been misinformed, you feel the same way."

The woman's eyes widened as they came to rest on me. "Your Highness," she said softly, lowering her weapon. "I'm so sorry, I didn't know that was you."

Thomas began to speak, but I interrupted him. I wanted to say this for myself. "I'm not the princess Juliana, Agent Dryden. My name is Sasha Lawson. I'm Juliana's analog. From Earth."

"Oh," she breathed. "I see. Come inside. We have much to discuss."

"I have a team with me," Thomas told her. "They're waiting for us down the road. We're all on the same side. We need sleep and food. We'll stay with you for just one night, I promise."

"This team," Dryden said. "You trust them?"

Thomas nodded. I stared at him, wondering if that was true. But my instincts told me to have faith. There was still so much I didn't understand about how his world worked and his place in it.

"All right," Dryden said. "Bring them in."

The house at Gorman's Gate was smaller inside than it seemed from the outside. All nine of us, counting Agent Dryden—or Constance Winger, as she called herself now—crammed into the tiny kitchen, sitting at the table or perched at the edge of countertops. Thomas stood in the doorway, watching everyone with incredible focus. Dryden couldn't take her eyes off Selene and me. We'd explained as much as we could, and because of her work on the many-worlds project, she understood what we were, but knowing isn't the same as believing. It was weird, but I was getting used to being stared at like that. As if we were something more—or less—than human.

"So what's your plan?" she asked.

"The princess is in the Tattered City," Thomas said. "With the prince of Farnham. They're hiding at the house of one of Juliana's friends, but she's made contact with the Castle, so we need to get to her before they do."

"Why? If the whole point of this escapade is to put Juliana on the throne, isn't the Castle exactly where she should be?"

"Not while the General is still in command," Adele put in. "If she takes over the regency now, he'll just use her as a puppet. We need to protect and hide Juliana while the Rowanites work to destabilize him."

"Rowanites?" asked Selene. All eyes fell on her. "What are those?"

"People loyal to the Crown. The General has been taking advantage of the king's weaknesses for decades in order to get a stranglehold on the country," Dryden said. "It's worsened since the queen's regency. The only way to end this hideous war is to remove the General from power and place it in the hands of someone who can really lead us."

"And you think that person is Juliana?" I shook my head. "I'm not sure she's your best bet." She had no more desire to rule the UCC than I did—less, maybe. At least I'd given it a shot, insofar as I could. But apart from Thomas and maybe Selene, nobody in that room knew that Juliana had betrayed her country, and it was probably for the best that it stay that way.

"She's our only bet," Rocko said, scoffing at my stupidity. "Eligible heirs to the throne aren't exactly thick on the ground."

"Well," Dryden said, more as an afterthought than anything else, "there is the bastard."

Rocko rolled his eyes. "I said *eligible* heirs."

"Wait, what? What bastard?" I asked.

"That's just a rumor," Thomas said.

"Oh no, it isn't," Dryden replied. "The king had a child out of wedlock, long before Juliana was born, before he even married her mother. A son: Christopher Turner."

"Not Kit Turner?" Thomas came closer and put his hands on the back of my chair, leaning forward with sudden interest.

"So you have heard of him."

"Uh, yeah, everybody's heard of him," Navin piped up. "I wouldn't exactly call him regent material."

"Who's Kit Turner?" I asked.

"Only the biggest traitor the KES has ever seen," Tim said. "He was a legend in the Service, probably one of the best shadow agents we ever had—until he got caught leaking intelligence to Libertas and the General locked him up in the Labyrinth indefinitely, with no trial. He was there for years, but eventually he escaped."

I remembered Thomas's saying that only one person had ever escaped the Labyrinth before. "Do you think the king helped him?"

Dryden barked out a laugh. "Certainly *not*. Turner was always making trouble for the king. He was . . . ambitious. He thought he should be crown prince, ahead of Juliana. He practically blackmailed the king into securing him a spot in the KES and helping him advance quicker than he should have, and then he spat in the king's face and sold the country's secrets to the highest bidder. Likely he thought that if he couldn't have the throne, no one should have it."

"Does Juliana know any of this?" I asked Thomas. Juliana had also given up her country's secrets—one of them, at least—to Libertas in exchange for something she wanted.

169

I wondered if he was the one who'd given her the idea in the first place. "Has she met him?"

He shook his head. "She knows he exists, but the king never let Turner anywhere near her or his other children."

"What happened to him?" Selene asked.

Thomas shrugged. "Nobody knows. He just disappeared."

Dryden stood. "All right, I assume you're hungry, and most of you look like you're about to fall asleep on your feet. Let's get some food in you and call it a night. Can't have you searching for the princess on half speed."

I was halfway done with my sandwich when I looked over at Thomas and realized I'd never actually seen him eat a meal. When I was in Aurora before, he lived and slept and did all his normal human things in the Tower, far away from me. There was so much I hadn't done with him and didn't know about him. There are a million different little things that make up a person, and I felt that I had missed so much.

Thomas noticed me watching and smiled, touching his knee to mine under the table. I wished I could spend more time alone with him. If I went along with Selene's plan, it meant separating from Thomas, at least for a while. Selene had no interest in bringing strangers into her universe. Who knew when we would see each other again?

After dinner, Dryden showed us where we'd be sleeping. Her bedroom was on the first floor, and there were three spares on the second: Cora and Adele were assigned to one, Selene and I to another, and Navin and Tim were sharing the third. Rocko and Sergei flopped on couches in the living room, and Thomas took the tiny attic alcove, which was big enough for just one person. We took turns showering. The hot needles of water worked miracles on the knotted muscles in my back and shoulders.

It was late when I finally settled down into my little twin bed and shut off the light. Selene was awake, staring at the ceiling, and when it was dark, she asked, "Are you afraid, Sasha?"

"No," I told her. It wasn't exactly a lie—she could see right through lies—but I was nervous. We weren't the only people on Juliana's trail, and I knew how bad things were likely to get before we found her—or when we did. The future was in no way certain, and that freaked me out. But it wasn't the same as being afraid. With Selene three feet away and Thomas pacing the floor above my head, I felt about as safe as I possibly could under the circumstances. "Are you?"

"No." The tether was giving off this ambient hum that was hard to interpret. "I'm uneasy. My faith is being tested. That's always an uncomfortable experience."

"How is your faith being tested?"

She sighed. "I thought it would be easier, that's all. The universe brought you straight to me. I knew we'd have to search harder for Juliana, but I didn't expect to need so much help."

"Neither of us is from this universe," I reminded her. "We should be grateful for the help."

"I know," she said. "I just wish we could have done this alone. You and I and Juliana. It's our destiny, not theirs. I worry all the time that we aren't strong enough."

I wanted to comfort her, but I had the same doubts she did. Selene promised that what we had to do to save her world would also break the tether, but all I had to go by was her word. What if she was wrong? But there was no point in saying that, so instead I said, "We are."

"Yes," she said, in this inscrutable tone that made my head hurt. The more time I spent with Selene, the more I liked her, but she was tough to figure out. One thing she, Juliana, and

I had in common was our stubbornness, but hers was more distant, more thoughtful, and much more difficult to interpret. *Sasha?*

Yeah?

Are you in love with Thomas?

"Um . . ." I paused. It wasn't the sort of question I would ever have expected her to ask, and I didn't want to talk about it with her or with anyone. I was having a hard enough time trying to figure it out myself. "Why?"

"Just curious. I think you are, but you didn't tell him earlier."

Of course. I should've known she'd be eavesdropping, but it was a waste of breath to tell her to stop. *I don't want to say something I can't take back.*

But if you really feel it, why would you want to take it back?

"I don't know." It was convenient to be able to talk to Selene in my head, but it made everything so slippery and hard to hold on to. The more we spoke through the tether, the less control I had over my thoughts and feelings.

Juliana's in love with the prince, Selene said. *It bothers her, because she's not entirely being her authentic self with him right now, and she's afraid he'll find out and hate her.*

I don't think Callum's very good at hating people, I replied. *He'll be hurt, though.* And that would be both our faults, not just Juliana's.

That sort of love seems complicated, Selene said, in a vague, evasive way that made me wonder why she'd brought it up in the first place.

"Selene—are *you* in love with somebody?"

The tether tightened, always a sign she was trying to hold something back. *Of course not,* she said, almost too quickly. *We don't "fall in love" in my society, I told you that before. Romance isn't even a concept I'm very familiar with, except for what I can feel through the bond from you and Juliana. I was only curious.*

And that guy I saw you with in your memories? You don't feel anything for him?

Leonid and I are a team. We work together. That's all.

I probably should've let it drop, but it was kind of great to see this vulnerable side of her. Selene put on a front with the KES agents, acted so powerful and untouchable, but she had her doubts and insecurities and soft spots like everyone else. *Then how come your light brightens every time you think about him?*

Selene yawned and turned over in her bed. "Good night, Sasha."

I smiled. "Good night."

One of the most annoying things about not sleeping well at night is that even when you're completely exhausted, you can climb into bed, turn off the light, close your eyes, and . . . nothing. I was still wide awake an hour after Selene's end of the tether quieted.

I slipped out of bed and took the stairs up to the attic carefully, not wanting to make any noise. Thomas's door was open a crack and the lights were on, but when I knocked, there was no answer, and the room was empty. I drifted around, picking things up off the dresser, examining the dusty artwork on the walls, fingering the ragged corners of the quilted counterpane. There was a window on the opposite side of the bed with a view through the surrounding treetops to a field beyond. In the sky, the aurora performed its usual nighttime acrobatics.

"The last battle of our revolution was fought on that field." I turned to see Thomas in the doorway, shirtless and wet-haired, with a towel hanging around his neck. I felt as if I had a swarm of butterflies living inside of me; I could almost hear the flutter of their wings as they hummed beneath my skin. He smiled, and my heart gave a sudden, hard jerk, as if it were trying to free itself from my body.

"Wow, do you look good without a shirt on," I said, doing my best to keep my voice steady, surprised I could even speak.

He walked toward me until we were separated only by inches. "So what you're saying is, you're not interested in the glorious history of this very important landmark?"

"Yeah," I said, grabbing both ends of his towel and using it to pull him forward. "Sorry, but I'm really not." He grinned, and I kissed him, feeling bold and inspired. He melted against me, and we settled comfortably into each other's arms. I unfolded as his lips skimmed up and down my throat, blooming like a night flower.

"I'm so happy you're here," he murmured. My skin was so hot I wouldn't have been surprised to see flames licking at my body. I dug my nails into his arms to keep myself steady; it must've hurt, but he didn't seem to notice.

"You are?"

He nuzzled my cheek. "I know I shouldn't be—it's so dangerous. But I am. I can't help it."

"It's okay. I'm okay. I want to be here, despite the danger."

"I wish you didn't have to leave."

"I know."

"But I think it would be best—for you and Juliana—if you find a place to hide until all of this is over. And if Selene is telling the truth about her world meaning us no harm, then maybe it's a good thing you're going with her. At least over there you'll be safe."

"She's telling the truth," I assured him. "You can trust her."

"I don't have to trust her," Thomas said with a shrug, as if it were obvious. "I trust you."

I rested my head on his shoulder, savoring the smell of soap and skin and the water still clinging to the ends of his hair. I ran my hand over his chest, lingering on the pink, puckered scar the bullet had left behind. He tensed when I touched it. "Is it still really painful?"

"A little," he said. "The exit wound hurts more than the entry wound, for some reason."

I turned him to look at the other scar below his shoulder blade and then spotted something just above it. "Thomas, I didn't know you had a tattoo!"

He glanced backward. "Oh yeah. I got it when I graduated from the KES Academy. It's sort of a tradition."

I circled him so I could see the design better: a gold heraldic falcon rising. I ran my hand over the ink, leaving a trail of goose bumps in the wake of my fingertips. There were three words scrawled beneath it: *In nocte consilium.*

"Most people get the KES seal, or motto, or both," Thomas explained.

I traced the edges of the falcon's outstretched wings. "So why did you choose this?"

"It's the charge and motto on Thomas Warren's family crest."

"In nocte consilium." I called upon all the high school Latin I remembered. " 'Advice comes overnight'?"

"Is that how it translates? I was told it means 'Tomorrow is a new day.' "

"Thomas Warren? As in Warren's Run?"

Thomas nodded. "He was John Rowan's right-hand man in the Second Revolution. A brilliant military tactician and an inspirational commander, *the* national hero to the people of the UCC. Rowan probably wouldn't have won the war and become king without him. He created the KES. I'm related to him on my mother's side. I was named after him," he finished proudly. "Thomas Warren Lebec."

"Lebec," I repeated. It had never even occurred to me that Thomas had had an original last name. To me, he was so thoroughly a Mayhew, albeit a reluctant one. "It's a nice name, Thomas."

"Yeah, I like it," he said, tossing the towel to the floor and coming in for a kiss. He ran his fingers through my hair, and it felt so good I let a deep sigh roll out of my throat. He kissed me in the soft, sensitive spot behind my ear, and I made the noise again. Thomas dropped his head and laughed against my shoulder. "You sound happy."

"I am happy," I said, hugging him tight. "So, so, so happy."

The knock on the door ricocheted through us like a bolt of electricity. I froze for a second and searched for an answer in Thomas's face, but he was just as bewildered as I was.

"Quick," he whispered in my ear. "Hide."

"Thomas!" I hissed. "I'm not *hiding*."

"You want whoever's behind that door to catch us together?"

"Fine," I said. The last thing we needed was a bunch of KES agents with something to prove knowing the truth about our relationship. "Where?" The room was so small, there wasn't anywhere to go.

"Behind the door."

I didn't like the idea of having to slink off into the shadows—it made me feel as if I were doing something I should be ashamed of—but it couldn't be helped. Thomas picked up a T-shirt from the back of a chair and tugged it on. Then he opened the door, squishing me into the wall.

"Adele," he said. I grimaced. Adele was all right, but she wasn't easy to fool. "What are you doing here?"

Adele laughed hesitantly. "I'm not sure. I was hoping we could talk."

"Okay." Thomas blocked the doorway, but Adele dipped under his arm and strode into the room. "Come in, I guess."

She sat down on the bed and looked up at Thomas with the sort of hunger in her eyes that I felt in my gut every time I saw him.

"What did you want to talk about?" he asked.

"I'm really glad you've come back to the KES," Adele began. "I thought about you every single day since you graduated from the Academy. Where you were, what you were doing . . . and then when I saw you again, I—I don't know. I was just so glad to see you."

"Uh, thanks. Me too. I, uh . . ." This conversation was making Thomas uncomfortable. He wasn't the only one. "Thank you. For helping me, I mean."

"Don't thank me," Adele said. "I'd do anything for you."

"Same here." I could tell he really meant it. But I did *not* like where this conversation was headed, and I wished he'd ask her to get out. "You're like family, Adele. You always were, even from the beginning. You're like my sister."

"A sister?" The bedsprings creaked as she rose to her feet. "Thomas, I don't want to be your sister." She ran her fingers up his arm. I couldn't see the expression on his face, only the turn of his head as he watched her do it. A blaze of jealousy shot through me. Who did she think she was? I didn't care if they were old friends. She had no right to hit on him. *She doesn't even know you're together,* the rational part of my brain whispered. The irrational part of my brain told it to shut up.

"I think you might have gotten the wrong idea," he said, stepping back. "I'm flattered, really, but—"

"Calm down, Thomas," Adele said. I'd never been a violent

person, but I wanted to punch her in her pretty little face. "I'm not proposing to you. I just think that, with all the stress, we could both use some company, you know?"

"I appreciate that," he said. "But I can't. Or . . . I don't want to. It's not personal. It's just . . ." The awkwardness was palpable, and I felt kind of bad for him. "I'm sorry. I can't."

"Why?" Adele was so close to him now. She could kiss him if she wanted to, and she did seem to want to. "Don't you think I'm attractive?"

"You're . . . very good-looking, Adele." Thomas sounded like he wanted to slam his head against a wall.

"Then is there someone else?"

"No?"

Adele made a fist and walloped him right in the arm. "I knew it! You are *such* a liar."

"What are you talking about? What did you hit me for?"

Adele put her hands on her hips. "Where is she? What did you do, hide her in the closet? Sasha, get out here."

"This room doesn't have a closet," Thomas pointed out, steering her toward the open door. "And I don't know what you're talking about. There's nobody here but me and you."

"You think I'm an idiot?" Adele flung the door closed. "Hi, Sasha."

"Hi," I said. This was so unbearably weird and embarrassing.

"I can't believe you lied to my face about this," Adele said, glaring at Thomas. "I was so sure there was something going on between the two of you, but I kept thinking, no, if Thomas was with somebody, he would have told me. We're such good friends! Just goes to show how much I know."

"I'm confused," I said. "What just happened?"

"She was trying to trick me into telling her about us," Thomas said. "Nice, Adele. Charming." Adele shrugged.

"So you're not interested in him?"

"No!" Adele rolled her eyes. "Ugh, it'd be like kissing my cousin. Just thinking about it makes me feel like I want another shower."

"Hey," Thomas snapped. "Some people think I'm a pretty great catch."

"Oh, did I hurt your feelings? Look, I don't care what you—either of you—do in your free time, but you've got to get your heads around the fact that you don't have any free time right now. There's a whole group of KES agents downstairs, and one of them straight-up hates you, Thomas. Rocko would drive over your cold, dead body in a tank for just about anything, and you better believe he'd sell you out in a second if he thought he had something concrete. We've all got a job to do, including me, and you two keeping secrets is getting in my way." Adele shook her head at Thomas. "I expected better of you."

"Careful. You might want to remember that I outrank you by about ten levels. You don't get to tell me what you expect."

Adele straightened her shoulders. "You know I'm right."

Thomas looked down at Adele, his expression a blank mask. "Was this the whole reason you came up here?"

"No," Adele said. "Dryden sent me to find you. She says she needs to see you as soon as possible."

THOMAS AT GORMAN'S GATE

Agent Dryden—Thomas couldn't think of her by any other name—was waiting for him when he came downstairs. She put her finger to her lips, and her eyes darted toward the living room, where Sergei and Rocko were snoring in perfect harmony. Then she set off down the hallway, pausing at the end to beckon him to follow.

The door at the end of the corridor looked out of place with the rest of the building; it was metal, with an LCD screen embedded in the adjacent wall. "You have a situation room?" he asked. Dryden pressed her hand against the screen. It turned green, and the door slid open when she typed in the code.

They descended into the basement. Dryden yanked a string dangling from the ceiling, and the room lit up. It was an impressive situation room for a rural, off-the-grid farmhouse. There was one whole wall of screens, each tuned to one of the UCC's six telebox stations, and another wall lined with metal filing cabinets. Dryden plucked two folding chairs from a rack near the staircase and handed one to Thomas.

"Sit," she commanded.

"I assume this is about the information Dr. Moss sent me

for," Thomas said. The physicist had been far from direct, but he'd been clear on one point: Dryden had a powerful piece of intelligence that, if released to the press and thus the nation, would bring about the ruination of the General's career. That was why Thomas had come. If he was ever going to be with Sasha, on Earth or Aurora, he had to make the multiverse safe for her. And that meant unseating the General by whatever means necessary.

"To tell you the truth, I never believed anyone would come for it," Dryden said, leaning forward on her elbows and looking him in the eye. "This isn't some public relations nightmare we're about to unleash here, Mayhew. This is a nuclear bomb; it will likely throw the country into absolute chaos, make the monarchy look weak, and open us up to further and escalated attacks from Libertas, which, as you know, has gained quite a bit of ground in the past few months."

"I understand."

"Do you?" Dryden sat back and folded her hands in her lap. "Do you know why Moss's code phrase was 'I've seen the face of God'?"

"No," Thomas said. "I didn't think he believed in God."

"He doesn't." Dryden laughed. "Believe me, he doesn't. I left the KES ten years ago, under very bad circumstances. I protested the actions taken by my superiors regarding an operative who reported to me, and as a consequence I lost my job. Due to the sensitive nature of my mission, I was placed under surveillance, had my assets seized. Eventually I had to go into hiding, change my name and move to the back of beyond, and still, I feel the eyes of the KES on me everywhere I go. This isn't a game, Thomas. Not to me, and not to Moss."

"Not to me, either." Nothing that put Sasha in danger was a game to him.

"The information I'm about to give you—Moss stole it and gave it to me for safekeeping. If the General knew I had it, Moss and I both would be dead. We worked on the many-worlds project for years; he's the only person in the government I trust. When I asked him what he wanted me to do with this information, he told me to sit on it, to wait. We needed the perfect moment, when the General was weak and the country was ready."

"I still don't understand what that has to do with Dr. Moss's views on religion," Thomas said, "or lack thereof."

"I was impatient," Dryden said. "I was sure that at any moment the KES would find me and kill me and I'd never get the opportunity to see the General fall. I wanted to know how long it would take for us to get to that moment—days? weeks? a year? Moss laughed at me. He said the right time was as likely to come as he was to see the face of God."

"So what's changed?"

Dryden shrugged. "The General made a mistake. He thought going to war with Farnham would strengthen his position, but he was wrong. The nation was enthralled with the princess's wedding; public opinion of the royal family was at an all-time high. Nobody can resist a young, good-looking couple in love."

"They weren't in love," Thomas pointed out. "They hadn't even met."

"The Castle media department was doing an excellent job of spinning that into a fairy tale," Dryden said. "Say what you will about those people, but they're very good at what they do."

"So what is this explosive information?" Dr. Moss was a strange character, slightly crazy, entirely paranoid. Thomas was starting to wonder if Agent Dryden was the same. What if there *was* no intel? What if he was putting Sasha's life at risk—not to mention his own or those of the junior agents who had followed him down into this foxhole—for nothing but the mutual delusion of two desperate people?

Dryden rose from her chair. She walked over to the wall of screens and pressed the power button on the only one that wasn't showing some kind of news report. Instead of turning on, the screen swung forward on a hinge, revealing a safe. Dryden opened the safe and drew out a thin file folder. "Do you know what a kill list is?"

"Exactly what it sounds like. A list of people to kill."

"Ten points, toy soldier," Dryden said. Thomas cringed. He hadn't been a toy soldier in years, and he'd sailed through the Academy so quickly he almost hadn't been one at all. "The thing about kill lists is that they're illegal. The government cannot simply execute its citizens in secret."

"For some reason, I don't find that comforting." He remembered the General's threat to send an exterminator after Sasha. There were things that went on in the KES that even a shadow agent like him could never guess at, each one more horrifying than the last.

"You shouldn't. The General is smart about how he uses the kill list. He doesn't just go around taking out people who disagree with him or cause temporary trouble. But he does do it, and the most recent name on this list is . . . ." Dryden shook her head. "I didn't even believe it at first, that's how shocking it is."

"You keep the kill list in a file folder? Shouldn't it be on some secure server somewhere?"

"Oh, why didn't I think of that? A server." Dryden frowned. "Because servers get hacked, even secure ones. The General doesn't keep the kill list on a *server*. The orders exist only in hard copy, on lightning paper, so they're incredibly easy to get rid of. You touch a flame to these things, and they'll go up in two seconds. Drop them in water and they dissolve instantaneously. Only two copies of each kill order are created: one that goes to the mission agent tasked with carrying out the assassination—which is destroyed as soon as it's read—and one that goes in the KES shadow archives in Subbasement H of the Tower. That's where these came from."

Dryden handed Thomas the folder. "The most recent kill order, the one you want, is on top. But you might want to flip through them. There's another one, from about a decade ago, that I think you should probably see."

Thomas opened the folder and forced himself to look at the top sheet. His eyes widened as he ran down the mission data sheet. "This can't be right."

"It's right," Dryden said. "It's real, it happened, and the General ordered it. Now do you see why we had to handle this thing like plutonium?"

"I don't understand," Thomas said. "Why would the General order this? How does this make his position stronger?"

"The General has been siphoning power from the king for almost his entire career. The arranged marriage between Juliana and the prince of Farnham was the General's idea. The king resisted at first, but eventually the General won. He always won with the king, in the end. I assume that once the treaty was signed and the marriage agreed upon, the king had finally outlived his usefulness."

"So what you're telling me—"

"I'm not telling you. That paper is," Dryden pointed out.

"The General had the king assassinated," Thomas finished. "That's what I'm supposed to believe?"

"Well, not exactly," Dryden said. "He didn't actually die, if you recall."

"Not yet. But it seems like he's getting there."

"If the General stays in power, this war with Farnham is only the beginning," Dryden said. "Are you sure you can do this? He is your father, after all."

"My father's name was Harper Lebec. He died on a military base almost fifteen years ago," Thomas said, staring at the king's kill order. "The General is just the man who raised me."

"Like that's such a small thing. And anyway, you say that now, but plotting against the king is high treason, and I'm sure you know what the penalty for that crime is in this country."

Death. The penalty for high treason in the UCC was death. Thomas understood, finally, Dryden's concerns. By turning the kill order over to the press, he was guaranteeing his father's execution, and she didn't think he was strong enough to do it.

Dryden tried to take the folder from him, but Thomas held on tight. "You don't have to do this," she said. "We can find someone else. I would understand."

But Thomas was barely listening. He had started to flip through the other kill orders, traveling years into the KES's secret, dirty past searching for what Dryden had told him to look for. He knew it as soon as he saw it. The very first field on the kill order form after the date was NAME—LAST, FIRST, and the last sheet from the bottom had ANDERSON, GEORGE typed across the top.

The General had ordered the murder of Sasha's father.

FOURTEEN

I couldn't sleep all night. When the first rays of sunlight pierced the curtains, I got out of bed, careful not to make any noise. I dressed and went downstairs to see if anyone else was awake. I found Agent Dryden in the kitchen making coffee and accepted a steaming cup.

"Nobody's up yet," she said. "Why don't you have a seat?"

"Okay." I blew on my coffee, trying to work up the courage to ask the question that kept pinging around in my head. "Agent Dryden?"

"You can just call me Dryden," she said with a smile. "It's what my friends used to call me, back when my name wasn't officially Constance. Back when I had friends. It's hard to be social when you're in hiding."

"Dryden." I took a deep breath. "Thomas told me you worked on the many-worlds project back when you were in the KES."

"That's true." She looked as if she knew exactly what I was about to ask.

"My father's name was George Anderson," I told her. "Did you know him?"

"I did," she said. "George worked for me. I was the one who sent him to Earth in the first place. I was very disappointed when he chose to stay."

"I'm not," I said. "If he hadn't, I wouldn't be here."

"Fair enough. What is it you really want to ask, Sasha?"

"What was my dad like?" I asked. "He and my mom died when I was seven, so I never really knew them. I hardly remember anything about them. I'd like to know if he was a good man."

"You have to understand—Anderson reported to me, but we weren't close in any sense of the word. I was his KES handler, but he wasn't an agent. He was a scientist. We didn't have all that much in common."

"But you talked to him," I pressed. "You knew him. You must have had some kind of opinion."

"Your father always struck me as a man of principle. It wasn't my decision to put him on the front lines of Operation Looking Glass; I thought it was an odd choice. He never seemed comfortable with the assignment, and it didn't surprise me when he defected. Is that what you wanted to know?"

"Not exactly," I said. "I was hoping you could tell me more about what he was like as a person."

"Does it matter? He was your father. Surely you would love him no matter what."

"Yeah. I just . . . I have a hard time picturing my parents. They're these very rough sketches, and I'm trying to fill in some of the details."

"Well, let's see what I can remember. He was very funny, your dad. Our meetings were businesslike and serious, because of the matters we were discussing, but he always found an opportunity to make me laugh. He liked classical music quite a bit, but he couldn't play any instruments, because he was tone deaf. He had a sister, I believe. He talked about her sometimes, how jealous she would've been if she knew he was living in another universe. He liked to say she was the adventurous one in the family."

"Did he have any other siblings?"

"I'm not sure. Like I said, we didn't often discuss personal matters. But it's possible."

I had an aunt. Maybe, if she'd married and had kids, I had an uncle and cousins. An actual, honest-to-goodness family in Aurora. I promised myself that I would find them someday. When all of this was over, I was going to track them down and meet them face to face, and I was going to bring Thomas with me. Maybe the big issue in my life wasn't choosing a universe to call home; maybe it was figuring out a way to balance them both.

"If Dad didn't want to participate in Operation Looking Glass, why did he take the assignment?"

"He was young and brilliant, and his country was asking him to serve," Dryden said. "What would you have done?"

Thomas entered the kitchen, rubbing his eyes. "Is that coffee?"

"Help yourself," she said. "There are mugs in the cupboard next to the stove."

Thomas leaned over the sink and splashed his face with cold water. "Everybody's up," he said, drying off with a dish towel. "We're going to leave in about thirty minutes."

"I'll go get Selene," I said, rising from my chair. Thomas looked out the window over the sink and stiffened. "What is it?"

"Motos coming up the drive," he said. Dryden stood so quickly her chair clattered to the floor. "They look like KES."

"How do they know you're here?" Dryden demanded. "Who did you tell?"

"Nobody!"

"Your moto? Could it have a tracker on it?"

"I looked carefully before we left Warren's Run. I didn't find anything."

"Amateurs," Dryden muttered. "Okay, get all your people together and go out the back door. There will be a path to your left that goes into the woods—take it. There's a van in a clearing half a mile from the house; the doors are unlocked, and the keys are under the driver's seat. The path will take you through the woods and dump you on a country road that leads to the Interdominion Roadway. Go *now*."

"What about you?" I asked. Thomas grabbed my hand, but I pulled away. "Come with us!"

Dryden shook her head. "I'll only slow you down."

"But they'll—"

"I know what they'll do," she said. Horror dawned on me as Thomas dragged me out of the kitchen and down the hall. The KES weren't coming for *us;* they were coming for *her.* Dryden had been hiding from them for ten years, and we'd led them straight to her.

"We have to help her, Thomas," I protested as he shoved me out the back door. Adele thundered down a nearby staircase with Cora, Navin, Tim, and Selene in tow, while Sergei and Rocko burst out of the living room clutching black duffel bags and hard briefcases.

"I know," he said, pulling out his gun. Adele did the same, but he shook his head. He repeated Dryden's instructions word for word. "You've got to get everyone out of here."

"We're not leaving you behind, are you crazy?" Adele demanded. I clutched Thomas's sleeve, but he stepped out of my reach. Panic flooded my body—this wasn't what I meant!

"I'll be right behind you," he said. "I'm just going to give her some cover, that's all."

"You can't do that alone, man," Tim said, pulling out his gun. "I'll help."

Thomas nodded, and Adele puffed up as if she was going to explode. "What, you're going to let him stay and you're ordering *me* off?"

"You're my second, Nguyen, and it's your job to get stuff done," Thomas snapped. "The most important thing is to protect the two of them"—he pointed to Selene and me—"so do it."

Adele took a deep, angry breath into her lungs, then expelled it in a huff. "Come on," she said, stepping through the back door. "Let's move."

I wanted to insist on staying with Thomas, but I knew I shouldn't. I didn't have a weapon or any sort of protection except the power, and a little energy wasn't going to stop bullets. Besides, Selene was running down the path to the trees, and I couldn't leave her alone with the KES agents. So I followed the group into the woods. We'd just reached the clearing and the van when we heard the loud report of a rifle echo through the still morning air.

"We have to go back," I said, grabbing Adele by the arm. "We have to help him!"

"You heard my orders," Adele said. "He wants us out of here."

"You can't just abandon them!" I started walking back in the direction of the house, but she motioned to Sergei and the team surrounded me. "Seriously? You're going to keep me here?"

"No," Adele said. "*Seriously,* I'm going to pile you and the rest of these people into that van and drive you to the Tattered City, because that is what I was told to do, and so help me, Sasha, if you get in my way—"

"You'll what? Shoot me?" I stared her down. "I'm not leaving him behind!"

"It looks like you won't have to," Selene said, pointing over my shoulder. I turned and saw Thomas and Tim running toward us. I broke into a smile, but Thomas's expression was grim, and when he reached us, he was all business.

"Let's go," he said, bustling Selene and me into the van. In seconds we had pulled out of the clearing and onto the small dirt path that wound through the woods. It was horribly quiet in the car; nobody said anything, but everyone was thinking the same thing. Everyone, maybe, except Selene, who stared out the window at the trees whipping by, lost in some kind of memory or dream of Taiga.

I couldn't stand the silence anymore. "What happened back there? Where's Agent Dryden?"

Thomas gripped the steering wheel so hard his knuckles turned a sickly shade of white. "They took her. She's gone."

FOR THE FIRST TIME IN

two months, when Juliana woke up, there was sun streaming into the room. She'd always been kept underground, never had a window. She closed her eyes and pretended that she was back in her own bed at the Castle. It worked—for about three seconds, and then there was a knock at the door. It was a porter with a lunch tray; she hadn't realized it until now, but it was after noon. Bless you, Sophie, *Juliana thought as she shoved food into her mouth in a most unprincesslike way—not that she cared.*

After she ate, she showered and dressed, and by the time Callum arrived, she was feeling almost human again.

"Hello," he said, leaning against the doorjamb with his hands in his pockets and smiling at her. "How'd you sleep?"

She shrugged. "I had a hard time turning my brain off. I keep thinking about my father."

Callum hung his head. "Me too. I know I only met him once, and he was already . . . ill. But I admired him."

"You did?"

"Why do you have that look on your face, like you don't believe me?"

"Because I don't believe you."

"Well, that explains it." He laughed. "Juli, your father's reign was not without its controversies, but underneath all the politics, I believe

he was a good man who cared about the people he was born to serve. You and I should consider ourselves lucky if we end up ruling with as much grace and character as he did."

"If we end up ruling at all," Juliana said. She still wasn't sure that she wanted to. After all she'd gone through to get away from that life, was she really going to walk back into the Castle and take her place on the throne as if nothing had happened? Even her feelings for Callum didn't seem like a good enough reason to spend the rest of her days doing something she hated.

"I'm willing to bet that we will," Callum replied.

"You're very optimistic, aren't you?"

"You've said that to me before. I liked it when you called me Cal. How come you stopped?"

Juliana looked away, her face flushed. "Why do you know so much about my father's reign?"

"I paid very close attention," Callum said. "I've always been interested in history and politics. Probably because I knew I'd never get to do any governing. In Farnham, the heir is the one trained to run the country; the spare just gets to stand in the background during photo ops and sit pretty for an official portrait once every ten years."

"Well, you are very pretty," Juliana said. He stepped into the room, closing the distance between them, and took her gently by the chin.

"Juliana?" The low, sexy way he said her name made her heart glow.

"Yes," she whispered.

"Do you really think I'm pretty?"

She burst out laughing, and he silenced her with a kiss. It started off insistent, almost too demanding and intimate—you belong to me, it seemed to say, which was not something Juliana was used to—but as the kiss deepened, and all the thoughts in her brain began to slough off and blow away, the chains around her heart loosened, and she felt capable of all those things Callum saw in her: bravery, goodness, strength. She wanted so badly to be the girl he thought she was. She wanted him to love her, the real her, and she wanted to be worthy of that love.

They pulled apart, breathless. He rested his forehead against hers. "There's something I have to tell you."

"Okay," she said, pressing a kiss against his cheek. "Tell me."

"Let's go for a walk," he suggested, taking her hand. "It's such a nice day outside. We might as well enjoy it."

Juliana and Callum strolled through the gardens of the congressional mansion hand in hand. At first they talked of inconsequential things. He told her funny stories about his brother, Sonny, who was an accomplished practical joker. Not wanting to be outdone, Juliana entertained him with a story of how she and Sophie escaped from their Lofton dorm and dodged all of her KES bodyguards to attend an underground concert in downtown Columbia City—only half of which was made up.

When they were far enough away from the house that Callum could be sure they weren't going to be overheard, he stopped and gestured for her to take a seat on a nearby bench.

"What's wrong, Cal?" she asked, giving the nickname a try. She almost didn't want to call him that, knowing Sasha had, but it made

him smile, and she figured it was worth the guilt and jealousy that tugged at her heart.

"I wanted to talk to you about what happened in Adastra," he said, sitting down next to her. She took his hand. He seemed so worried, she almost didn't want to hear what he had to say. It wasn't possible that he knew what she and Lucas had done to Thomas, was it?

"Can I ask you a question first?" It was a pretty transparent attempt to change the subject, but she wasn't quite ready to talk about Adastra.

He cocked his head inquisitively. "Sure."

"When we were in those cells, why did you tell me your name was Peter?"

"I didn't think it would be smart to tell a stranger who I was."

"No, that I understand," Juliana said. "I mean, why Peter?"

"Oh," he said with a laugh. "It's my middle name. After Peter Corbit, the founder of Farnham. Why did you tell me your name was Sasha?"

"Not sure. It was just the first thing I thought of." Great, yet another line of questioning she was eager to avoid. "You were saying? About Adastra?"

"Right." He cleared his throat. "I wanted you to know . . . I mean, I wanted to tell you that when my mother threw you into the Hole, I . . ." He squeezed his eyes shut, as if trying to push away the memory. "I worked so hard to get you out, Juli. You have to believe me, I did everything I could, but she refused, and you can't make my mother do anything she doesn't want to do. I tried bribing the guards, but they're too afraid of her, and when she found out about it, she locked me in my bedroom and posted armed men outside my door."

"Oh, Cal," she said, rubbing his arm. "It's all right."

"No, it's not!" He took a deep breath. "I couldn't forgive myself for leaving you. And now that I know where you ended up, I feel even worse. Every time I think about you down there in the dark, afraid and alone, I just . . ."

"Callum," she said, putting a firm hand on his shoulder. He hadn't done anything to her, and she couldn't let him keep beating himself up over it. He could apologize to Sasha someday if he wanted, although if Juliana had her way, he would never even know she existed. "We're both okay. I think, when it comes to all this, we should let the past be the past."

"You can do that?" he asked, as if he couldn't believe she would ever forgive him. What had she done to deserve someone this good?

"I absolutely can."

He smiled and kissed her. "I love you, Juli."

"I—" she began, but at that moment, Sophie came rushing up, looking frantic.

"Juli," she said, breathing hard, "you have company."

★

FIFTEEN

"Where is she?" Selene asked. We were all in the draw-ing room at the congressional mansion in the Tattered City. Thomas and Adele had flashed their KES badges at the guards and gotten us in easily; Selene and I had slipped in among the group of KES agents, who took care to shield us with their bodies as we trooped past servants and staffers in the hallways.

"She'll be here in a second," Navin said. Selene's restless-ness was making everyone kind of jumpy, me most of all, since I could feel her emotions lighting up the tether like fire-works. "Keep your sandals on."

Selene glanced at her feet. "They *are* on."

"Oh boy," Tim muttered. "Here we go."

Selene, it's okay, I said. *You can relax. We found her.*

I don't know, Sasha, Selene replied. *I don't like this place. I don't like having all these people around. They want to take her away from us.*

First of all, nobody can make Juliana do anything she doesn't want to do. They work for her. And second . . . Thomas wants her to go to Taiga. He told me they need a place to hide Juliana until the Rowanites can bring down the General.

She gave me a sharp look. *He said that?* The tether loosened a little.

Everything is going to be fine, I assured her. Call me selfish, but Juliana was far from my biggest concern at the moment. Thomas hadn't spoken more than two words together since Gorman's Gate, and now he was standing apart from everyone else, staring out the window, lost in thought. Under normal circumstances I would've tried to talk to him, but we were still tiptoeing around each other in public, and this did not seem like the right time for me to show more interest in him than was appropriate. But I couldn't stop watching him and wondering what was going through his head.

The doors opened, and we all stood as Juliana strode into the room. She still had that awful blond hair, but in all other ways, she looked the same as I remembered her—the same as Selene, standing right by my side. Each of the KES agents, including Thomas, took a knee in front of her, something I'd never seen them do before, even when I was pretending to be Juliana. I glanced at Selene, who was curious but not surprised, and then I understood, with gut-wrenching certainty, that the king had died. Juliana was the queen presumptive of the United Commonwealth of Columbia.

It happened this morning, Selene explained. *There wasn't time for them to tell us before we had to leave Gorman's Gate.*

Then how do you know? I demanded. *Wait, no, let me guess— listening.*

That's right. I wasn't sure if I should tell you.

Why not?

I was afraid it might upset you. Selene put a hand on my shoulder. *I know how attached you were to Juliana's father. I assume that's why none of the KES agents told you, either.*

I stepped away from her, feeling betrayed. Just because the

KES agents didn't want to tell me about the king—for which I blamed Thomas, the only person in that group who cared how I felt about anything—didn't mean she should have kept it from me. We were supposed to be a team. Grief washed through the tether, soaking it all the way through, and it was hard to find the boundary between the sadness I felt over the king's death and the devastation Juliana was experiencing.

Her face was a dark mask of anguish, and in spite of all she'd done, I felt an overwhelming desire to comfort her, even as the repulsion that struck whenever I met one of my analogs pushed me away. What we'd been through mattered—I wasn't naïve enough to think that it didn't—but it seemed so small in the face of this enormous, unprecedented moment. We were together, the three of us, and it felt as right as it did wrong. The tether writhed with emotion and power; it was a struggle to stand still and say nothing.

"No," Juliana croaked. "No, no, no—get up! I'm not your sovereign. Do not kneel in front of me."

"Your Majesty," Thomas began, but Juliana covered her face with her hands and shook her head. Her shoulders trembled with everything she was trying to keep inside, but I could sense it all through the tether; it seemed as if the universe were crumbling to pieces. Selene grabbed my hand, and I squeezed her fingers. I was so sorry for Juliana. Everything she'd run from was staring her right in the face.

"Don't call me that!" Juliana snapped. "What are you even doing here?"

"Juli," Callum said, in a voice so soft it was almost a whisper. He put an arm around her. "It's going to be all right."

"No, it's not! Look at them, Callum. *Look.* What makes you think that anything is ever going to be all right?" Juliana pointed at Selene and me, and Callum noticed us for the first time. Confusion flashed across his face as he tried and failed to make sense of what he was seeing.

"What's going on?" he asked, although it was hard to tell whom he expected answers from. Thomas's shoulder brushed mine as he stepped past me to stand in front of Callum and Juliana.

"Your Highness," he said to Callum. "I'm not sure if you remember me. My name is Thomas Mayhew, and I'm an agent with the King's Elite Service."

"Of course I remember you," Callum said coldly, but he seemed relieved to have someone to direct his anger toward. "You're Juliana's bodyguard. I'd like to know where you and your friends were while Juliana was being held against her will by Libertas."

"Callum . . ." Juliana put a hand on his arm, then snatched it away. In a few seconds he would know everything. She was afraid that when he did, he would hate her. "There's something I have to tell you."

"Who are they?" he demanded, staring at Selene and me.

Juliana knew she had to explain, but she couldn't find the words. Her mind reached out to me, pleading for my help. She didn't even know she was doing it, but the dark red of her presence smoldered like burning coal at her end of the tether, and her desperation pummeled through my brain.

"Callum," I said, venturing a tiny smile. This was going to be so hard for him to understand. I wanted to show him, in whatever way I could, that he had nothing to fear from me. It surprised me how happy I was to see him again. "My name is Sasha Lawson. The girl you met at the Castle wasn't Juliana—it was me."

"That's ridiculous! Juli, tell her that's ridiculous." He glanced at Juliana, but she wouldn't meet his eyes. "Juliana, please."

"It's true," Thomas said. "Juliana went missing three weeks

before the wedding was supposed to take place. She turned herself over to Libertas in exchange for help escaping her life at the Castle. I took Sasha out of her world—a universe parallel to ours called Earth—and forced her to act as the princess while the KES looked for Juliana. It was Sasha you spent time with and Sasha you ran away with. It was Sasha your mother threw into the Hole."

"Out of her *world*? Do you know how crazy that sounds?" Callum couldn't stop looking at me. All the scrutiny made me nervous—reminded me, in a way, of having to perform as Juliana back at the Castle. Now I had to perform as myself, to prove who I was, and I found I knew how to do that even less.

"And what about her?" Callum pointed at Selene. "Don't tell me she's from a parallel universe, too."

"I am." Selene was irritated at having to deal with all of this. Callum meant nothing to her. But Juliana was an entirely different story. This was the first time Selene was meeting her, I realized with a start. She was absolutely thrilled. "Juliana, I've come a very long way to find you."

Juliana shook her head. "This is not happening."

"Let me get this straight," Callum said. All the color had drained out of his face, which made his blue eyes seem even brighter. "*You* were the one I was . . . with at the Castle. You're the one I almost married." We never would've gotten married, but it wasn't the time to quibble over details. "The one who almost *poisoned* me."

"What?" Juliana glared at me. "You poisoned him?"

"Please note that he said 'almost,'" I shot back. Who was she to get on her high horse after all the trouble she'd caused and all the people she'd hurt? Anger was quickly burning away any sympathy I'd felt for her. Typical Juliana, still out to save her own skin.

"And *you*." He turned to face Juliana. "You lied to me. You pretended it was you I'd been with at the Castle. You let me apologize for leaving you behind in the Hole when the entire time it wasn't even you who got thrown in there!"

"I didn't want you to hate me," Juliana said, clutching his arm desperately. He shook her off and refused to look her in the eye. "I like you so much, Callum, and I didn't want you to know what I'd done."

"This is absurd," Callum said. "I can't believe it."

"Believe it," Selene said impatiently. "I can appreciate that you're getting a lot of new information all at once, but to be honest, this has very little to do with you. You're just one small piece of a large puzzle, and we don't have time for you to come to terms with this slowly."

"And which one are you?" Callum demanded. "The one I kissed on the beach or the one I danced with at the gala?"

"Neither," Selene said with a haughty glare. As if she would *ever* have allowed some strange boy to kiss her. Leonid's face flashed across the tether.

"You kissed him?" Juliana asked me.

"Oh my God," I exclaimed. "I didn't kiss him, he kissed me, and by the way, let's not forget that I never would've been here in the first place if you hadn't run away from your own life!"

"You should be thanking me," Juliana snapped. "If I hadn't left, you never would've met your boyfriend."

"Hey," Thomas said, stepping in between us. "Don't start with that, Juliana."

Callum tossed me an exasperated look. "So you *were* with him. I knew it."

Adele cut us off: "You're acting like a pack of children. We have a war going on here and a brand-new queen who needs protection. You're just going to have to work out your messy emotional issues later."

"Adele is right," Thomas said. "We have to—"

But we didn't get to hear what Thomas thought we had to do, because the door opened and Sophie barreled through.

"Juli," she said, her eyes wide with panic, "there's a whole group of Libertas agents at the door. They're demanding that we release you to their custody."

"How did they know I was here?" Juliana asked.

Sophie's face fell. "It must have been the guards. Everyone in this city is in Libertas's pocket. You have to get out of here, now!"

Thomas surged forward. "Is there a second exit that would allow us to avoid a shootout?"

"I—I think so," Sophie stammered. "There's a hidden door in the back garden wall. My father uses it all the time when there are riots outside the front gates." Her eyes landed on Selene and me. She looked absolutely floored to see us there, wearing her best friend's face. "Who are they?"

"Forget it," Juliana said, grabbing Sophie by the arm. "We need you to show us where this gate is. Can you do that?"

Sophie nodded. "Come with me."

Sophie led us through the mansion and into the gardens. The KES agents flanked Selene, Juliana, Callum, and me as we made our way through a maze of rosebushes.

It's going to be all right, Selene said. Juliana stiffened; I was getting so used to talking to Selene in my head, I'd sort of forgotten just how strange it could be the first time. However good at shutting us out Juliana had been before, that was all shot to hell now. The power had weakened whatever defenses she'd constructed against our minds. It was just as Selene said it would be: the closer we were and the longer we remained together, the more entwined our minds were becoming and the better we got at using the tether.

He hates me, Juliana thought despondently. *It's entirely my fault.*

It doesn't matter what he thinks, Selene told her. She was trying to help, but that wasn't what Juliana needed to hear. *All that matters is that the three of us are together.*

Juliana glared at Selene. *I don't even know who you are!*

Juliana, I said. *Callum will forgive you. It's obvious he cares about you a lot—he's just having a hard time coming to terms with all this.* I had no idea why I was trying to help her. What did I care if Juliana was upset? She was only getting what she deserved. But there was the tether, tugging at me, reminding me that whatever my opinion of her was, she and I were connected. Until we broke it, I was going to feel every awful thing she felt.

Regardless of my motivations, the rosy light of her mind brightened, and I felt the tether relax. *You really think so?*

I had no idea if Callum would ever forgive her, but the force of her emotions made my brain feel like it was going to explode, so if it calmed her down, I'd tell her anything she wanted to hear. *I do. You have to admit, if the tables were turned, you'd be angry, too.*

Sasha, I . . . I'm so sorry. I recoiled in surprise. The last thing I expected to get was an apology from Juliana. *I didn't realize how many people would suffer because of my choices.*

I hesitated. *It's okay. I know what it's like to live a life you don't want.* I didn't think I meant it, but by the time I finished saying it, I realized it was true.

"It's here," Sophie said, pushing her way through a gap in the hedge and disappearing. We followed her and found ourselves standing in a tiny stone alcove. There was a door in the wall, fitted with an LCD lock. It scanned Sophie's palm, and she punched in the code, a process that was far too familiar to me by now. The door slid open, and when I peered through, I saw a quiet, nondescript private street on the other side.

It felt as though we were walking right into a trap.

"Thomas," I said. He turned to look at me; so did Sasha and Juliana, perhaps sensing my nervousness through the tether. "I don't think—"

"Let's go," Adele said, waving the KES agents forward. Thomas put a hand on her shoulder to hold her back, but she shook him off. "We don't have time for any of your petty personal crap, Mayhew. We're going."

She barreled through the door with her gun raised, and there was nothing for the rest of us to do but to follow her.

"Where are you taking us?" Callum demanded.

"Our moto is just up the street," Thomas explained. "We're going to a KES safe house, and then we'll discuss what to do next."

Selene's green light danced happily on her end of the tether. *We're almost there,* she said. *Oh, Sasha. Taiga is almost saved.*

What are you talking about? Juliana asked. I was just about to respond when a bullet whizzed past my head and shattered the glass of the car window directly behind me.

THOMAS IN THE TATTERED CITY/1

"Get *down*!" Thomas grabbed the person closest to him—Adele—and pulled her to the ground, rolling away so he wouldn't flatten her. Bullets zipped through the air like rocks in a landslide, pinging against the metal siding of the motos that lined the street. The violent sound of glass breaking filled the air above his head, but time seemed to slow as the shards fell; they floated down like snowflakes, weightless and sweet. This happened sometimes: when the adrenaline started flowing, the world decelerated, as if someone had pulled the fabric of the universe tight around him. All at once he felt his senses heighten and his mind quiet as his training kicked in.

He pulled out his sidearm and pressed his back up against the nearest moto, then glanced around to assess the situation. To his left was Sergei, peeking through a blown-out window, with Juliana cowering in his shadow. To his right—he let out a deep sigh of relief—was Sasha, pressed against the concrete sidewalk, with Navin and Selene at her side. Cora and Rocko had dragged Callum behind another moto, and Tim was standing against the mansion's garden wall, hidden in the shadows. Everyone was alive and apparently unhurt. Well, almost. Adele pulled herself into a seated position beside him, clutching her knee.

"A little gentler next time, Mayhew, if you don't mind," she grumbled.

"Maybe next time I'll take a pass on saving your life," he returned. Adele laughed.

Without agreeing on it or sharing anything more than a glance, he and Adele rose to their feet and began shooting at the windows of the building on the opposite side of the street. Rocko, Cora, Sergei, and Tim followed suit, returning fire with an exactness that was indistinguishable from instinct. They discharged their weapons without hesitation, until the dark figures behind the empty eyes of the building stopped moving and disappeared. Breathing hard, Thomas exchanged looks with his team; there was a subtle gleam in their eyes that hadn't been there before, and he remembered how young they all were, himself included. They were still getting used to the exhilaration of fighting the bad guys and winning.

The bullet wound in his shoulder ached with the echo of his gun's recoil. He did a quick sweep of the street, narrowing in on Sasha, who had her hands pressed against her face. Selene touched her back; she jumped, startled, and looked up, spotting Thomas. He crouched down to examine her, brushing the hair away from her eyes and taking her hands.

"Are you okay?" If there'd ever been any hope of hiding the way he felt about her from his fellow agents, it had evaporated; Juli had done a fine job of unmasking their relationship, and although the words *boyfriend* and *girlfriend* seemed both too casual and too definite to describe what he and Sasha were, he was proud to wear the label, insofar as it meant anything at all.

She gave him a weak smile. "I'm fine. Just a little shaken up. No worries."

All he had was worries, but he didn't say that to her. Instead, he helped her to her feet and took her in his arms, because, really, what else could he possibly do?

Then she stiffened, and he knew she'd seen something, or heard something, or felt something he couldn't access. The tether linking her mind and those of her analogs sometimes seemed like a third person standing between them, always transmitting, always watchful. But he made a mistake. He misinterpreted, read the signal wrong.

"Gunner, Patel, bring the moto around," he said. He wanted away from this bullet-riddled, too-exposed street immediately. More than anything, he wanted to make them all safe, even the ones who didn't think they needed his protection.

Then he heard Juliana scream.

He whipped around, drawing his weapon again, even though he'd wasted all his bullets on the Libertine shooters. A dark green van with the ten stars of the Libertas insignia screeched to a stop at the intersection, pulling up just as a man in black dropped a sack over Juliana's head and looped an arm around her neck, dragging her toward the vehicle.

Sergei grappled with three other Libertines, fighting them off as best he could, but they overpowered him quicker than Thomas could run, knocking him unconscious with a hard blow to the head. He dropped to the ground, and his attackers ran off, jumping into the van as Juliana disappeared into its belly and shutting the door behind them.

Thomas sprinted after the van as it sped down the street. He ran harder than he ever had before, flying so fast over the broken asphalt that the soles of his boots barely touched the ground. The driver of the van stomped on the gas pedal;

he would lose them in seconds if he didn't do something. He leapt onto the back of the van, scrabbling for purchase on the bumper as his fingers closed over the hot metal handle. He felt it turn, and then the door opened, sending him soaring; he held on tight as he dangled off the back of the van. The road rushed like a river beneath his feet.

The van took a sharp turn and he swung back. Somehow Juliana had gotten the hood off, and he caught her terrified expression, heard her voice—so nightmarishly like Sasha's, threaded with panic—as she screamed his name. Then someone stepped between them and pointed a gun at his hand, still gripping the handle.

"Nice try, toy soldier," the man said with a self-satisfied grin. "Next time you might want to pay a little bit more attention." Then he fired the gun and Thomas let go, tumbling to the ground. The asphalt tore up every inch of exposed skin as he rolled to lessen the impact of the fall. He came to rest in a gutter, choking on a puddle of dirty, stagnant water. By the time he managed to stand, the van was nowhere to be seen.

Juliana was gone. "Thomas," Sasha said as he limped back to where he'd left the group. They were huddled together, talking in frantic, hushed voices. Sergei slumped against the moto, awake but injured; Cora held a ripped piece of fabric to his head in an attempt to staunch the bleeding.

Sasha rushed to Thomas's side and put a light hand to the cuts on his face, but he winced at her touch and jerked away. There was no part of him that didn't feel the hot, dark burn of shame at losing Juliana to Libertas—*again*—and he couldn't stand her kindness. Just looking at her reminded him how badly he'd failed, and for the first time he understood how much of a liability having her there was. She was a distraction, one that had cost him his mission and put his queen in terrible danger. Sasha never should've come to Aurora. It had been so stupidly selfish of him to see it any other way.

"Everybody, get in the moto, *now*." Nobody bothered to argue with him; the whole group was shaken up about losing Juliana, even Adele, Tim, and Cora, who'd all seen combat before. Even Rocko, who under most circumstances would've died rather than betray fear. They piled into the moto, all except Sasha, who hung back and fixed him with a searching look.

"Are you okay?" she asked.

He rubbed the back of his neck. "Yeah, I'm fine. It's just a couple of scratches."

"That's not what I meant." He stared at her blankly, and she stared right back. Finally she broke her gaze. "All right. I know, I know," she said as he gestured at the open moto door. "I'm getting in."

It had been just six weeks since he'd last seen the safe house on Eugenie Street, but he felt like an entirely different person. As they pulled up in front of the squat redbrick building amid the jungle of run-down high-rises that lined the block, he recalled, with perfect clarity, the person he'd been back then. Devoted and careful, he'd spent almost all of his time thinking about the KES and his mission, plotting the shortest route to success. It had never been about rising in the organization, not really. He'd been raised to believe he was built for greatness, and his whole life centered on realizing that potential.

But the safe house was the place where all of that focus and determination began to break down. Or maybe it had happened just a few hours earlier than that, on Earth with Sasha. Sometime between leaving his world and returning to it, a crack had formed inside of him, small at first, then gradually widening until it became an enormous canyon that split his heart in two irreconcilable pieces: the part that loved and would do anything to be with Sasha and the part that still wanted to serve his country, the people he'd pledged his life to protect. When he'd survived his execution and Sasha had returned for him, he'd thought, briefly and foolishly, that there was something he could do to bridge the gap, so that he could have both things. Now he knew that was impossible. He would have to choose, and soon, or else he would lose them both.

"What are we doing here?" Sasha asked. "I thought this place was compromised."

"It wasn't," Thomas replied. Distance, that was what he needed—to put as much space between himself and Sasha as possible so he could make his decision with a clear head. "Let's go."

"Where are we?" Callum demanded. "Where have you taken us?"

"This is a KES safe house," Adele explained. "We'll hunker down here until we can figure out what to do next."

"We have to find Juliana!" Callum insisted. "How much time do you need to figure that out?"

"It's not as simple as that," Tim replied. "We need strategy, tactics. We can't just go in there swinging our fists. We'll be crushed."

"Not to mention, we don't even know where they've taken her," Rocko pointed out.

Callum was quiet for a moment. "I think I might be able to help a little bit on that score."

"Great," Navin said. "Where is she?"

"Not here," Thomas said. "Let's get everyone inside.

Gunner, ditch the moto somewhere and meet us back here. Rocko, you go with her. I don't want anyone doing anything alone, you got it?" Libertas would never have been able to get their hands on Juliana if Sergei hadn't been the only agent guarding her when they pulled up. Thomas wasn't going to make the same mistake twice.

Everyone murmured in agreement, even Rocko. They all seemed wary of Thomas, as if they weren't sure what he would do next. He had to get himself together. He couldn't have his team doubting his leadership abilities, especially not while everything else was so uncertain. He'd put himself and his desires before his mission for far too long. It was time to give some thought to what everyone else needed from him.

He stood guard while the rest of them descended the stairs to the basement entrance. Sasha put her hand on his arm as she went by, but he let her pass without acknowledgment. Guilt plucked at him—she'd done nothing wrong, and she didn't deserve to be frozen out—but he didn't know what else to do. He was Agent Thomas Mayhew now, and Agent Thomas Mayhew didn't allow himself to get sidetracked worrying about other people's feelings. Emotions were poison to careful planning; he couldn't feel and think at the same time. Thinking was what the situation called for, so he put the half of his severed heart that cared only for her in the same dark cabinet where all of his secret pains and weaknesses lived, then shut the door.

As soon as Thomas stepped over the threshold, a familiar voice greeted him. "Well, if it isn't my favorite toy soldier," Fillmore said, grinning from his seat on the only chair in the room. The place had not changed at all since Thomas had last been there. It was still the bed and the metal munitions locker, with a tiny bathroom to the left. Sasha stared at the bed as if she expected it to come alive and bite her, and Thomas forced himself not to remember her lying there the night he brought her through the tandem.

Thomas glared at Fillmore. "That's enough."

"And look! You've brought my favorite fake princess with you," Fillmore continued, bowing low to Sasha, who looked so disgusted that Thomas had to smile. She really hated Fillmore, with good reason. "Who are the rest of these—?" His brow wrinkled as Selene stepped out from behind Sasha. Fillmore shot Thomas a confused look. "Where did you find *another* one?"

"Doesn't matter," Thomas said. Cora and Rocko came through the door. "We need your help. Libertas has the princess—"

"Queen," Callum supplied. "She's your queen now."

Leave it to the only royal in the room to insist he use Juliana's proper title in the midst of all this chaos. "Libertas has the queen, and we need a plan to get her out."

"Happy to be of service," Fillmore said. "Things have been a little dull around here since Operation Starling ended. How can I help?"

"I'm not sure yet," Thomas said, kneading the back of his neck. Fillmore could indeed be very useful, in spite of the fact that he was disrespectful and highly insubordinate at even the best of times. He knew the Tattered City better than anyone, and he'd been involved in several ops involving Libertas.

"You don't have a plan?" Callum asked. "Can't you just negotiate for her return?"

Rocko barked out a laugh. Thomas shot him a warning look, and Rocko scowled.

"No," Thomas said. "Libertas wouldn't release her if we offered to sell them the Commonwealth for a string of jade beads. We'll have to extract her."

"First you've got to know where they're keeping her,"

Fillmore pointed out. "Libertas has little hidey-holes all over this city. How do you plan on finding out which one they've taken her to?"

"I'm pretty sure Prince Callum can tell us." Callum looked at him through narrowed eyes. "You were held in the same place she was. You escaped Libertas with her. You must know something about where they kept her the first time. Maybe they'll bring her back there."

"That's a big maybe," Adele said, folding her arms across her chest. "They'd be pretty stupid to do that."

"Not if there's a reason they had her there in the first place," Callum said. He sat down at the foot of the bed and rubbed his temples, as if doing so would coax the memories out. "The whole time Juliana and I were in those cells together, there was one guy in particular who paid her a lot of attention. A Libertas leader called the Shepherd."

Sasha nodded. "He spent a lot of time with her before, too. When she was their ally instead of their prisoner."

Callum drew a sharp breath, as if he were only just re-membering what he'd recently learned about Juliana's be-trayal. "He was obsessed with her. I don't know why."

"Well, she is kind of hot," Tim said. He turned to Sasha and Selene and said, "Sorry if that was rude, but I mean, you guys *are* kind of hot."

"Thanks," Sasha said flatly. Selene shot her a bewildered look, but she just shook her head as if to say, *Ignore him.*

"I don't think that's how it was," Callum said. "It defi-nitely wasn't romantic. But it was intense. He would come to her in her cell and spend hours just talking at her. She never responded or really listened, but it was like he just had to have her in the room for some reason. He hated her, but he wouldn't leave her alone."

"Of course he hated her," Navin said. "She was the princess

of a country he and the terrorists he works for are hell-bent on destroying."

Callum shrugged. "I don't know. It just always seemed more personal than that. But I never saw them together or even met him myself. I only heard them through the wall."

"Is there anything you can tell us about the place they were holding you?" Thomas asked.

"They kept us underground, in this maze of rooms and hallways they call the catacombs," Callum said. "When we escaped, we took a staircase up to the street and we saw Thirteen Bells—that's what it's called, right? That huge bell tower in the middle of the City Center?"

Thomas nodded. "What else? Did you get a good look at the building itself?"

"No," Callum said. "We ran away so quickly, I didn't get a chance to look around. All I know is that it's near Thirteen Bells, and if the catacombs are anything to go by, the place is enormous. Our cells were near the kitchens, so we could smell the food being prepared."

"Tell us everything you remember," Adele said. "You never know what kind of small details will make a difference."

"I'm sorry, but there isn't anything else." Callum sank into a chair and covered his face with his hands. "We were so close to being free. To being safe. I should have protected her." He looked up, searching for a friendly face, and his gaze landed on Sasha. "I couldn't protect her. I couldn't protect you. Why can't I ever protect anybody?"

Sasha sank to her knees in front of him. "It's not your job to protect her, Callum." She gestured around the room at the KES agents. "It's theirs."

"I hate to agree with the analog, but she's right," Rocko said. "This is all Mayhew's fault."

"That's not what I meant," Sasha said, shooting Rocko a

cold stare. A wave of tenderness washed through Thomas's heart. He didn't need Sasha to defend him, but it made him feel better that she did.

"Maybe not, but it's the truth."

"There is one other thing," Callum said. "Late at night I could hear this thumping noise coming from upstairs. Juliana and I could never figure out what it was, but it happened all the time."

"Thumping?" Cora's face screwed up in confusion. "What kind of thumping?"

"I don't know," Callum said. "It sort of sounded like music, but why would they be playing music in their headquarters in the middle of the night?"

Fillmore's face lit up. "I know where they're keeping her. There's a huge nightclub in the City Center across the street from Thirteen Bells. It's called Martyr. Used to be a cathedral before the Church abandoned all its holdings in the Tattered City, and it's rumored to be owned and operated by Libertas."

"A nightclub." Thomas smiled. He couldn't help it. This was the very best piece of news he'd received all day. He glanced at Adele. "You know what that means, right?"

Adele nodded. "Carnival Columbia."

"Carnival Columbia," Thomas repeated. "We might just have found our way in."

"What's Carnival Columbia?" Sasha asked.

"It's a national holiday in the UCC," Callum explained, doing an admirable job of hiding his contempt. The prince likely had no respect for Commonwealth Independence Day celebrations, and Thomas didn't blame him. It wasn't as if Thomas had any interest in marking the day the people of

Farnham had seceded from the UCC and declared themselves their own country, either. "It's tomorrow."

"And what about Carnival Columbia is supposed to help us find Juliana?" Selene wondered. She'd been silent for quite a while, Thomas noticed. He wouldn't have thought it possible for her to be overwhelmed, but the farther they traveled from the Labyrinth, the less in control and confident Selene seemed. She depended on Sasha more and spent much of her time lost in thought. But she was still formidable when she set her mind to something, and he felt her eyes boring into him now, searching for answers.

"Carnival Columbia is kind of an antiquated name," Cora said. "Most people just call it the Night of the Masks."

Sasha's expression changed as understanding dawned on her, and then Selene. The way they shared information along the tether was incredibly unnerving. "Why?" Sasha asked.

Navin, who was a history buff, jumped in eagerly. "Well, back in 1789, John Rowan—he was governor of the New York Colony at the time—held a masquerade in honor of the new prince regent over in England."

Tim laughed. "Now you've got him started, he's going to lecture you on the last two hundred years. Buckle up."

"I'll keep it short," Navin said with a roll of his eyes. "Anyway, everyone who was anyone was at this party—the governors of all the other colonies, most of the high-ranking military officers, global ambassadors—and they were wearing masks. John Rowan's personal militia provided security, which should've tipped everyone off right away, but they trusted Rowan; they thought he was one of them.

"About halfway through the party, just about the time people realized that John Rowan wasn't actually *there*, word began to spread that armed insurgents had begun a siege of both Boston and New York, overpowering the British troops. Meanwhile, most of the influential people in the colonies were trapped at St. Lawrence, at the mercy of John Rowan's guard."

"St. Lawrence?" Sasha repeated. "Didn't Juliana's mother give her St. Lawrence?"

Thomas nodded. "Rowan gifted St. Lawrence to the Deforts after the Second Revolution. Lionel Defort—Juliana's very-great-grandfather on her mother's side—played the part of John Rowan on the Night of the Masks and kept everyone from escaping or being smuggled out."

"You said 'most' of the powerful people in the colonies were at St. Lawrence," Sasha pointed out, turning to Navin. "Who wasn't?"

"Well, John Rowan, for starters, but also Thomas Warren," Navin said. "They were in Columbia City—which was still called New York back then—claiming it in the name of the new United Commonwealth of Columbia. Once the war was over, people started celebrating the Night of the Masks every July seventh."

"With masquerades?" Selene guessed.

"That's right," Adele said. "They'll have a Night of the Masks celebration at Martyr—every bar and restaurant and club in the whole country does—and as long as we're on the guest list, we should be able to get in without anyone seeing our faces."

"I'm sorry, but why would Libertas throw a Night of the Masks party?" Sasha asked. "For that matter, why would anyone who lives here, considering how much they hate the UCC?"

"Well, first of all, not everyone in the Tattered City is in league with Libertas," Thomas said. "And it's not easy to get people to let go of their traditions. Libertas has only been around a quarter century; the UCC is eight times that old. Besides, holidays are lucrative opportunities, and if there's anything Libertas likes more than stirring up conflict, it's making money."

He turned to Fillmore. "This is where you come in. We need tickets to the Martyr masquerade, clothes, and masks. Can you do that?"

Fillmore shot him a frog-faced grin. "This is what I was built for, Mayhew. Give me a couple of hours and I'll have everything you need." Fillmore hopped to his feet, and in a matter of seconds he was out the door.

"So we're supposed to spend the next day and a half in this tiny room?" Callum asked.

"Oh no, Your Highness," Tim said. "This is just the antechamber. It's only for short-term stays. There's much more to this safe house than that." He strode to the bed and twisted the finial off one of the posts, exposing a small control panel. "Behold."

There was a door in the wall right next to the bed, and when Tim pressed a button on the control panel, it slid open, revealing the cavernous interior of the safe house beyond.

"After you," Tim said grandly.

SOMEONE WHIPPED THE

hood off Juliana's head, and she realized with sinking dread that she was right back where she started: a dark, damp cell in the catacombs of Libertas's headquarters. But this time she wasn't alone. In fact, she was the furthest thing from alone: the room was full of people, but it was so dimly lit that she couldn't see any of their faces.

"Who's there?" she demanded.

"Turn on the light," said a disembodied voice. Its owner was shielded by the darkness of the room, but she recognized him anyway. She'd spent so much time with the Shepherd over the past weeks, she heard him in her dreams. "I want to get a good look at her."

Suddenly it was so bright she had to cover her face with her arm. Tears pricked at the backs of her eyes; she bit her lip to keep from shedding them. Crying in front of Callum was one thing, but no way was she going to do it in front of the Shepherd.

She was surprised to see Lucas among the crowd. So much had changed after what happened in that Farnham prison. She'd become an inconvenience to Libertas instead of an asset, and Lucas had paid the price for it. He'd visited her sometimes, but he hadn't dared to speak to her. He'd seemed so broken. She'd understood why he felt the need to sit with her, though: she was his coconspirator, someone who knew the size and shape of his guilt because it haunted her, too.

Lucas was silent as death in the corner. He looked like death, his skin pale and sallow, with sagging dark bruises under his eyes, his lips chapped and bitten. He'd lost so much weight in the past weeks, his clothes hung wrong on his bones. He'd never been very strong to begin with, and Libertas was a demanding mistress.

There were a half-dozen other Libertines in the room, men and women. The Shepherd circled her slowly, taking special note of her face and hair, even going so far as to reach out and touch a lock of it.

"We'll have to fix you up," the Shepherd muttered. He gripped her chin in his hands and canted her head back and forth, side to side. "She's bruised—who did this?" He threw an angry glance toward his cohorts, who shrank back and shook their heads: Not me. *"Nobody touches her anymore, understand? We'll have to cover what's already here with makeup. Go tell Makenna." The Libertine closest to the door—one of the men—hurried off with a sigh of relief. The Shepherd's hold slackened, and Juliana ripped away, stumbling back. He caught her by the wrist, steadying her. She wrenched away again.*

"Strip her down," he said. He was, as always, dressed head to toe in black, every inch of skin covered by fabric except for his face, neck, and hands. She wondered what this getup was hiding; there was some faint pink puckering of the skin between the ear and shoulder of his right side: burns, long healed but permanent. She was so focused on the marks that it took a few seconds for his words to sink in.

"No!" she cried, wrapping her arms around her chest.

The Shepherd ignored her, addressing himself to the remaining Libertines in the room, Lucas exempted. She had a feeling he was there only to witness her humiliation, perhaps as his own punishment. "I want to see where we stand."

She fought them, but they overpowered her, and soon she was shivering in only her underwear, which had grown too big for her. She was skinnier than she'd been when she left the Castle, and she could tell from the way his eye roamed the landscape of her body that this was what the Shepherd meant to discover from her nakedness. There wasn't any lust in his eyes. To him, this was business.

221

"She looks like a prisoner of war," he barked at nobody in particular.

"I am," she reminded him, biting the ends of her words in fury. "Now give me back my clothes!"

He jerked his head, and one of the Libertines rushed forward with her rumpled things.

"We can't put her on the box looking like that," the Shepherd said. "Clean her up. Fix her hair. Find her some decent clothes, something that doesn't make her look like she hasn't eaten in three weeks. The people won't like it if they think we've let their little princess starve." His eyes flashed with menace, and he corrected himself: "Forgive me—their queen."

"The box?" Juliana asked.

"Yes, Your Majesty, don't you see? You're one of us now. And I mean for the people to know it. You're going to deliver a live, public statement of support for Libertas tonight."

"I won't," she said fiercely.

He paused for a moment. "Everyone, get out."

The only person who hesitated to follow orders was Lucas, who lingered at the door. "Out, Janus!" the Shepherd shouted. Lucas scurried away.

"You must think you're very clever, escaping from us like that," the Shepherd said, pacing the floor in front of her. "Care to tell me how you managed it?"

Juliana said nothing. She wouldn't have known how to explain what happened even if she'd wanted to.

"No? Fair enough. It doesn't matter now. We got you back." The Shepherd stared at her. "The king is dead—but you already knew that, right?"

"Yes," she said. "He's dead because you murdered him. So if you think I'm going to let you primp me up and push me onto some stage so you can get a sound bite of me praising Libertas, you're insane. I would never, ever support my father's killers. The people know that."

"The people." The Shepherd laughed. "The people think you're a spoiled, simpering child, and they don't trust you to lead them. We know what they want. We know how to protect them from the real threat."

"Which is what?"

"Those corrupt bloodsuckers you call a family and that rabid bulldog you've unleashed on this country," the Shepherd spat. "The General won't rest until he's killed every single one of his citizens to win a war nobody even wants to fight!"

She had no wish to defend the General, but she wasn't going to let him talk like that about her father. History would remember him however it wanted to, regardless of who he really was, but he wasn't even buried yet. "My father didn't want this war! He did everything he could to prevent it."

"He did nothing," the Shepherd shot back. "That joke of a royal wedding was a distraction, not a solution. The king was either too weak to bring the General to heel or he was unwilling. It doesn't matter which. He was a cancer on this country, and now the cancer has been cut out. I wish I could say Libertas was responsible for that act of patriotism, but unfortunately we didn't kill him. That honor belongs to the General."

The Shepherd smiled at the look on her face. "You don't seem shocked to hear that. Suspected it all along, didn't you? I knew you would. You're a pragmatist, Juliana. We're very similar in that way."

"You and I are nothing alike," she said.

"Oh, you would be surprised to discover how much we have in common," the Shepherd said. Juliana narrowed her eyes at him. The Shepherd had always been calm and composed with her in the past, but now he was impatient. There was something he was bursting at the seams to tell her. She decided to save him the trouble.

"And you would be surprised to discover how good my memory is," Juliana said. "I know who you are, Kit." She was proud of how she kept her voice from quavering. She wanted him to think she'd *always known, that she'd been playing her own game, but it wasn't until she'd heard him call Thomas "toy soldier" in the van that she started to suspect. It was a KES term, one that told her he was a defector. And the burn . . . everyone knew the traitor Kit Turner had escaped the Labyrinth by setting a fire in his cell. It had been a long time since she'd last seen a picture of him—years, in fact, almost ten—but as the pieces fell into place, memories began to rise to the surface, and finally everything clicked.* My brother, *she thought.*

"Blood does tell, doesn't it?" Kit said. "You realize that all your problems would've been solved if the king had just recognized me as his heir, right? You would've been like that Farnham prince you were supposed to marry: powerless, with nothing expected of you. You could've lived any life you wanted, within reason."

"That's why you turned your back on your country?" she demanded. "Because Dad wouldn't let you be king? If you ask me, that was the smartest thing he ever did."

Kit shrugged. "You're probably right. This country doesn't need another king. It needs a real leader, someone who's willing to put the power in the hands of the people."

"And you're that someone?" She laughed. "I'm sorry, but that's the most ridiculous thing I've ever heard."

"Not me," Kit said with a knowing smile. "Not yet. The Monad is going to turn this world upside down and make it new. I'm just his humble servant."

"The Monad," Juliana scoffed. "I'm starting to think he doesn't even exist."

"Oh, he exists," Kit said. "Resist all you want, Juliana. The world will change. And I'm going to make sure you get a front-row seat when it does."

224

SIXTEEN

"Sasha?"

Selene and I opened our eyes. Cora was standing at the door. "Food's ready. Thomas asked me to see if either of you were hungry."

"We are," I said, getting up off the bed. I knew Selene was just as starved as I was. We'd spent the last several hours trying to tune in to Juliana, and I felt as if I'd run a marathon. I turned to Selene and said, "Next time we do that we've got to carbo-load beforehand."

You're elated, she said as we followed Cora through the halls of the safe house and down the narrow back staircase that led to the kitchen.

I just can't believe it worked! But the tether was stronger than ever before, and a combination of chaos and exhaustion and fear had weakened Juliana's mental defenses enough that Selene and I working together could see through her eyes.

My first instinct was to tell Thomas about it, but he'd been acting weird around me ever since we lost Juliana to Libertas, and I got the sense—as much as I tried to ignore it—that he blamed me, somehow, for the fact that she'd been recaptured.

I blamed myself, too. I should've known what was happening before I did, but I was too focused on Thomas, too busy trying to push away the panic of the previous moments, that I wasn't listening. I wasn't paying attention to anything but him and me, and because of that I missed the warning. Finding Juliana wasn't just about saving Selene's world now, or breaking the tether, either. It was about making things right.

We found everyone already gathered in the big living room on the ground floor of the safe house, spooning pasta into their mouths. I sank into a chair and gratefully accepted a bowl from Navin.

"Sasha and I have something to tell you," Selene said, ignoring the food. "We were able to tap into Juliana's mind through the tether, and we saw the Shepherd tell her that he was going to put her on some kind of— Sasha, what was it?"

"The box," I told them. We'd decided without even discussing it not to tell the KES agents that the Shepherd and Kit Turner were the same person. Something about that information felt like a bargaining chip, and no matter what, we couldn't be sure what any of their loyalties were. I wasn't even sure if I should share the information with Thomas. Selene would certainly be angry if I did, and she would know. "He's going to force Juliana to go on television and deliver a public statement of support for Libertas tonight."

Several of the KES agents groaned. Thomas shook his head. "I should've known they'd try something like that. Now that the king's dead, she's the official voice of the Commonwealth. If the people think she's on Libertas's side, it validates whatever they're planning."

"The people despise the royal family," Callum said. "Won't Juliana's 'support' just make Libertas look worse?"

"Not if she comes out against the war with Farnham and

the actions of the UCC military," Adele said. "Juliana's approval rating shot up when everybody thought you two were going to get married, and then again when everybody thought she'd been kidnapped. My bet is that they're counting on people's newfound affection for her to turn the tide against the General once and for all and make it possible for them to do what they've always wanted: bring down the entire government."

"And then what are they going to do with her?" Callum demanded. Nobody answered him. "How do we even know she'll still be alive by tomorrow night?"

"Sasha and Selene will keep an eye on her," Thomas said. The certainty in his voice made me proud. It was easy, in a group of armed guards, to feel useless, but Selene and I had our talents, too. "If they get the sense that she's in imminent danger, we'll speed up our timeline and go in there by brute force." The agents exchanged looks—that wasn't something they thought had even the slightest chance of working.

"Somebody turn on the box," Rocko said. "Sounds like there's something we've got to see."

At eight o'clock sharp, we all gathered around the television to see Juliana deliver her public statement of support for Libertas. Her hair hung dark and silky over her shoulders. This cheered Selene up. *She looks like us again,* she said.

"Good evening, Columbia," Juliana began. Her voice was steady and calm, though both Selene and I could feel the fear vibrating like a high, shrill note along the tether. Selene squeezed my arm so tight she was cutting off my circulation. "I know that you're all frightened by the recent turn of events that has led to the invasion of our neighboring kingdom of Farnham, and unsure of what the future holds for our great country. My heart goes out to the family and friends of all the soldiers who have died in the past weeks, fighting for what some might call the preservation of our freedom and the reclamation of the lands that were lost to us in the Great War with Farnham.

"But I must also disavow the actions of the Columbian military leadership in launching this war. It has become clear to me that no longer do those who are commanding our armies and negotiating our diplomacy have any desire to work toward the benefit of our people. There is, however, one group that has always been fighting for you—for us, all true Columbians everywhere—and that is Libertas. Tonight I throw my full support behind Libertas and declare them my ally. I can only hope that you will do the same."

The screen faded to an image of the Libertas flag, a triangle of ten gold stars on a forest-green background. Adele punched the off button angrily with her thumb. I searched the room for Thomas and found him standing near the kitchen. His hands were balled at his sides, his knuckles practically white. The other agents began muttering to each other in low voices.

"The General is not going to like that," Tim said darkly. "I don't know about the rest of you guys, but I'm really glad not to be at the Labyrinth right now."

We all jumped when we heard the commotion coming from the safe house antechamber. Thomas went to the door.

"It's just Fillmore," he called over his shoulder. "And he's brought us some stuff."

"Some stuff," Fillmore muttered as he waddled into the room, arms stacked high with boxes. "I've got all your mission necessities right here, and not one of you ingrates has offered to help me carry them."

Sergei, Navin, and Cora got up to unburden Fillmore.

Navin rifled through his box and pulled out a handful of bright plumage. "Feathered masks? Fillmore, we're going to look like a real flock of idiots in these monstrosities."

"That was all that was left," Fillmore snapped. "You think it's easy to find nine masks this close to Carnival? You're lucky it's not worse."

"Did you get us on the Martyr guest list for tonight?" Thomas asked. Fillmore nodded. "How?"

"I've got my ways," Fillmore said, settling down in one of the fat-cushioned armchairs and sighing contentedly. "Now, which one of you wants to rub my feet?"

"And the rest of it?" Thomas prompted. "Did you get everything we asked for?"

Fillmore shrugged. "Sort of."

Thomas yanked open two large, bulky cotton bags and began rooting through them. He pulled out a variety of clothes—jeans, dark button-down shirts, and light jackets for the boys; jeans and black camisoles for the girls—all of which seemed to satisfy him. Then he went over to examine the contents of Navin's box, and his face fell.

"What are these?" Thomas asked. "I told you to get a bunch of different ones. They're all the same!"

"Not all," Fillmore protested. "There are a couple different options for the men."

"It's the *girls* we need to look different, Fillmore!" Thomas turned the box upside down and shook; about ten feathered, spangled masks tumbled onto the coffee table. There were a few different large masks, clearly meant for the boys, but the girls' masks, which were smaller, were identical: bright blue feathers, plenty of sequins, and short beaked noses that suggested the face of a tiny bird.

The sparrow, the starling, and the lark, I thought. But Selene and I were missing our sparrow. I could see why Thomas was so annoyed. It would be easy to differentiate between petite, long-haired Adele and tall, curvy Cora, with her auburn curls; but in similar clothes, wearing the same mask, Selene and I would be indistinguishable from each other. In the midst of a huge club, with people swarming all around us, drunk and disorderly and dancing to deafening music, it was going to make things difficult.

Thomas kneaded the back of his neck. "There's still time. You'll just have to go out and get another mask. We have to be able to tell the difference between them."

"Can't you do that already?" Selene asked. He shot her a dirty look, but she wasn't trying to be sassy; she was honestly wondering how he could mistake one of us for the other.

"I was talking about everybody else," he said. "They need to be able to know at a glance which of you is which."

"Are you hearing me, Mayhew? There are no more masks left," Fillmore whined. "The whole city's been cleared out. I had to show my badge just to get these!"

"Your KES badge helped you get something in the Tattered City?" Cora asked, flabbergasted. "I'm surprised you're not sitting in the same Libertas oubliette as the queen right now."

"Not exactly . . ." Fillmore trailed off. Thomas folded his arms across his chest and glared at him until he confessed. "I've been here for years. You can't have expected me to just *resist*, could you?"

"Oh, please tell me you didn't," Adele groaned.

"Didn't what?" I asked. "What did you do?"

"He joined the Blackmarket Runners," Rocko said, in a bored sort of way, as if he couldn't see what the big deal was. Callum glowered in Fillmore's direction; clearly, this was an Aurora thing.

"What are those?"

"Smugglers," Tim explained. Selene was confused, so he explained what smugglers were.

"He betrayed you," Selene told Thomas, in her usual straightforward way. "What are you going to do with him?"

"I didn't betray you! I swear, I've never done anything for the Runners that went against the KES," Fillmore insisted. He was trembling now, afraid of Thomas, who was looming above him looking very pissed off.

"*Everything* the Runners do is against the KES," Thomas said. "You know that, Fillmore. How could you be so stupid? Do you realize how tightly woven the Runners and Libertas are? You might as well have had the ten stars tattooed on your forehead!"

The Libertas symbol is a tetractys? Selene asked me, shoving her way through the sound of Fillmore's squalling to the base of my brain.

How did you know that?

I saw the shape of it in your head just now. Ten stars in an equilateral triangle. The green light of her mind grew stronger and began to pulse; it was so bright, it eclipsed Juliana's. Selene was getting worked up—odd for her.

What's wrong? I asked, but she didn't respond.

"Tell me none of your Runner friends know about this safe house," Thomas said.

"Of course not," Fillmore told him. "I'm not stupid."

"I disagree," Adele said.

"Tomorrow is going to be a very long day," Thomas said. "I want everybody to get a good night's rest. We're going to need it." He glanced at Selene and me. "You guys let me know if anything changes with Juliana."

The KES agents began filing out of the room, heading for

the sleeping quarters on the second and third floors. I was hoping Thomas would stay behind, that I could get a moment alone with him, but he fell into deep conversation with Adele as they hiked up the stairs, and I held back, feeling left out, as if someone had slammed a door in my face.

"Hey." I turned and found Callum standing right beside me. "Can I talk to you?"

"Sasha?" Selene said, pausing on the landing. "Are you coming?"

"I'll be there in a second." I gave Callum a tentative smile. "What did you want to talk to me about?"

He ran his hands through his dark curls, staring at the floor. "This is weird. You. Her. *Her*," he said, pointing in the direction Selene had just gone. "You were really the one I met at the Castle?"

"Yeah," I said. "I know it's hard to understand. Sometimes I still can't believe it, and it's happening *to me*. But I never meant to hurt you, Callum. I didn't want to lie to you. I just didn't have a choice."

"I'm having such a hard time wrapping my head around the fact that it was *you* at the Castle but *her* in the catacombs. I look at you and I see her. I know you're not the same person. I could tell when I met her that something had changed. But it's so improbable, my brain can't accept it. You know?"

"Totally," I said. "What changed?"

"Huh?"

"I mean, when you were with Juliana—how was she different from me?"

Callum gave the question careful consideration. "I guess I always felt like you were keeping me at a distance. You were so nice and polite and gracious, and I liked that about you, especially after the things I'd heard about Juliana. She has a reputation, you know. But I could tell you were performing for me. I ignored it, because I wanted so badly for everything to work out, but it drove me nuts. I almost would've rather had you be mean to me, which was what I'd expected."

"Sorry I wasn't enough of a jerk," I joked. He fixed me with a blue-eyed stare.

"I just wanted you to be who you were," Callum said. "To not be so cautious around me. But Juliana . . . she's not great at hiding how she feels, or who she is deep down. I like that I can tell when she's scared, or angry, or sad. She is who she is, you know? No varnish."

"That's for sure." I, for one, thought Juliana could use a little varnish; then again, I wasn't well on my way to falling in love with her. Callum had it bad for Juliana, and part of me wondered if he didn't enjoy the challenge best of all. But that was none of my business. I was only too glad that he had no lingering feelings toward me. "If it helps, I was being myself at the Castle, as much as I could under the circumstances. I liked you. I still like you. Juliana's lucky she met you. It's probably better than she deserves."

"Did she really run away?" Callum asked. I could tell this question was nagging at him. I nodded. "You're angry with her, aren't you?"

"Well, she's the reason I ended up here in the first place, and she tried to steal my life, so yeah, she's not my favorite person. But it doesn't matter." I could feel about Juliana any way I wanted, but it didn't change the fact that I needed her.

"I think it does," he said. "I've been watching the way you and Selene act around each other. You react to each other's emotions. Whatever that bond is between the three of you, it seems pretty intense."

"You have no idea."

"Then Juliana must know how mad you are," he went on. "She must be able to feel it. Maybe one of the reasons you find it so hard to connect with her is because she's afraid of what you'll think if she lets you into her head. I'm not going to make excuses for her. She's done some bad things. But if I know her at all, she's plenty ashamed. If you try to forgive her, maybe things will get easier."

He leaned forward and placed a soft kiss on my cheek. "Good night, Sasha. Sleep well."

I turned his words over in my head as he started up the stairs. I called his name, and he paused on the landing. "Thanks," I said. "For the advice. You're a good person, Callum. Better than the rest of us, I think."

"I'm not particularly good, actually. And I'm not being selfless. I have a stake in this, too. I want Juliana back, and you're the best hope of finding her." He looked away, carried off by his thoughts. He appeared changed somehow, made older, maybe, or ever so slightly less handsome by his time with Libertas. Sadder, too, but then, Callum had always been sad deep down, under the layers of optimism and hopeful cheer.

"We will find her," I said, even though I had no business promising him that. There were so many ways we could fail, but I didn't want to let him down.

"You have to. You owe me, Sasha. I saved your life once."

"I know you did." If there was anything that moving through worlds had taught me, it was that debts had to be repaid in full. "I want us to be even."

"Help me find Juliana," he said, "and we will be."

SEVENTEEN

I followed Callum up the stairs, trying not to worry about what the next day would bring, but it was hard not to imagine all the things that could go wrong. The KES agents were trained, armed guards, but they were also flesh-and-blood people—they could be hurt or killed, and I was afraid for them. It didn't even come close to how worried I was about my own friends, though, and Thomas most of all.

Selene had chosen a room for us on the third floor of the safe house, and I gravitated toward it without even thinking. It was still so strange, the way the tether tugged at me when I was near her, reeling me in like a fish. Sometimes it was as if the universes wanted us to find each other; other times it seemed so obvious that we were dangerous together, meant to be separate for our own good and the good of the world.

I wanted to be rid of the tether, but I was also becoming dependent on it and attached to the way it bonded me to my analogs. Things with Juliana were complicated, but I *liked* being close to Selene, no matter how much I tried to resist it. The thought of losing that connection was just as terrifying as the thought of merging with my analogs even further. The more I tried to understand it, the more confused I became.

It didn't help that things were so clearly weird with Thomas. I wanted to talk to him, but I had absolutely no idea where he was—in one of the bedrooms, I figured, trying to get some sleep. It wasn't like before, at Gorman's Gate, when I knew he'd be happy to see me; if I sought him out now, I had the sinking feeling he'd blow me off so he could keep a tight focus on the mission ahead. Something had changed between us in that moment when concern for me kept him from protecting Juliana. It had only been a few seconds, a couple of heartbeats, but in that time a key had turned and set us on a different course.

A creaking sound came from somewhere behind me. Someone had left a door ajar, and it was swinging in a light breeze. I pushed it open and found myself facing a staircase leading up to a glassed-in roof deck. Someone had gone outside. I knew I should ignore it and go to bed, get some rest before I collapsed on the floor from exhaustion, but I was a slave to my own curiosity, and I had a pretty good idea whom I would find up there.

Thomas was sitting on the roof with his head tipped back, looking at the aurora through one of the open skylights. I called his name softly. His face fell when he set eyes on me, and every trace of tranquility in his posture disappeared. And yet it was still there, that charge between us. He was happy to see me, too. He was just afraid to admit it to himself.

"You're still up?" he asked, shoving his hands into his pockets. I sat down beside him. "I thought everyone had gone to bed."

"They have," I said. "What are you doing up here?"

He shrugged. "Oh, nothing. Just thinking. I like watching the aurora. Calms me down."

"It is kind of hypnotic," I agreed, letting my gaze drift

up toward the sky. Apart from Thomas, the aurora was my favorite thing about his world. I'd missed it back on Earth. Something about it made me believe that the universe wasn't completely indifferent to us, that it was watching and that it understood. I almost said that to Thomas, but I thought it might make me sound a little nuts.

"So," I said.

"So." He shifted uncomfortably. "Sasha, I'm sorry about before, when I was kind of distant. There's a lot going on, things are getting so complicated, but I don't want you to think—"

"I don't," I said, resting my head on his shoulder. "I get it. You're worried about Juliana."

"No," he said. "I mean, yes, I am. It's more than that, though. It's . . . it's everything. I thought I could find Juliana, like that would be so easy, and then get out, but I don't think I can. I have to see this through. Even if we rescue her from Libertas, there are still so many things that need to be done. I can't walk away, no matter how much I wish I could."

"What are you trying to say?"

"I can't go with you, wherever you go," Thomas said in a rush, as if he thought if he didn't say the words quickly, he wouldn't be able to bring himself to say them at all. "I want to, but I can't. I have to stay here."

"I don't think you were invited," I said. Bringing Thomas along with us to Taiga had never been part of Selene's plan, and we would definitely have a problem if I tried to suggest it. The better I got to know Selene, the more ridiculous the General's fear that she and her people were trying to invade Aurora became. From what I could tell, she was far more concerned about keeping outsiders away from her universe than about invading anybody else's.

"You know what I mean," he said with a sad smile. "After.

When you've done what you have to do. I want us to be together—believe me, that's all I want—but I have obligations here. I have a duty."

"To the KES?"

"No," he said. "The KES is corrupt. I think we can agree on that. Even if the General thinks he's protecting the country, or the world, or whatever, it doesn't justify his methods. People are dying on the battlefront and rioting at home. Someone has to take him down if we even have a chance of putting the UCC back together and Juliana on the throne."

"Just because someone has to take him down doesn't mean it has to be you," I argued, though I knew I was wasting my breath. There was no way to talk him out of what he intended to do, whatever that was. Maybe he'd convinced himself it was about duty, or honor, or patriotism, but in the end, it was personal. Thomas needed to destroy the General because his father had spent over a decade fashioning Thomas in his image. I would've bet my life Thomas needed to prove to himself that he was something more than just the sum of the General's expectations. That he was his own person.

But he *was.* Risking—or sacrificing—his life to bring the General's tyranny to a halt wasn't going to make that more true, just as failing to do so wasn't going to make it false. Someone had to say it, and if not me, then who?

"I don't trust anyone else to do it," Thomas admitted. "If I went back to Earth with you, I would always wonder if there was something more I could've done. I don't think I could live with the guilt."

"It's not your job to save the world," I told him.

"Says the girl who's about to follow her analog into another universe *in order to save the world*," Thomas pointed out.

"That's different," I protested. Okay, so he wasn't wrong,

but if he kept making decisions based on his father, he was never going to step out of the General's shadow.

"Maybe you're not the only one with a destiny," Thomas said. "Maybe I'm supposed to do something important, too. And maybe this is it."

"Do you really believe that? Or are you just saying it so I'll get out of your way?"

Thomas gave me a look as if I'd hit him. "We're on the same side here, Sasha. If I wanted you out of the way, I'd ask you to move."

"It doesn't feel like we're on the same side." I could feel the gulf between us growing wider even as we sat there, staring at each other, half in love and half lost. "It feels like you're telling me to leave you behind. That *is* what you're telling me, right?"

Thomas hesitated. "I think, for now, that's the safest thing to do. Let me deal with my own universe's problems. If Selene wants to drag you into hers and you're willing to go along with it, that's your choice. But I need you to do me a favor."

"Oh, you mean besides deserting you to fight the General by yourself?"

"I want you to promise you'll take Juliana with you to Selene's universe."

"What makes you think she'll even go?" I was getting pretty tired of people talking about Juliana as nothing more than a bargaining chip, a pawn on a chessboard to be moved around and captured by whoever had the most guns and the best advantage. The worst part was, Selene and I had been doing the same thing. We'd been thinking about her only in terms of what *we* wanted, but we knew, better than anybody else, that she was a real person, and she deserved to make her own choices.

"Let's say I have a feeling she'll take the first opportunity to save herself," Thomas said.

"You might be underestimating her."

"If I promise to help get Callum across the border into Canada, I bet she'll go," he said. "They really seem to care about each other, bizarre as that is, and Callum's not politically important without her. Once he's gone, nobody will bother looking for him. But I don't know if there's a place on this planet we could hide Juliana for long. On Taiga, no one will be able to touch her, and with the two of you, I'll always know she's protected, even if I can't be there to do it."

"You'd trust me with that responsibility?"

"I'd trust you with anything." He scooted closer and cupped my face in one hand. "Like I told you before, you're my true north," he said matter-of-factly. "You haven't steered me wrong yet."

I closed my eyes and let him put his arms around me, though I wasn't sure that was a very good idea. *We're breaking up*, I thought, which was strange, because the thing we had between us was never very defined. It didn't have a name or boundaries; it didn't look like much from the outside. But inside, it felt infinite, and it seemed impossible that something so vast could ever crumble.

240

"But I'm always getting you into trouble," I said, pressing my face into his shoulder.

"Maybe," he whispered. "But it's my favorite kind of trouble."

He shouldn't have kissed me, but he did. It would've been so much easier if he hadn't. If he'd released me and moved away, said good night and gone to bed, it would've been hard, but it would've been the right thing, for both of us. He kissed me anyway. It started off slow, just a tentative brush of his mouth against mine. I tried to pull away, but I was never very good at taking orders, even from myself. I let my hands wander across his shoulders and back; the bare skin of his arms was hot. He cradled the nape of my neck with his hand and wove his fingers through my hair. I shut my eyes and let myself fall. The hard part would come soon enough; I was happy to put it off for just a little while longer.

In quantum mechanics, there's this theory that says a particle exists in all possible locations simultaneously until someone measures it. The mere act of *looking* forces the particle to take its place in the world. My life held endless prospects, and I could've lived it so many different ways. But in that moment, all those other possibilities fell away, and my life, the one I was choosing to live, narrowed to a finite point. Being with Thomas felt like being seen; but more than that, it felt like being *observed*.

Thomas placed a gentle kiss on my cheek. "Sasha?"

"Yes?" I felt as if I were going to topple over, like one of those toys with the round bottoms that can never stay up straight. If this was what it felt like to break up in theory, what was a real goodbye going to feel like?

"What exactly does Selene want you to do to save her world? She must have a plan."

"I don't know," I told him. "Why don't you ask her?"

Thomas glanced over my shoulder. I turned to see Selene, just as I expected, standing at the top of the steps. Thomas helped me to my feet.

"I'm sorry," she said. "I'm interrupting."

"It's okay," I replied. "Stay. Answer Thomas's question. I'd like to know, too."

"How did you know I was there?" Selene asked me.

I tapped my temple. "Listening."

Selene grinned. "You learn fast." She walked over to us. "To understand what it is I need Sasha and Juliana to do, I'll have to tell you a little bit about my world."

"So tell me," Thomas said.

She paused for a moment, then told him about Typhos, the asteroid that had decimated her planet, and Kairos, the sacred text whose prophecies had saved her people.

"Recently, Kairos's prophecies have mostly been about one thing," she went on. "Blueprints for the construction of a machine we call Terminus. The reason we can't leave Home is that Taiga can't sustain us. All the plants are gone, all the animals, with the exception of what we were able to preserve. But the planet isn't completely dead. It's been a hundred years—the sun has started to emerge from beyond the dust cloud that covers the sky, and the soil still contains the essential nutrients for things to grow. The water is clean, the air is clearing up . . . now is the time to bring Taiga back to life."

"How is a machine supposed to do that?" Thomas asked.

"Electroculture," Selene said. "If we can divert enough energy into the ground, we can accelerate plant growth and revitalize the planet. That is what Terminus will do. It will take the energy we feed it and distribute it into the ground that surrounds Home. We have been constructing it for a quarter of a century, and now it is complete. Except for one thing."

"Where are you going to get all that energy?" I wasn't an expert on biology or engineering, but even I knew that electroculture on that level would require a pretty big battery.

Selene held up her hands. "Where do you think?"

"The power." I understood now why Selene kept insisting that she and I wanted the same thing. Pouring the energy from our metaphysical bond would activate the Terminus machine, but it could also—if I was lucky—be a large enough release of power that it would overwhelm the tether and break it, just as Dr. March predicted.

"That's right. But you and I can't do it on our own," Selene said. "It has to be the three of us. *The sparrow, the starling, and the lark.* Kairos wouldn't have said it if it weren't true."

"Let's say Sasha and Juliana both agree to help you," Thomas said. "Can you guarantee that they'll be safe in your world? That nobody will come looking for them?"

"Yes, of course," Selene said with confidence. "No one in your world has ever been to Taiga. They don't know how to get there."

"How do you get there?"

"Do you know what ley lines are?" Selene asked. I shook my head. "They're natural paths over the Earth that are suffused with mystical energies. Ancient cultures knew of them and designated them with monuments and markers. Birds and other migratory creatures follow them when they move from north to south and back again. But they can also be used to move between worlds. We call them transits."

"And they just . . . exist?"

"They're built right into the fabric of the universe," Selene said, "no technology required. There are doors everywhere, Sasha. You just have to know how to find them."

She walked over to the wall of windows and looked out at the sliver of the lake we could just barely see through the buildings. "There's a transit near here—they often occur close to water. That was the one my ancestors stumbled on by accident. It's not very far from there to Home, on the other side."

"After you activate this Terminus machine, what happens to Sasha and Juliana?" Thomas asked.

"They'll have a place with us as long as they wish to stay. And when they want to leave, they'll be free to go." Selene frowned. The idea of Juliana and I going back to our own worlds made her sad—Selene was happiest when we were all together. But I caught a glimpse of Leonid in her thoughts, and the tether practically sighed with a deep yearning for home.

"Are you sure it's going to work?" I asked.

Selene nodded. "I've never been so sure of anything in my entire life."

EIGHTEEN

It wasn't until I woke up the next morning that I realized something was wrong.

Selene? Her eyes were still shut, but I could sense her mind opening. *Can you feel Juliana anywhere?* The last time I remembered sensing her presence on the tether was back during her interview, when it was flashing like a strobe light with anxiety and regret. Now it had faded to almost nothing, just the slightest pale flicker that on the one hand proved she was alive but on the other hand told us something was dangerously off.

"I think she's unconscious," I said. "Like they drugged her or something."

"Whatever it is, it's deeper than sleep." Selene rubbed her eyes. "Even when she's sleeping, I can tell."

"Me too." Worry jangled against my rib cage. What was Libertas planning to do with Juliana now that she had served her purpose? I wouldn't put it past any of them to kill her, especially not Kit, who seemed to hate her with an intensity I wouldn't have thought a sibling could feel. Then again, Lucas had betrayed Thomas; as an only child, what did I really know about brothers and sisters, anyway?

But I was beginning to know a little through Selene. My attachment to her grew deeper by the minute, and I knew without question that I'd do anything to help her. Juliana, too, if it came to that, even after everything. The strength of these protective feelings frightened me, but they also made me feel important. There were people in the world who counted on me. I didn't want to let them down.

"We'd better tell the others," I said. We found the KES agents gathered downstairs in the living room, sipping mugs of coffee and talking in low voices. Thomas was in a corner conferring with Adele. I searched for Callum but didn't see him; he must not have woken up yet. Either that or he was avoiding everyone. The safe house was packed with people he'd been raised to see as his enemies; this new situation probably wasn't doing a whole lot to change that way of thinking.

They all looked up as Selene and I descended the stairs. "What's wrong?" Navin asked. "You two look like you've been punched in the gut."

"We can barely sense Juliana on the tether," I explained. "I think Libertas knocked her out after the interview." This didn't seem to surprise anyone.

"She escaped them before," Thomas said, rising from his seat and moving closer to me—but not too close. "I bet they're not going to take their chances on her doing it again."

"Smart," Rocko said. He shrank beneath the weight of a half-dozen glares. "What? That power they have is spooky. I wouldn't want anyone using it on me if I could help it."

"We were just going over our plan for tonight," Thomas told us. "Gunner, go into the antechamber and see if you can find adrenaline in the supply locker."

"Adrenaline?" I asked as Cora disappeared into the adjacent room.

"It can counteract most of the sedatives in use today," he said. "I used it on you once. Do you remember?"

"No," I said. "Wait—back at the Tower? After I passed out in the Tattered City?" When I woke up in the Tower, I felt much better than I had when I'd lost consciousness in the alley, after our scuffle with Libertas, except for a tiny pinprick on my finger, which I instantly wrote off. "You injected me with adrenaline?"

Thomas nodded. "You passed out because of the tandem sickness, and I kept you under artificially until we got to Columbia City. I thought it'd be easier, under the circumstances." *Since you kept trying to run away* was what he meant. "But then I had to wake you up, so . . ."

"Aren't you clever," I said flatly. The memory of that day had faded, pushed aside by more urgent concerns, but now it flooded back. I remembered how lost I'd felt in this new, dangerous world, how much I'd hated Thomas for bringing me through the tandem, how the fear at being separated from my true home had hollowed me out. So much had changed in the months since I woke up to find myself in Aurora, but the scars of that first time lingered, and they ached now as I realized that getting used to something wasn't the same thing as getting past it.

When Cora returned, she was carrying a small metal suitcase packed with black foam. Inside were six vials of adrenaline and a package of hypodermic needles sealed in plastic.

"That should be enough," Thomas told her. "Everybody take some."

"What if one of us finds her first?" Selene asked, either reading the question in my mind or thinking of it on her own.

"You'll each be with an agent," Thomas said. He hesitated. "Unless you'd be willing to stay out of this completely. Hear me out," he went on as Selene and I started to protest. "Libertas would like nothing more than to get their hands on all three of you. Having the queen in their custody is a victory, but capturing her two look-alikes as well would be even better, especially considering how the General used Sasha to thwart their first attempt to use Juliana as leverage. They don't understand what you are, but they must see that you're dangerous.

"Also," he said as Callum appeared on the stairs, "I'd rather not bring the prince if I can help it."

"Yeah, right," Callum said, staring Thomas down. "I'm going. Juliana is *my* fiancée. I'm not going to just sit around like some pampered baby waiting for you all to rescue her. I've been in the catacombs before. I can help guide you through them."

"You need us, too," Selene said. "Sasha and I have a direct connection to Juliana. It's the fastest and the easiest way to find her. If you leave us behind, you'll be searching for her blindly, and you'll likely fail."

"All due respect, Your Highness, the wedding is off and the treaty has been broken," Thomas reminded Callum. "Juliana isn't any more your fiancée than Tim is." Tim rolled his eyes. Thomas turned to Selene and me. "And, yeah, you might be able to help us find her faster, but we're all trained agents of the King's Elite Service—we're more than capable of extracting Juliana without your connection, which, let's be honest, you might not even be able to use if they're keeping Juliana sedated."

"They're what?" Callum snapped.

"I'd feel much better about all this if you three stayed here while we look for Juliana," Thomas said. He looked at me with a silent plea in his eyes, as if he thought I would back him up. He was probably right: we were a lot safer right where we were, and if I were him I would suggest the same thing. But there was no way Selene and I were going to let the KES rescue Juliana without us. She was one of us—it was our duty to help her—but more than anything else, we just didn't trust them enough. If we stayed behind, who was to say we'd ever see them—or Juliana—again?

I shook my head. "We're going."

Thomas sighed. "It was worth a try."

The Night of the Masks didn't properly start until late in the evening, so at eleven p.m. we donned our masks and party clothes and headed out into the Tattered City. As it turned out, Thomas did decide to leave someone behind; he'd assigned Rocko to stay at the safe house with Fillmore in case things went bad and extra help was needed. Fillmore seemed happy to be kept out of the fray—as a support agent, he couldn't have gone with us anyway, even if he'd wanted to—but Rocko was livid. He spent most of the afternoon crashing around the safe house, glaring at Thomas and muttering mutinous things under his breath.

The revelry had begun as soon as the sun dipped below the horizon, and the blocked-off streets were teeming with people on their way to clubs and parties. They were drunk and lively, and I wondered if they all suspected, somehow, that this was their last Carnival Columbia, that the world was changing and soon they wouldn't recognize it.

We walked to Martyr, which was only ten blocks away from the safe house. Thomas had instructed us not to call too much attention to ourselves by clumping together—"Big groups are bad signs, and Libertas will be on alert more than usual tonight"—so we kept our distance, threading into the crowds as if we, too, were just looking for a good party. The tether was humming like a beehive, which made it easy to keep track of Selene even though I couldn't see her. I kept my eyes on Thomas's golden head about ten feet ahead of me. The only person I was afraid of losing in the scrum was Callum, so I slipped my hand into his and squeezed. I half expected him to pull away; Callum had avoided me all day, and I got the feeling he was still mad at me. But he squeezed back.

"You nervous?" I asked.

"No. Why would I be nervous?" His mask covered only the top part of his face, so I could see his false smile in the undulating light of the aurora.

"Right. Me neither," I lied. As if he sensed my anxiety, Thomas turned and met my eyes; we might have been wearing masks, but concern for me showed all over his body. I nodded at him, and he smiled, too; I was too far away to tell if he meant it or was just pretending everything was fine for my sake.

Martyr had been built in the hollowed-out remains of a neo-Gothic cathedral. The stone spires rose above the surrounding structures. The stained-glass windows winked in the light thrown off by firecrackers blossoming in the distant sky, and, as always, the aurora threw a faint green wash over everything. The line outside Martyr snaked around the block, and Thomas's team, now deployed on their mission, began to snuggle into its folds two by two, like animals boarding Noah's ark.

"Are you religious, Sasha?" Callum whispered as we took our places.

"Not exactly," I told him. I believed in something greater than myself, but I still wasn't sure what that was. Maybe I would never know.

"I am," he told me. "I'm trying to take it as a good sign that this is all going down inside a church."

"I hope you're right about that," I said, gazing up at the massive stone arch that guarded the door to Martyr. "We need all the help we can get."

THOMAS IN THE TATTERED CITY / 2

Thomas shoved his hands into his pockets and felt the small bulk of his KES ring. He couldn't wear it inside Martyr; a hawk-eyed Libertas agent could pick it out in seconds, and it would blow their cover. He watched from the other side of the street as Sergei, playing just a little drunk, ushered Sasha into the line, leaving Callum to Cora; the crowd quickly engulfed all four of them. Thomas took Selene's hand, careful not to imagine it was Sasha's, and led her to the back to wait their turn. He hadn't wanted to leave Sasha to someone else's care, but the need to keep a close eye on Selene trumped the urge to fasten himself to Sasha's side. The more space there was between them, the easier it would be to say goodbye; at least, that was what he told himself.

"Your world is very strange," Selene said, her eyes wide as she took in the high-spirited tumult all around them.

"Is it?" he asked. He was barely listening to her, too busy surveying the scene. There were Libertas agents everywhere, some obvious in their black clothes and green armbands, with rifles hoisted on their shoulders. Some were more discreet, dressed as partygoers, but he knew they were agents from the way they held their heads, the way they appeared stiff and alert—just like him. If he was lucky, they would mistake him as one of their own. Then he could get close enough to take one of their guns and make better use of it. The bouncers at the door were patting everyone down, so they'd had to come to Martyr unarmed, but he felt naked without a weapon.

"So many people," she said. "So much noise. It's very quiet where I come from."

"Oh yeah?" If he was going to let Sasha go, watch her slip into yet another world, he wanted to know as much about that world as he could.

Selene nodded. "It's very far away from here."

"How can you know that?" There was no way of measuring distance between universes. It was quite possible they existed one on top of another, like layers of cosmic sediment.

"Oh, I just mean . . . it's not like here. Nothing like it at all." She lowered her voice. They were standing close together, trying to feign some kind of physical affection that would sell them as a couple. The temptation to treat her like Sasha was difficult to beat back, but she wasn't Sasha. She wasn't even Juliana. She was her own person, and she was not someone who belonged to him. He had to keep reminding himself of that.

"They told me that, of course, but some part of me couldn't quite believe them," Selene went on. "How could a world so accessible to us be so different from ours? But it is. Your father's fear that we want to invade this universe is absurd. How would we live here? Look around you: there are no trees, no open spaces. No vestiges of what we lost so long ago. It would only be exchanging one broken world for another."

"We have trees," Thomas said. "And open spaces. Not right here, but in other places in this world. You saw that in the woods beyond the Labyrinth. It's not all broken."

"Well," Selene said, smiling, "maybe we will invade, then."

Thomas laughed in spite of himself. Selene wasn't as strange as he thought she was, and anyway, he was ninety-nine percent sure she was kidding.

It took them nearly an hour to get inside Martyr. By the time they walked through a small entrance that had been carved into the enormous wooden cathedral doors, Thirteen Bells was chiming the hour—midnight, not that it was possible to tell from the number of times the bells tolled. They always rang thirteen times, regardless of the hour.

The last time Thomas had been in a club was the night he received his KES assignment, and it'd been nothing like Martyr, just a seedy place with loud music and watered-down drinks. Martyr was a work of art, if a club could be called that. The light in the place was crimson, the color crawling all the way up the vaulted ceilings and hanging there like a ver-milion fog; the walls were covered with enormous paintings, each depicting the bloody torture and death of a saint, with a wide gold banner across the top informing casual observers which martyrdom they were viewing. To Thomas's left, St. Stephen endured a plague of arrows buried to the shaft in his flesh; to his right, Joan of Arc strained against her funeral pyre, eyes lifted toward the sky as flames engulfed her.

"This stuff is horrible," Thomas said. He had a strong stomach when it came to gruesome things, but the idea of hundreds of people partying under the tormented gaze of all these suffering saints made his skin crawl.

"Oh, I don't know," Selene replied. "There's something romantic about dying for what you believe in, isn't there?"

"There's nothing romantic about dying," he said tersely. Had the king's death been romantic? Or those of Thomas's parents? He was starting to wonder what point there was in being a hero. He used to think it was the most important thing in the world. He'd wanted nothing more than to fight for the country he loved, under the command of a man he worshipped. Now it was only his conscience that drove him to fulfill his duty. Pride had nothing to do with it.

"You may be right," she said. Her voice was dreamy, as if she was lost in thought. "But there's nothing romantic about living the way we do, either."

"The way *we* do?"

"All alone," she said, "separated from everyone, serving a future we have to believe in or else we'll crumble to dust." She looked him straight in the eye, her gaze strong even through the distraction of her blue bird mask. "We're very similar, you and I."

"I don't think so," he said. Hoping to avoid further conversation, Thomas took Selene's hand and guided her toward the center of the churning dance floor. At one point, Selene grabbed his arm and jutted her chin to the right.

"She's over there," Selene said, taking for granted he knew who she meant. Sometimes it seemed as though Sasha was the only "she" there was. He knew he shouldn't steer Selene toward Sasha and Sergei—it had been his command, after all, that the groups separate so as not to look like a unit and to provide better coverage in the sea of people. But he did so anyway, drawn to Sasha like a moth to a flame.

She and Sergei were dancing awkwardly together, neither knowing where to put their hands or how close to stand. Sasha didn't move like that with Thomas. He remembered prom night as vividly as if it were yesterday: with him, she was a dash of quicksilver, as lithe and radiant as the aurora in the sky. It wasn't because he was a better partner. It was because with him she was herself, even if she didn't notice it.

When had *he* started to notice? Admiration had blossomed suddenly and unexpectedly when they first met, and attraction had followed quickly after, but it wasn't until she went back to Earth that he realized the feelings were much bigger than that.

"I can tell you care about her," Selene said. "But you must realize that the two of you can't possibly last. Some walls are too high to climb."

For the first time, Thomas saw something besides confidence and calm cross her face, a fleeting expression of regret beneath eyelashes as black as coal. "Speaking from experience?"

"No." The look was gone, and she was Selene again, as inscrutable as ever. Maybe they weren't as different as he thought. "We should dance together. That's what everyone else is doing. It will seem strange if we don't."

"I don't like dancing." He scanned the room. Sound tech didn't work in a place like this. The music was too loud and variant for the mikes and earpieces to filter, and forget about hearing each other the old-fashioned way: Selene was standing right next to him, her mouth only inches from his ear, and still he had to strain to make out what she was saying.

He didn't like being caught without comm in an enemy space, but though his ears were failing him, he could still count on his eyes.

It wasn't hard to identify the Libertas guards throughout the club: they were the only ones carrying weapons, and they displayed them openly, daring someone to try something. The Night of the Masks was the rowdiest Columbian holiday of the year, and they had to know something might go down with the KES after Juliana's broadcast. He spotted a young Libertine hanging in the back of the club, near the altar, and identified him as the most likely to give up his gun at the slightest provocation.

Selene drew Thomas toward her. For all her confidence, Thomas could tell that she had little hands-on experience with men and wasn't sure how to behave around him. But she had a spy's instincts, and she understood the necessity of putting on a good show. She wrapped her arms around his waist, her hips swaying from side to side in a decent approximation of the music's rhythm. For a second, just one fleeting second, he let his heart believe what his eyes were seeing and held her close, pretending she was Sasha.

"You're not *that* bad," she murmured, but despite the way her body moved—she had the same fluid grace as Sasha and Juliana—it was easy to see that she wasn't used to dancing, either. The music bewildered her, and Thomas wondered if she'd ever heard anything like modern rock.

Who are *you?* he thought. But there was no point in asking. She wasn't going to share any more with him than she had already. He surrendered to the moment, clutching Selene under the strobe lights and watching Sasha over her shoulder.

Suddenly, Selene gripped his arm.

"Thomas," she hissed in his ear. "Juliana is waking up."

NINETEEN

A crimson light, faint and far away, glimmered at the edges of my consciousness. I sagged against Sergei in relief, feeling the sudden sense of release that came with exhaling after holding your breath.

"What?" Sergei asked, speaking into my ear so that I could hear him over the blaring music. Why were all KES agents so *tall*? Sergei was even taller than Thomas, almost six five. My neck was sore just from looking up at him all night.

"Juliana," I said. "She's coming to."

She wasn't fully conscious, but whatever sedative they'd given her was wearing off, and she was slowly swimming out of her stupor. This was good news. If she would just open her eyes, we might have some sense of where to look for her. We'd have to get into the catacombs beneath Martyr, then count on the strengthening bond to tell us whether we were on the right track or not—which meant that either Selene or I, or both of us, had to be with the KES when they went below. "Where's Thomas?"

"Right behind you," Sergei said.

I turned my head and caught sight of him, green eyes skimming the crowd. The minute his gaze found mine, it stopped wandering. There wasn't anything I could say—he was too far away—but he understood. Selene must've told him. There was a glint in his eye, a determined set to his jaw. Thomas was on the hunt.

But first he made a beeline for me, shoving people out of the way to reach me. He wrapped his arm around my shoulder and pulled me in.

"Look who it is," he said. I followed the trail of his gaze to the back of the club, where our old enemy Stringy Hair, one of the Libertas commandos who'd ambushed me in the Tattered City six weeks earlier, was standing. He wore no mask; many of the Libertas agents had failed to follow the dress code, which I had to imagine was on purpose. People needed to know they were being protected—or threatened, depending on who they were.

"Make sure your mask stays on, okay? He can't see your face. Or yours, either," he said to Selene, who appeared next to me. She took my hand.

Very soon, she said through the tether. Her mind was taut with concern; it made me tense up, eclipsing all the comfort I felt in Thomas's presence. *We'll find her, Sasha.*

I know we will. Thomas grabbed my other hand, and suddenly I was the rope in a game of tug-of-war between the two people to whom I was most loyal in this world.

And then this world exploded, and I was plunged into darkness.

"JULI! JULI, WAKE UP!" A

brief pause, then a stinging slap on her cheek. Someone shook her. "Wake up, goddamn it! We have to go!"

"What?" Her eyes felt as heavy as marble. The last thing she remembered was eating breakfast, a nasty gruel she'd refused until hunger threatened to carve out her insides. And now . . . what time was it? How long had she been out? She knew enough of Libertas's tactics to gather that she'd been sedated. It had happened once or twice before, when she was being uncooperative, but always via injection, never knockouts slipped into her food. Kit had reached a new low. She hadn't even been making a fuss this time.

"Come on, Juli!" Lucas handled her roughly, trying to prop her up against the wall. "You've got to wake up!"

Her eyelids fluttered closed. He grabbed her chin in one rough palm, his fingers digging into the soft flesh above her jaw so hard that her eyes popped open, her brain roused by pain and terror.

"I'm rescuing you, you spoiled brat," he hissed in her ear.

She tried to stabilize her jellied spine into something tough—steel or wood. She would even have settled for a strip of weak, bendy plastic. Anything but the wobbly pudding her bones seemed to be made of. "Help me."

"I'm trying!" Lucas kept looking over his shoulder as if he expected to see someone standing behind him. If she didn't get stronger,

strong enough to run, he would leave her behind. He wasn't going to sacrifice himself, not for her, not for anyone. Why had he even thought to free her in the first place?

It was Thomas, of course. As much as Lucas envied him, as small as he felt in his brother's shadow, Lucas couldn't despise him. Lucas believed Thomas to be dead. News of his execution had reached Libertas ears; there was no way Lucas hadn't heard. Now he was doing what he thought Thomas would do. It was sweet, in a way, if one could ignore the events that had come before this change of heart, but Juliana couldn't. But she wasn't above accepting his help, if it meant getting her life back, in whatever ruined state the General and Libertas and she herself had left it.

She took a deep breath and gave over to survival instinct, forcing her body to right itself.

I can do this, she assured herself. She flexed and straightened her limbs, made them hard and wooden with sheer force of will. She felt unmoored, her mind floating up, up, up to the ceiling as her doll body assembled into something human-shaped and ambulatory. She felt Sasha's cool blue light and Selene's bright green one hovering somewhere very far away, but she knew they were close. She understood that somehow, despite the fact that her head was too filmy, full of cobwebs and candy floss, to figure out exactly how close, exactly where they were. How was she going to get to them?

She wondered if Callum had come, too. She was almost glad she'd been sedated, so she didn't have to feel all the pain and misery of missing him. He knew everything now. He probably hated her. And Thomas . . . she'd seen the way he looked at her at Sophie's house, as if she were some sort of monster. He would never look at Sasha like that. She'd lost Thomas to her analog completely.

The thought crashed over her like a pallet of bricks.

Lucas had to help her stand, then help her walk; it was impossible to accomplish anything without leaning on his shoulder. This slowed *them down, and they'd barely made it out the door before a loud crash above caught their attention and arrested their progress.*

"What's happening?" Juliana demanded.

"I created a diversion upstairs in the club," he said, dragging her along the long, empty corridor. "It was supposed to draw everyone out of the catacombs so we could make it out the back way without being seen."

"And then what?"

"I don't know. I haven't thought that far, okay?"

"What kind of diversion?" she asked, thinking, somewhat hysterically in her half-drugged state, of the time her cousin Roman had set a large flock of pigeons loose in her father's Counsel Room, painting every member of his cabinet with droppings and feathers. Only the General had managed to emerge unscathed. It was the first time she considered the possibility that the somber, imposing man her father trusted above all others might truly be invincible.

"This is Libertas," Lucas said, as if the answer were obvious. "What else? I set a bomb."

TWENTY

The bomb rent a huge tear in the festivities, scattering party-goers in all directions, stirring up the Libertas guards and bouncers like a drink shaker. Nearly everyone who wasn't racing for the doors was on the ground, struggling to get their bearings in the wake of the blast. Something heavy was lying on top of me, making it hard to breathe. I panicked, thinking I'd been crushed by a piece of stone from the ceiling, but then I realized that the weight was human: Thomas.

Memories of him shielding me from the blast came rushing back. I shook him by the shoulder, and he grunted, rolling off me and inspecting me for signs of damage. "I'm fine, I'm fine," I said. He helped me sit up. His heart was hammering, and his breathing was labored.

Selene was lying a few feet away, with her arm over her eyes. I crawled over to her and checked her pulse, which was weak but growing stronger; she was coming around. Sergei was to our left, eyes open and alert, keeping low to the ground. He and Thomas shared a look, and I knew without being told what they were thinking. Someone else's chaos had offered them a window, and they would be foolish not to take it.

"Help me find the others," Thomas whispered. The explosion had taken all the lights down, and it was hard to see much in the dark except for vague shapes. We'd left Tim outside Martyr to patrol the perimeter and look for escape routes. With Rocko back at the safe house with Fillmore, that left us with four people missing: Callum, Adele, Cora, and Navin. We'd spread out in Martyr, so they could be anywhere.

"I don't see them," I said.

"I'm jealous of the connection you have with Selene," he said. "It'd be so much easier if I could communicate with my team telepathically."

"It's not all it's cracked up to be," I told him. "But, yeah, it can be pretty convenient at times."

Then I noticed a small plastic nubbin in Thomas's ear. "Maybe you *can* talk to them," I said, pointing to it. "The music's off. Maybe your comm will work."

He spoke into the tiny microphone in his mask. "Nguyen? Gunner? Patel? Can anyone hear me?"

Adele's voice came crackling over his earpiece, audible even to me. "I can hear you, boss."

"Me too," Cora replied. "And I've got Callum." Soon Tim and Navin checked in over the comms as well.

"And," Navin said, "I've got a gun. Took it off a dead Libertine."

"Good work," Thomas said. People were starting to get up, wandering around, dizzy and disoriented, searching for the nearest exit. "Okay, it's time to move. Mac, what's it look like outside?"

I leaned in close to hear what Tim was saying. At my feet, Selene stirred and opened her eyes. *Did you see Juliana?* she asked. I nodded, holding up a finger. I could only concentrate on one conversation at a time.

"It's chaos out here," Tim said. "I can hear sirens in the distance. If you're going to make your move, it has to be now. They've got to be regrouping."

"Who set that bomb?" I asked. Thomas shook his head.

"Not us, that's for sure," he said. "But this is Libertas, and it's the Night of the Masks. I should've at least factored in the possibility that there might be another attack other than our own. But it's too late for that now. We've got to move."

Thomas helped me haul Selene to her feet. She seemed shaken, but she was trying to hide it behind that calm determination she feigned so well. Thomas adjusted the mask on my face.

"As soon as we're underground, take the masks off," he instructed us. "They'll make you too conspicuous. But not until then." Selene and I needed to hide our identities as long as possible, and so did Thomas. After all, most of the Libertines probably supposed him to be dead.

"All right, team," he said clearly into his comm. "Let's do this."

We're not the only ones on the move, Selene said. Juliana was awake and running, but the information trickling through the tether was too fuzzy and incomplete to give us a real sense of her intentions or her progress. I wanted to tell Thomas what I'd seen while I was unconscious, but he was shoving his way through the mob; I had no choice but to follow him.

Sergei ushered Selene in a different direction, but we were all headed to the same place: the back of the club, toward an enormous painting of St. Thecla enduring her sentence of being eaten alive by wild beasts. An angel hovered in the upper right-hand corner of the painting, ostensibly to save the young martyr from her horrible fate, and I couldn't help but wonder who was going to save us. The painting served as a giant scrim, hiding the back of the club from view, though it was clear from the way the vaulted ceiling receded from us that the cathedral was much deeper than it appeared.

"Where are you going, little lady?" A hand grabbed my arm and spun me around; I found myself face to face with Stringy Hair. He jerked his head in the opposite direction, toward the front door. "Exit's that way. Better get out quick. No telling what's going to happen next. KES bastards."

My mind careened back in time, flashing to the alley in some other part of the Tattered City, to this man's arm wrapped around my throat, crushing the life out of me. People churned all around us, bumping into us on every side. One knocked me into Stringy Hair's embrace; he clutched my elbows hard to keep me steady.

"Take off the mask," he said, in a voice that was almost . . . *kind*. "It'll make it easier to see." When I didn't, he plucked it off by one of its feathers, and his eyes widened as he got a good look at my face. His fingers dug into my flesh, and I yelped in pain. "It's *you*."

"Get your hands off her," Thomas growled. Stringy Hair pulled me closer, crushing me to his chest with one arm as he reached for his gun. *"Now."*

Stringy Hair pulled out his sidearm and pointed it at Thomas. "Take off the mask or I'll shoot you." Thomas held up his hands in a gesture of surrender. *No, Thomas, don't,* I begged him silently, knowing that once Stringy Hair knew his true identity he really *would* shoot him, and happily. But Thomas didn't have a choice; as soon as the mask was gone, understanding bloomed across Stringy Hair's face.

Sensing that now was my only chance, I lifted my foot and brought it down hard on Stringy Hair's, crushing the man's toes with my sharp heel. He cried out in pain and lowered his gun. Thomas sprang forward and took it, twisting the man's arm so hard I heard it crack. Stringy Hair sank to the ground, clutching his broken arm to his chest, his eyes streaming with tears, his face torn apart with agony. He couldn't even find the breath to speak.

Thomas didn't hesitate; he took me by the hand, holding Stringy Hair's gun in the other, and tugged me forward. I stumbled over Stringy Hair's body but didn't fall. Familiar masks emerged in my peripheral vision: Adele and Navin, Cora and Callum, Sergei and Selene. Thomas and I made eight, Tim outside made nine. And Juliana would make ten.

A tetractys, Selene thought. *It bodes well.*

What? I asked, but then everything exploded again. Not a bomb this time but bodies, flying at us from all directions, surrounding us on all sides. Libertas. They weren't all down for the count, not by a long shot. We were almost behind the painting; I was close enough to peek around it, and sure enough, there was a door embedded in the center of the golden retabulum that stood behind the ornate altar.

Someone grabbed me from behind and wrapped an arm around my throat. I couldn't get the image of Stringy Hair squeezing me to death out of my head, though it couldn't be him. I fought against my captor, swinging my arms, kicking my legs, anything I could do to sink a hard part of my body into a soft part of his—or hers.

I felt the power surge through me, roiling and ready just beneath my skin. Selene and I were close enough for it to be truly destructive, but I tried to stay calm, to channel it, swiveling in the Libertas agent's arms and placing my hands flat against his chest like the paddles of a defibrillator. Breasts swelled under my palms—it was a woman.

I pushed the power through my hands, knocking her off her feet and tossing her, limp as a towel, on a heap of rubble.

267

I looked at my hands, then at her; the jolt had hit her hard, and she was perfectly still. I caught a glimpse of her gun in its shoulder holster; that could prove useful to me or to someone else. I went to retrieve it, but however badly the power had hurt her, it hadn't knocked her out completely. She snatched at one of my ankles, and I shook her off, grinding her fingers under my foot as the sound of splintering bone echoed through my body. She yowled in pain, but I felt nothing but numbness. I took her gun, not sure what I would do with it, only sure that she shouldn't have it, then moved as far away from her as I could get, leaving her to be gobbled up by the dark.

"Sasha, where are you?"

Sasha, where are you?

Thomas's voice, Selene's thought, simultaneous and confusing. Libertas had done the smart thing: they'd kept the lights off so that it would be harder for us to find our way while we fought with them in our search for the door. Shots rang out in every direction, clips emptying with brutal speed. There was too much motion; it was like being stranded at sea during a hurricane, solid things eluding me with the fluidity of water. Then I saw it: a bright glow in the shape of a door. Someone had reached the entrance to the Libertas catacombs. Someone had found the way.

I hoped it was someone on my side and not the other.

The Libertine girl's gun was cold and heavy in my hand. I shoved my way toward the door, stepping on toes, elbowing stomachs, frantically straining toward the only source of light in the cavernous cathedral. I sensed Selene beside me; she, too, had a gun in hand, but she looked even more bewildered than I was to be holding one.

We don't have these on Taiga, she explained, but she didn't ask what it did or what she should do with it. Selene was nothing if not adaptive.

We were feet from the door now. I could hear the sounds of people grappling, fighting, fists on flesh, skulls on metal, the sounds of turmoil and hurting all around me, but I couldn't see anything except that door, that door that looked a lot like the other door, the one Callum had drawn: a door into the unknown. My mind was in two places: in the dark with Thomas, desperate to know what was happening to him, and in the catacombs with Juliana, whose frightened thoughts and emotions were pouring through the tether in flashes like Morse code.

Limping down a hallway, feeling heavy and weak, but she had to keep moving, they were coming, they weren't far behind. . . .

Leaning on him through the tangled, musty corridors. He was drenched with sweat; she could smell his fear rising off his skin, sharp and acrid. . . .

A door at the end of the hall, ten gold stars in an equilateral triangle shining against a backdrop of black steel. That was their way out. . . .

A shot, two shots; they hit him in the back and he fell, taking her down with him to the cold stone floor. . . .

"Sasha!" Callum came out of nowhere and seized me by the arm. His lip was split wide open, seeping blood, and his eye had already started to swell from where he had been punched, but one look at his knuckles showed that he'd done damage of his own. I looked at him in surprise, and he shrugged.

"Boxing lessons," he said. "I told you I had a lot of useless talents." He had told me, a long time ago. "Turns out, that one wasn't so useless after all."

"No kidding," I said, giving him a quick hug. "Where is everyone else?"

"I don't know. I lost Cora," he said, looking back into

the dark where the others were still presumably fighting. "I thought I heard Sergei and maybe Adele, but I'm not sure."

"We have to go. We can't wait for them," Selene insisted, heading for the open door. If it hadn't been a KES agent who'd opened it, then there were Libertines down there, lying in wait. Selene and I were armed, but we had natural weapons, and Callum was without protection. I thrust my gun at him, and he took it with a trace of uncertainty.

"Hey!" Adele came out of nowhere and shoved us all through the door to the catacombs, shutting it behind her. Then she turned to us, glaring at us one by one. "What the hell do you think you're doing, just standing there like that? If we want to get out of here alive, much less find Juliana, we have to go *now*." She snatched the gun from Selene's hand. "Give me that!" She took off the safety with a snap. "I had one, but I lost it. Come on, let's move. Do either of you know where Juliana is?"

I shook my head. We were standing at the top of a staircase, but from what I could tell from Juliana's mind, we were about to descend into a winding maze of tunnels and corridors and windowless cells. The only thing I could remember of any particular significance was the door with the tetractys on it, the Libertas symbol. I told Adele this, adding, "And she's with someone. A man, I think."

"Who?" Adele demanded. I'd never seen her so fierce; she was in action mode, and she wasn't looking to make any friends tonight.

"The god with two faces," Selene said. "Janus."

"Janus? You mean Lucas," I said. But Selene wouldn't know about Lucas. She might not even know that Thomas had a brother at all.

"Who's Lucas?"

"Never mind. He has Juliana?"

"He's helping her escape," Selene said. "But he's been shot."

"Lucas? Lucas *Mayhew*?" Adele asked. "What's he doing here?"

"Mayhew?" Callum searched my face for information. "Isn't that Thomas's last name?"

"Will you all just shut up and stop asking questions?" I snapped. "We're wasting time." I turned to Selene. "Janus's real name is Lucas." Then to Adele: "Yes, Lucas Mayhew. He's a member of Libertas, has been for a while." Then to Callum: "Lucas is Thomas's brother. Now, are we all caught up?" They nodded. "Great. Selene, since you apparently know the most about where Juliana is, you tell us where to go. Adele, since you're the best shot in the group, you go first."

"Hey, who said you could give the orders?" Adele said with a weak smile. "I'm the only KES here."

I pointed down the staircase. "Go."

We crept through the hallways, which were disconcertingly empty, like the pathways through a maze where monstrous creatures lay in wait. When had these catacombs been built? Surely not with the original church, or perhaps partly, but this extent of winding corridors and barricaded chambers implied a more ambitious purpose, one that could only belong to Libertas.

Adele took the lead, prowling along with gun in hand, on high alert for anyone who might want to stop us, but Selene and I were just as dangerous. I'd seen what my bare hands did to that Libertas girl. Perhaps it was naïve, but I felt safe and self-assured with my new power. I just hoped I could use it to protect others as well as myself.

Callum, though also armed, seemed to me particularly

vulnerable, and I made sure I stayed near him. Selene had her internal radio tuned to Juliana's frequency and was impatiently parsing it for information in her head, but I knew—because I was doing the same thing—that there was no more to learn. Something had made Juliana go silent again. We were afraid for her, but we knew she wasn't dead; that was something we would feel if it happened, I was sure of it.

We passed a set of swinging double doors that looked like they might belong to a kitchen. The sudden sound of glass breaking made us all jump, and Callum, who had been going through the hallways with his finger resting on the trigger, accidentally pulled it in alarm and embedded a bullet in one of the doors.

"Shit," Adele muttered under her breath. None of us moved, waiting to see if someone would come marching out of the kitchen to see who was there. Adele turned on Callum, incensed. "What the hell do you think you're doing? Hand it over." She thrust her palm out, and Callum gave her the gun, still shaking from having fired it. He rubbed his shoulder and grimaced in pain.

"Whose idea was it to give the little prince a gun?" Adele glared at Selene and me.

"Hey!" Callum hissed. "Don't call me that."

The sound of more breaking glass reached our ears, and then an unintelligible shout. Selene's head snapped up.

"That's Juliana," she said. Adele glanced at me, and I nodded to confirm. I'd heard her, too, in my head. It wasn't a word or an image, just an amorphous, frightened burst of emotion, a flare of red at the base of my skull. "She's in there."

"Okay," Adele whispered, clutching a gun in each hand and crouching just outside the double doors. "On the count of three, we're going in. You two fire up whatever the hell kind of freaky power you've got going on, and Prince Callum, you stay back as far as you can."

Callum was uncertain. "What if it's a trap? What if they're trying to draw us in there just to make it easier to pick us off one by one? If that room really is a kitchen, there'll be knives and glass everywhere. It's like a murder factory."

"If you're scared, you can stay out here," Adele said.

"I'm not—forget it. You're not leaving me behind," he said.

"It probably is a trap," Adele told him. "But we don't have a choice. Don't worry, I won't let you die."

"Thanks," he said, rolling his eyes. I put a hand on his arm and gave him the warmest, most hopeful smile I could.

"We're going to be fine," I told him.

"I'm sure that's true," Callum said, with more certainty than he probably felt. But he always was an optimist.

"Okay, people—one, two, three!" Adele said in a voice just below a whisper.

Hearts racing, we burst through the doors, the tether swinging and thrumming with the force of a high-velocity wind.

THOMAS IN THE TATTERED CITY/3

The door was closed. The light was gone. Bodies littered the ground near Thomas's feet. The tranquilizer gun he'd snuck into the club taped *very* snugly against the inside of his upper thigh had done its job, but he'd emptied two clips bringing the Libertines to their quiet rest, and he was out of ammo. He had a handgun jammed into the belt of his jeans; he took it out, standing silent and still, daring someone to come at him and force his hand, but no one came.

His head was bleeding from a three-inch gash near his hairline, and two fingers on his right hand were probably broken; his nose was most definitely so. He wiped his mouth and drew his hand away covered in black liquid. It tasted like metal on his tongue. There were claw marks on his neck where a Libertine's fingernails had punctured the skin in places, his wrist was sore, his head was pounding like a jackhammer, but he was alive. He could work with alive.

"Mayhew?" The voice, which belonged to Navin, came through the comm. Thomas found him moments later, slumped against the altar, clutching his upper arm. The moon, which had been hiding behind a thick blanket of clouds the entire night, finally shone through the windows, and Thomas could see that Navin was bleeding.

"Is it bad?" Thomas asked, kneeling beside his friend.

"Just—grazed—me," Navin lied, a full-body shiver slicing his words up with pauses. Thomas ripped the T-shirt off the nearest unconscious Libertine and wrapped it around Navin's wounded arm, hoping to staunch the flow of blood until he could seek medical attention—although that might be hard to find for a KES agent in the Tattered City. But one problem at a time. Navin couldn't stay at Martyr. If he was going to live, he had to leave.

Thomas helped the agent to his feet and turned him in the direction of the front door. The ruined church was empty now except for the victims of the blast—ten or twelve, civilians mostly, though Thomas saw one or two commandos sprawled there, too—and the casualties of the fight between the KES and Libertas. Thomas searched the blank faces of the dead for someone he knew and found Cora's bloody face half covered by a fallen tapestry. His gut turned inside out at the sight of her. Her eyes were open, blank and unseeing, and there was a dark spot right in the center of her abdomen. Navin groaned and slipped a little, sliding down the side of the altar; Thomas turned his attention back to him, clutching him under the arms to prop him up.

"I can't help you out," Thomas told him, thinking of Sasha and the others who were missing. They must've gone down below; he had to follow them.

"Leave me," Navin insisted. "I can't walk. I can barely stand. I think my ankle's broken, or sprained, or"—he sucked in a labored breath—"something."

"No," Thomas said. "You need to get to Tim. He can help you, find someone to patch you up, but you have to get to him."

"Can't, boss," Navin said with a tight, grim smile. "No chance in hell."

"I'll get you out." Thomas and Navin turned in the direction of the voice and saw a very battered Sergei, stumbling like a drunken dragonfly but managing to stay upright. He had a gun in his hand, but he dropped it, letting it clatter to the ground. "Clip's empty."

Thomas reached over and plucked a replacement from the shoulder holster of one of the Libertas guards. Weapons were plentiful now. He tossed it to Sergei, who caught it with one hand; the other was plainly broken, perhaps all the way up to the elbow. Sergei's face was calm and expressionless; he was in shock. How was Tim going to handle two people who might die before he could get them to help? Thomas knew he ought to go with them, but he couldn't abandon the rest of his team. When they had Juliana, he would send Adele and Rocko back to help Tim. Yes, that was what he would do. It was as good a plan as any, under the circumstances.

Cora, he thought. *God, Cora.* But there wasn't time to grieve.

"All right, then get going," Thomas said. He hoisted Navin off the ground and propped him up on Sergei's good shoulder, then watched his two friends limp in the direction of the front door, hoping against hope they wouldn't be gunned down by any remaining Libertines outside the entrance, knowing they had no other option. When they were out of sight, he turned back to the door, checked his gun, and walked through.

Left or right? Which way would they have gone? He couldn't decide, didn't know the answer. For the first time tonight, he felt both helpless and alone. So many people he cared about, gone or lost or far away. Which way to turn? He had no idea.

When in doubt, always go right, his favorite instructor, Captain Barrick, had told him once after a sim in King's Town. So he went right. He walked through the abandoned catacombs, peeking around corners and pausing whenever he heard a sound, making his way through the brightly lit corridors, encountering nobody and nothing. Until the fourth turn, when he was faced with a motionless body on the ground, two bullets in its back. He decided to leave it—if the man wasn't dead, he soon would be—but instinct made him look back at the last second, and when he did, the man lifted his head and Thomas found himself staring into his brother's eyes.

"T," Lucas croaked, reaching out a tentative hand.

Thomas fell to his knees. His hands hovered over his brother's back; he wanted to help, but there was nothing to be done. He swallowed the grief and the terror and took Lucas's trembling hand in his own.

"I'm so sorry, Lucas," Thomas said. Lucas's eyes closed, and Thomas thought that might be the end. He was grateful for the chance to apologize, for things that he'd done and hadn't done, said and hadn't said. They might have been rivals, but Lucas was his brother, and Thomas loved him. That was something no one, not even the General, or Lucas himself, could destroy.

Then Lucas's eyes struggled open again. "One . . . one . . . two . . . ," he struggled to say. Thomas attempted to comfort him, to stop him from speaking—it would only make it hurt worse, prolong the inevitable—but Lucas tried again, heedless of Thomas's advice, perhaps impervious to the pain now.

"One . . . one . . . two . . . three . . . five . . . eight," Lucas managed to say, after many pauses and horrible, wheezing breaths. "Ahead."

"One, one, two, three, five, eight?" Thomas repeated. The first six numbers of the Fibonacci sequence, the king's code,

Sasha's magic numbers. How could Lucas possibly know them? And what did he mean by saying them now? And "ahead"? Ahead to *where*?

Lucas lowered his head and pressed his cheek against the cold stone floor. "Ahead." The word came out with a long exhale, and then Lucas was still. Thomas reached out and closed Lucas's eyes, then placed the palm of his hand on his brother's dirty brown head in benediction. It was a church, after all, and Lucas deserved a blessing, even—perhaps especially—in death.

Then he rose to his feet and took off in the direction of an enormous crash.

TWENTY-ONE

A bullet whizzed past my head. I threw myself flat against the floor, not sure which direction it was coming from. We were in an industrial kitchen; there were half a dozen metal islands in each direction and several racks of hanging pots that made it hard to see. Selene was to my right, Callum to my left, and Adele was standing near the door, half-protected by a huge refrigerator, trying to get a clear shot at whoever was shooting at *us*.

Shards of glass littered the floor, and I could see where they'd come from; there were milk crates full of drinking glasses stacked one on top of another in a nearby corner, and several of them had tipped over. There was blood, too, enough to indicate that there'd been a struggle. I knew it was Juliana's blood; it sang to me, with that same trilling note that traveled along the tether. She was somewhere nearby.

Silence descended. Adele gestured for us to get up, and we rose to our feet. She advanced through the kitchen, taking corners with her gun pointed straight ahead, her finger motionless on the trigger, her face set into a stony expression of determination.

Out of nowhere, a body sprang from the shadows, careening right into Adele and knocking her off her feet. Her gun went flying and clattered to rest under a nearby table, far out of her reach. But she was wrestling with the Libertine who'd attacked her, throwing punches and aiming kicks at delicate areas, but the Libertine was ferocious. I couldn't see a way of getting my hands on him to administer the power without hurting Adele. I looked to Selene, helpless, but her eyes were trained elsewhere, somewhere off to the left. I turned and caught a blur of movement, a curtain of dark brown hair swinging in the strange blue light of the kitchen: Juliana.

Selene took off running, and Callum and I followed. But instead of Juliana, we found three Libertines waiting for us around the next turn, guns trained on us.

"Hands up," one of them demanded breathlessly. "Don't do anything stupid."

"Okay," Callum said. "Don't shoot." He glanced at Selene and me; we all slowly lifted our hands, palms forward. The Libertines advanced; the one who'd spoken removed plastic zip ties from a hidden pocket and slipped them over Callum's wrists first, perhaps considering him the biggest threat. The other two kept their guns on us.

The Libertine with the cuffs turned his attention to me, grabbing me by the hands and pulling me forward. I resisted but not too much, just enough that my hands were in the right position.

"I really wouldn't do that if I were you," Callum warned him.

"Oh yeah? Why—" But he didn't get a chance to finish his sentence. I closed my eyes and focused on opening up the tether, letting the power pour through my body, head to heart to wrist to fingertips, until it shot out of my palms like twin beams of a lighthouse, catching him hard in the chest and throwing him to the ground. Selene turned to the Libertine to her right and did the same, this time to his stomach; the power slammed him up against one of the metal tables and sent a leaning stack of bowls crashing to the ground in a shower of ceramic shards.

"What the—?" The third Libertine's eyes widened in shock, but he didn't hesitate. "Backup!" he shouted into an invisible mike. "I need backup in the kitchen *now*!" He reared back and slammed the butt of his weapon into Callum's cheek, sending him flying. I opened my mouth to scream Callum's name, but no sound came out. Using the power had wearied me, and I wasn't sure if I could do it again so soon, but there were more of them coming, lots more, streaming through another set of doors and converging on us.

Don't worry, Selene said, but the tether shrieked with our combined terror—hers, mine, and Juliana's. *Just get as far away as you can.*

I didn't want to leave her, but the certainty in her voice convinced me. She was planning something, and I was only going to get in her way. I grabbed Callum and dragged him to the opposite side of the kitchen. We crouched behind a tall metal island, peeking out from behind.

As the Libertines closed in, Selene sank to one knee and placed her palms flat against the linoleum floor, closing her eyes and hanging her head. At first nothing happened, and I was sure she would be killed, but then Selene began to glow, her whole body engulfed by a warm white light, like a small, dense star giving off a last brilliant gasp of fission.

"What's happening?" Callum asked.

"I don't know," I whispered. "It's Selene. She's . . ." I looked over my shoulder. The Libertines had forgotten their guns and were staring at her in awe. They ought to have run, because the glow grew stronger and brighter and larger until it exploded, throwing all the Libertines clear across the kitchen and blinding the rest of us with light. I pressed my face into Callum's shoulder. What had Selene *done*? And, more important, what had it done to her?

The glow receded, and the kitchen was silent. All I could hear was Callum's breathing in my ear. I rose to my knees and looked back toward where Selene had been kneeling, not expecting to see her there at all, as if I thought the power would have consumed her like a fire, leaving behind a pile of charred ashes. But she *was* there, whole and alive. The Libertines lay in a circle around her, motionless. I rushed to Selene's side and put a hand on her back; it rose and fell with the force of her breath, which was coming heavy and fast.

Are you okay? She winced, and her end of the tether curled up in pain. A sharp ache spread through my body, but I tried to ignore it and focus on Selene.

"Are you okay?" I asked again. She nodded and forced a smile. I put my arm around her. It had cost her so much to do what she'd done. I could *feel* her pain—it was physical and psychic at the same time, and it throbbed through the tether like a deep stab wound. She was trembling, and when she lifted her head I saw tears in her eyes.

"It hurts," she gasped. I helped her to her feet. Adele, who'd escaped her own Libertas attacker, was sawing through Callum's cuffs with a knife she'd found on one of the counters. His wrists were covered in chafe marks from where he'd tried to wriggle out of them.

"Are you all right?" he asked me.

"Yes," I said. "But Selene . . ." She was standing off to one side, looking lost.

"We have to find Juliana," Selene said, staring at the inert bodies on the floor as if she couldn't believe what she had done. Her voice was hollow and strained.

"We don't know where she is," Adele pointed out.

"I *saw her*," Selene said. "She has to be close. She was with only one man; they couldn't have gotten far."

We left the kitchen with Adele once again in the lead. She hadn't seen much of what happened with Selene, hadn't seen the power she'd released, and was calmer and more self-assured than I'd ever seen her; clearly, she thought we'd already won, though we had no idea where Juliana was, not to mention Thomas or the other KES agents.

That problem was solved as soon as we stepped into the hall. Thomas stood at one end, and we were at the other; in the middle was Juliana, in the Shepherd's clutches. Even though I knew his name was Kit, that he was Juliana's brother and the king's son, nothing seemed to suit him except his Libertas handle.

The Shepherd had the muzzle of a gun pressed to her forehead, and Thomas had a gun trained on him; they were at a stalemate. Thomas was covered in blood, breathing heavily in anger but apparently fine. Whose blood was he wearing, then?

"Don't move," the Shepherd growled. "You move and I shoot her. She's not important enough to me not to kill her right now, but I can see that's not the case for you."

"You're right," Thomas said. "I don't want anyone to get hurt." At this, his gaze flickered to me, traveling up and down my body to assess whether I was okay. When he was satisfied, he turned his attention back to the Shepherd. "What do you want? I'll give you anything if you'll just let her go."

"I want to get out of here unscathed," the Shepherd said. "With her."

"No deal," Thomas told him. "But I'll let you walk out of here if you release her. That's your only choice."

"Don't talk to me about *choices*!" the Shepherd shouted. "I'm the one with the leverage here, toy soldier, and don't you forget it. I don't take orders from people who work for the General!"

"Then I guess we're at an impasse," Thomas said. He was playing it cool, calm, like a man who was holding all the cards. But it was the Shepherd who had the real bargaining piece, the thing we all wanted. Juliana's eyes were wild, her expression a tumult of fear.

Sasha, she said. The tether trembled at the sound of my name. *Help me, please.*

"Let her go!" Selene commanded, lifting her hands.

"Selene, no!" I cried. I was afraid of what another surge of the power would do to her.

The Shepherd turned his head, distracted by the sound of Selene's voice echoing through the corridor. When his eyes landed on us, they widened, and his jaw dropped. "What are *you* doing here?"

284

Thomas raised his gun and pulled the trigger. Three shots rang through the air; one of them landed in the center of the Shepherd's forehead. His eyes dimmed as the life left them, and then they closed. The Shepherd fell to the ground, pulling Juliana with him. We all raced forward, too late to catch her, but Thomas reached her first. Juliana jerked out of the Shepherd's grasp and stared into his lifeless face.

"He's dead!" she cried. A high-pitched, keening noise ripped through the tether. "He's dead! He's dead!"

"Shhh," Thomas said, gathering her to his chest. My heart

felt as though it was being shredded to pieces, but I couldn't decide, in the madness, what hurt more: Juliana's pain or Thomas's tone as he soothed her. He still cared about her. Not the way he cared about me, but he couldn't abandon her. It just wasn't in his nature. Callum stood to the side, staring at the two of them, looking just as left out as I felt. "It's okay. You're going to be okay."

"Mayhew," Adele said in a low voice. She was crouched beside the Shepherd as if feeling for a pulse, but he was clearly dead.

"What?"

"Look." Adele pulled back the collar of the Shepherd's shirt so we could all see what she saw: the KES seal, tattooed right over the Shepherd's heart. "He called you 'toy soldier.' He was one of us once." Thomas swallowed hard but said nothing.

"It's Kit," Juliana said. "He's Kit."

"Your brother Kit?" Thomas glanced up at me. "Did you know about this?"

"Yeah," I said.

"And you decided not to tell me?"

"Would it have made any difference?" I demanded. Why hadn't I told Thomas about Kit Turner? I should have, but for some reason, I never did. Selene shrugged at me. *Some things just aren't his to know,* she said. *We're allowed our secrets.* But that didn't seem right, either.

"We have to get out of here," Callum insisted. He crouched down and smoothed the hair back away from Juliana's face. Her cheeks were starting to show some color, and her presence along the tether was strengthening. She was going to be fine. "He can't be the last of them."

"Callum is right," Thomas said. "We have to go—*now.*"

Adele nodded, getting up. Thomas turned his attention back to Juliana. "Can you stand, Juli?" She shook her head. He stood and hoisted her up, throwing her over his shoulder, then considered his options—left or right?

He muttered under his breath, something that sounded like "Always go right." And then he charged toward us, choosing left. Not knowing what else to do, we followed him down the hallway, shaking and almost delirious with fatigue. Soon enough, we came to a door that I recognized, with the ten stars of the Libertas symbol emblazoned on it. Adele tried the door, but it was locked.

"One, one, two, three, five, eight," Thomas said. He looked behind him, as if expecting to see something—or someone—there, but the corridor was empty, except for a large, dark pool of blood on the floor. "Ahead."

"What?" Callum grabbed my hand in surprise. Those were the king's numbers, the magic numbers, the first six numbers of the Fibonacci sequence: one, one, two, three, five, eight. He recognized them as well as I did.

"Sasha," Thomas said. "Come here, please." I stumbled forward, not entirely in control of my limbs, running on very little fuel and desperate for something—anything—that would allow me to rest.

"What do you need me to do?"

"You can press the stars," Callum said. "This is the door Juliana and I used the first time." I saw that he was right—they could be pushed, like typewriter keys.

Thomas looked in my eyes. "One, one, two, three, five, eight. Remember?"

"Yes, I remember," I said. Then I reached up and pressed the stars in sequence: one—the top of the pyramid. Then one again, then two—the star right below it, to the left. Then three—the star next to two. Then five, to the bottom left of three. Then eight, to the bottom left of five. Left, left, left. One, one, two, three, five, eight. Magic numbers.

The door slid open, and we found ourselves facing another tunnel, and at the far end of the tunnel, another door. And beyond that door, a staircase. And at the top of that staircase, freedom.

TWENTY-TWO

I barely remembered returning to the safe house. We had to take detours to avoid Libertas patrols, police, and first responders; halfway there, Juliana demanded that Thomas put her down. As soon as he did, she gravitated to Callum's side; whatever strangeness still existed between them was put aside, and she leaned against him the rest of the way. I expected Thomas to move to the front of the pack, to lead, as was his instinct, but instead he came and put his arm around me; I rested my head on his shoulder and relished the feeling of having him close, knowing that we would be separated sooner than I wanted and longer than I hoped.

Fillmore took one look at our bedraggled state and set to work treating our small wounds, administering a shot of adrenaline to Juliana to chase away the remnants of the sedative and patching cuts and scrapes. Rocko helped, too, making pots of coffee and heating up soup for whoever was hungry; it sat cooling on the table, since none of us could bring ourselves to choke anything down.

Thomas asked after Navin, Sergei, and Tim and got blank looks in return. Silence settled over us. "Maybe they went to the hospital," I suggested. The broken look on Thomas's face was unbearable; I didn't even know if I believed what I was saying, but I wanted so badly to make him feel better.

"Yeah, maybe," he said, rubbing the back of his neck. "We should get some sleep. Tomorrow is going to be difficult. We need to get out of the Tattered City, but Libertas will increase security on the city borders."

"I assume you have a plan," Adele said.

"I will," he said. "Just give me a couple of hours."

"I'll help you," she offered. "I'm not tired."

"Okay," he said. "Everybody else, head upstairs. We've got plenty of empty rooms, Juli. Pick whichever one you want."

"You can sleep with me," Callum said. His ears turned pink when he realized how it sounded. "I mean, in my room. I'll take the floor. Or not. Whatever you want, Juli."

She smiled and kissed his cheek, which only made his blush deepen. "Thank you," she said. "But I want to stay with them." She glanced at Selene and me. "Is that all right with you?"

"Of course," Selene said. It had been just Selene and me for so long, I wasn't sure if I could let Juliana in. I was still so angry with her, and even though my mind was attached to hers—even though I'd seen so many things through her eyes—I felt that I barely knew her. But I didn't want to ruin what was probably our only opportunity to persuade her to come with us to Taiga. My goals had not changed: help Selene, break the tether, be with Thomas. Some part of me would miss the tether when it was gone, but if that was the price I had to pay to live my life the way I wanted to live it, it was a sacrifice worth making. And I needed Juliana for that.

"Sasha?" Juliana knew what was going through my head. It had become impossible to keep my feelings from them. For better or worse, we were fused together. All I could do was hope that activating the Terminus would cleave the tether and give us our independence back.

"Of course," I said. "Whatever you want, Juliana."

"I need you to explain what it is you want me to do," Juliana said when we were alone in our room. Selene and I were sharing a bed; I'd given up mine to Juliana. "I know you didn't help rescue me out of the goodness of your hearts."

"That's not fair," Selene protested. "We care about you, Juliana. All we want is for you to be safe. You're one of us."

"Sasha doesn't think so," Juliana accused. "Right, Sasha?"

I sighed. "How can you expect me to trust you after what you did?"

Juliana twisted her hands in her lap. "I don't. But I know you know that I'm sorry, about everything. You can feel it, can't you? You can read it in my thoughts."

"That's not good enough," I replied. The truth was, Juliana's thoughts were a complete jumble. She wanted to stay with Callum, and she wanted to run from him, afraid of the strength of her feelings, worried he wouldn't be able to forgive her old sins. She wanted to help her country, and she wanted to flee from her responsibilities, afraid that she would fail everyone and make herself miserable in the process. She couldn't make up her mind about anything, so she was letting us make it up for her.

"Apparently not." Juliana hung her head. "You know, all I ever wanted was to be normal. All the pressure of being a princess—and now a—a queen . . . it was just too much for me. I don't think I was built right for it. I always felt I was meant for a different life." She raised her eyes to look at me. "Your life."

"So you decided to steal it. Totally understandable."

"No," she said. "I didn't even know you were real until the Shep—Kit told me. He was my brother, you know. And now he's dead. Just like Dad." She took a deep breath and kept going. "But I saw you all the time in my dreams, and I wanted so badly to have what you had. A life without expectations. Freedom. You must know what I'm talking about, Selene."

Selene shrugged, avoiding our eyes. "I've always taken great pride in my responsibilities," she said softly. "I don't even know what I would do with a 'normal' life."

"Normality is way overrated," I said. Once I'd had a taste of what an abnormal life might be like, I never could get used to being a regular person again. Still, I understood what she meant, probably far better than Selene ever could.

"Okay, well, anyway," Juliana continued, "normal just isn't an option for me. It's way too late for that. Maybe it was too late the second I was born."

"We were born," Selene corrected her.

"Right. My point is, I want to help. I don't want to feel like everyone in every world is braver than me. Callum, you know," she said, "he believes in me, in himself. He thinks we matter, that we can still do good, even though the world is falling apart. I'd like to live up to that faith." She stared at us. "So what is it you need me to do?"

"Sasha." I opened my eyes. The room was still dark. Selene and Juliana were standing over me. I sat up and yawned.

"Did I fall asleep?"

Selene nodded. "A few hours ago. It's time for us to leave. Thomas and Adele have gone to bed, but they'll probably be awake again soon and we'll have lost our chance."

"How do you know they're asleep?" Juliana asked.

"Listening," Selene and I said in unison. She looked confused, but she didn't press the point.

I turned to Selene. "Thomas *wants* us to go to Taiga. Don't you think it's smarter to have his help looking for the transit?"

"We don't need help," Selene said. "I know how to find the transit." She pulled up her sleeve and showed us her tattoo. Juliana, who'd never seen it before, stared at it suspiciously.

"Is it just me, or is it glowing?" she asked. Selene's tattoo, which used to be silver, had changed to a greenish color, sort of like the aurora. It was faint, but it did seem brighter than it should have, considering how dark it was in the room.

"That's how it works," Selene explained. "The ink is infused with a phosphorescent mineral compound called diastium that turns green in the presence of transits. We're not that far away from one—that's why it's starting to light up. The closer we get, the brighter it will become. And I already know where to look for it."

"I have to say goodbye to Thomas," I insisted. "I can't leave without telling him. Who knows when I'll be back?" I gave Juliana a hard look. "Don't you want to say goodbye to Callum?"

Juliana shook her head. "It'll just make things harder." She was struggling to be brave, and she thought that was what it meant: turning off your feelings and walking away. That struck me as cowardly, and not unlike what she'd done to get herself in trouble in the first place. But I was too tired to argue with her. I couldn't control either of them. In some ways, we were still so separate, which was a relief.

"You can't tell Thomas we're leaving, Sasha," Selene said. "He might try to stop us."

"He said he wouldn't," I reminded her. "You were there!"

"Just because he said it doesn't mean he meant it. The only

people I trust are the two of you." Selene smiled at me. "Besides, I think he'll understand. He has his own battles to fight. It's important that none of us get in the way of that."

I hesitated, turning over my options in my head. In a million years, I never thought I would end up having to choose between my analogs and Thomas. How easy such a choice would've been only a few days ago. Now it seemed impossible.

"All right," I said. "Let's go before I change my mind."

I probably should've guessed we'd end up at Oak Street Beach. Everything kept leading back to that stretch of sand, as if there were a magnet buried deep underneath it that constantly pulled at me. The three of us stood side by side at the water's edge, staring out at the gentle waves as they rode in to the shore. Selene's tattoo shone like a beacon. She pointed out to where the water was high enough to reach our knees.

"There it is," she said, her voice soft with reverence. "Do you see it?"

"Not really," I said, squinting. "What's it supposed to look like?"

"It's hard to describe," Selene said.

"I don't see it, either," Juliana piped up. "Are you sure it's there?"

"Yes, I'm sure," Selene told us. "The traveler's mark doesn't lie."

"Maybe you just need to get a little closer," came a voice from behind us. We turned with identical expressions of surprise. Thomas took a step back, as if we'd startled him instead of the other way around.

"Whoa," said Callum, who was standing beside him. "That was really creepy."

"What are you doing here?" we demanded all at once.

"Just when you thought it couldn't get creepier," Thomas muttered.

Juliana glanced at Selene and me. "We've really got to work on not saying the same thing at the exact same time."

"What are you doing here?" I asked.

"I followed you," Thomas said.

"And I followed him," Callum said.

"I think she meant why are you here?" Selene replied, but the boys didn't answer that question. Thomas reached for my hand and dragged me far enough away from the others that no one could overhear our conversation. Well, nobody except for the two girls with whom I shared a consciousness.

"You know that if they want to, they can listen to everything we say, right?"

"I don't care," Thomas said. "I didn't want everybody staring at us while we talked."

"Okay."

"Why did you leave like that?" he asked. I held his hands and forced myself to look him in the eyes, even though the pain I saw in his face made me want to run away. "You were just going to go off without saying goodbye?"

"I thought it would be easier," I admitted. "I'm not always as brave as you think I am."

"That's okay," he said. "Neither am I. I wouldn't have stopped you. I hope you know that. I meant what I said before. It's your choice what to do with your life. I'm not going to get in your way any more than you're going to get in mine."

"That's the thing, though. I was afraid that if I said goodbye, I would *choose* to stay," I told him. "Leaving you doesn't feel right. But letting them go to Taiga without me . . ." My eyes flickered over to Juliana, who was having an intense conversation with Callum, and Selene, who was standing by herself, gazing out at the lake with a homesick look on her face. "That doesn't feel right, either. Is it possible for someone to have two fates?"

"I don't know. I'm not the expert. Maybe you should ask Nostradamus over there." He smiled. "There's one thing I do know, though. You and I—it's not going to end here, on this beach, not like this. I'm not ready to give up, are you?"

"No," I said. "But I'm not really sure what the future is going to look like, or when it's going to come."

"Me neither," Thomas said. "I have absolutely no idea what's going to happen, to this world, or to us, or to everybody we know. But I believe there's something between us worth trying to save. I know we can't be together today, or tomorrow. Maybe not for a while, even. But someday we'll be together again, just like this, except then we will get to decide, and neither fate nor duty will have a damn thing to do with it. Even if we decide it's not worth it, we deserve a better ending than this."

"It's worth it, Thomas," I said. "To me it is. When we're done on Taiga and the tether is finally broken, I'm coming back to Aurora. To you."

"Then I guess I'd better clean up this mess while you're gone, huh?"

"Yeah, you'd better," I said, wrapping my arms around his waist and laying my head on his chest. "I love you, Thomas." I looked up at him and watched as a grin spread across his face.

"Finally," he said. "I was wondering if you'd ever say it back. I was kind of starting to feel like an idiot."

"I'm sorry," I said. "I was scared, I guess. Of what saying it would mean, especially if I was going to have to leave you. But it's not the saying it that matters. It's the feeling it. The words just put it on the record."

"Well, I'm happy to have it on the record," Thomas said. He glanced to his right, where Juliana and Callum had gone from arguing to kissing. Poor Selene was sitting in the sand now, staring sullenly at her traveler's mark. The tether whipped back and forth with her impatience to get home, but she knew that dragging us away from Thomas and Callum prematurely would only make things more difficult for her later on.

"So what are your next steps?" I asked. "After we're gone."

He took a deep breath and lowered his voice before speaking. "Dryden gave me a piece of intelligence Dr. Moss stole from the classified archives at the Tower. It proves that the General ordered the murder of the king." He seemed to want to say something else but then thought better of it. I bit my tongue to keep from pressing it. Our time together was growing short.

"Are you serious?" He nodded. "What are you going to do with it?"

"I'm going to turn it over to a reporter I know at the *Columbia City Eagle*," Thomas said. "And the president of the Congress, Nathaniel Whitehall. You remember him. Hopefully, this will be the key to toppling the General and putting Juliana on the throne."

"Wow, Thomas," I said. "That's big-time whistle-blower stuff. Espionage, even. If the General survives this information leaking out, he could have you executed."

"He won't survive it," Thomas said. "The people are ready for change. Libertas wouldn't be as strong as it is if they weren't. This is the end of the General. And I'm going to make damn sure it happens." Thomas caught my expression and narrowed his eyes. "What? Why are you looking at me like that?"

"You're a hero, you know that, right?" He shrugged and

looked away from me. I put my hand on his cheek and turned his face back toward mine. "A real-deal, actual hero."

"Stop saying *hero*," he said. "It makes me sound like a cartoon."

"Hey." I grabbed him and brought him so close our lips were almost touching. "You're not a cartoon. Cartoons don't bleed." I touched the cut on his forehead. He winced, but he didn't pull away. His eyes were locked on my face. "And they don't cry." I traced my thumb over the dried tears in the indigo-colored hollows beneath his eyes. "And they don't tremble when they're afraid." His hand was shaking. "You do. And you helped save us all. Some of us more than once."

"Lucas is dead," Thomas confessed. Though I'd just been through the slaughter and carnage in the club and catacombs, I was surprised. In all the chaos, I'd forgotten that Lucas was even there and hadn't thought about what might've become of him. "I couldn't save *him*."

"Did you . . . ?" From the expression on Thomas's face, it seemed like a possibility that it'd been Thomas who killed Lucas.

"No," he said, nearly choking on the word. "But I would have. If I had to." *If it meant saving you,* the look on his face told me. But knowing that I was the only person he'd sacrifice his brother for wasn't heartwarming or comforting; it was just sad. He shouldn't ever have to make a choice like that. "I found him down there. He was helping Juliana escape, and they shot him in the back." I nestled closer to him, sensing his need for physical comfort. He curled his body around me.

"He told me the code for the door," Thomas said. "He helped me, in the end. Helped us. He wasn't all bad, you know. He was just lost."

"I know," I said. Lucas had done some awful things, but he

was dead now, and he'd given Thomas his last breath. It didn't erase what he'd done, but it did lessen the debt a little.

Thomas checked his watch. "You'd better go, and so had we. Callum and I have to get back to the safe house before Adele and the others realize that we're gone."

"Too late," Adele said. I caught a glimpse of her over Thomas's shoulder and saw that she'd brought Rocko with her. "What's going on here?"

"Adele," Thomas said. "Selene is going to take Sasha and Juliana to her universe. It's the perfect place to hide Juliana until we can bring down the General."

"Nobody's going anywhere." Adele and Rocko pulled out their guns and trained them on us. Everyone took an involuntary step back. Thomas reached for his own weapon, but Rocko pulled his trigger and sent a bullet flying over Thomas's shoulder. It never would've hit him, but it was a warning: *Don't you dare move.*

"Put your hands up," Rocko growled. Thomas raised his palms in surrender, and we all followed suit.

"What are you doing?" I demanded. I blinked hard, as if by doing so I could banish the sight of Adele—Thomas's *friend*—standing before me with a gun pointed at my chest. Her jaw tightened, but Adele said nothing. It didn't matter. No explanation was going to make this better.

"Her job," Thomas said, his voice hollow. "That's right, isn't it? Cora, Navin, Sergei, Tim, Rocko—they were never my team, were they? They were yours."

"How the hell do you know that?" Rocko snapped.

"I should've known the General was never going to let me take a crew fresh out of the Academy on such an important mission unless he had a ringer or two. Or more. Did they all know who they were really reporting to, or was it just Rocko?"

"Does it matter?" Adele asked with a shrug, her voice steady and calm. That blank KES mask I'd seen Thomas wear so many times had slipped down low over her face; I couldn't read her at all. "I've got my orders. I have to bring you back."

"No!" Selene cried, surging forward.

"Stop or I'll shoot you!" Rocko shouted. He knew about our powers, and they frightened him. Thomas pulled Selene back.

"Don't," he warned us. "What happened to you owing me one, Adele?"

"What?" I asked, but Adele and Thomas weren't paying attention to anyone except each other.

"I could've stopped them from escaping the Labyrinth, but I didn't," Adele replied. "As far as I'm concerned, we're even."

"How did you find us?" Thomas asked.

"The KES ring you're wearing," Rocko said smugly. "It's got a tracker in it."

"So that's how they found us at Gorman's Gate," Thomas said. Every time he thought he'd outsmarted the General, it turned out his father was one step ahead.

We can't let this happen, Selene thought frantically, grabbing my hand. *We have to go through the transit while there's still time!*

Thomas will figure this out, Juliana thought in confident defiance. *He won't let them get the best of him. He's too good for that.*

We have to help him, I told my analogs. *We have the power. They can't stop us if we use it. They're helpless against it. You've seen what it can do.*

Can it stop a bullet? Juliana asked, her end of the tether sticky with sarcasm.

Maybe, Selene said. Then she fell silent and retreated behind the mental scrim she put up when she needed privacy to think. Juliana and I exchanged a fearful look. As connected as the three of us were, it wasn't always easy to predict what

Selene was going to do, and the tether was still throbbing from her massive power deluge in the catacombs. She couldn't withstand another one, not so soon.

"How are you going to bring us back to the Labyrinth? We outnumber you almost two to one," Callum pointed out, ignoring for a moment the fact that the two of them were holding us at gunpoint.

"I have reinforcements coming," Adele said. It was so easy to see why the General trusted her—she was so capable, so unflappable, in the face of all of this. I was shocked to discover that her betrayal didn't actually shock me at all. I should have known. When had anyone in Aurora ever been loyal to us? "We had a contingency plan, in case not everyone made it out of the club. They'll be here any second."

"Is the KES really that important to you?" Thomas asked her. He was wearing his KES mask, too, but he had to be devastated, despite his assertions that he'd had a feeling this was coming. It was one thing to believe something to be true, another thing entirely to realize you were right. "You know what the General will do to them. To all of us."

"It's the most important thing to me," Adele said quietly. "You know that." Then she squared her shoulders, not taking her eyes off us for a second, not lowering her weapon an inch. "Back up, all the way to the rock wall, then turn around and put your hands behind your backs." When we didn't move, she raised her voice. "Do it!"

We had no choice; we had to follow her orders. We stood with our faces pressed against the sharp rock embankment, blind now to what was going on around us. I tried to turn my head so that I could see better, but in a second I felt the cold muzzle of Rocko's gun at my temple. "Don't even think about it."

They're going to tie us up, Selene said. *I can use the power without my hands, but I don't think either of you will be able to.*

You can't use the power! I insisted. *You're still in too much pain.*

The tether contracted as Selene winced. Using it at all, even to talk, was still difficult for her, but she was pushing through the misery. *Then it will have to be you, and it will have to be now. Are you ready, Juliana?*

The tether bobbed up and down, a psychic nod. *I can feel it in my fingers,* Juliana thought.

So can I, I said. The power surged through us like a lightning storm. We could cause a lot of damage with the voltage we were carrying. I hesitated. What would be left of Adele and Rocko when the three of us were done with them?

Who cares? Juliana hissed. She was itching to release the power. It was awful and uncomfortable, having all that energy writhing within you and having to struggle to contain it. All you wanted to do was to let go, to let it possess you and become you. I was more certain than ever that *this*—the power, and the way it grew stronger and more ferocious when we were together—was the reason why analogs weren't meant to meet, to touch, to find each other. How long would it be until there was no looking back? And did it even matter? Either way, it was too late now.

On three, I told Juliana, and though we couldn't see each other, couldn't look into each other's eyes, I knew she'd heard and that she was right there with me. *One—two—three!*

It happened in one achingly slow moment. Juliana and I, turning, raising our hands, our palms and fingertips shining like filaments in the hot, bright heart of a lightbulb—the glow of the power traveling up our arms, our necks and shoulders, down our spines and through our legs, engulfing us in halos of light that burned white at first, then blue as the power intensified—Thomas shifting, calling out my name in warning—the terrified faces of Adele and Rocko as Juliana and I rushed forward like pillars of fire—Rocko pressing the trigger of his gun, once and then again—the bullets racing toward us, then *bending* as they came close, whispering past our heads as if we were supernovas and they were asteroids that had ventured too close and become trapped into orbit by the pull of our gravity.

Adele was my target, but the power reached her before I did, hitting her squarely in the chest. Out of the corner of my eye, I saw the same happen to Rocko, and in an instant they were in the air, and then in another, as the world sped up again, lying flat on their backs on the hard-packed sand.

I stood paralyzed as the power drained away and left an awful pulsing ache behind. I was trembling down to my very atoms, and the tether swung crazily.

"You did a good job," Selene said, putting her arms around me. Relief flowed through the tether like water. Juliana kept her distance, and for the first time I wished I could hug her.

When I found the strength to look up, I noticed Thomas and Callum hunched over Adele and Rocko, feeling for pulses that I knew they might not find. I stepped out of Selene's arms and made my way toward Thomas, but the look in his eyes stopped me. He and Callum wore matching expressions of terror on their faces. I closed my eyes, couldn't bear to look at them. Were they afraid for us, or *of* us?

"Are they dead?" I asked, terrified that we'd gone too far, that we'd killed them both.

Thomas shook his head. "No, but they're out cold. No telling for how long, so you have to go *now*."

Selene was halfway to the water. Juliana looked over at me, and I felt the tether grow bright with the strength of our connection. Selene was up to her calves in the lake now, the sleeve of her shirt pulled up, her tattoo on full display. I could see it glowing faintly in the distance, the same green color as the aurora overhead.

Juliana and I were only a few feet away from Selene, water licking our ankles, when a loud shout behind us caught my attention. I turned to see Thomas coming for me. He called out my name—once, and then again, an agonized, frantic cry—and then he was pulling me into his arms, crushing me, kissing my cheeks, my forehead, my lips.

"Don't go," he whispered, taking my face between his palms and touching his nose to mine. "Don't go, please, please, please don't go. Stay with me." He pressed his lips hard against mine. I felt the fabric of the world slip out from under me. How could I leave him? It seemed more impossible than ever. But there was no looking back. We'd come so far, done so much to get here. Our fate was calling, and we couldn't turn away.

"Sasha." Selene's hand on my arm, calling me back. "We have to go."

I placed one last kiss in the center of Thomas's brow. "I love you."

He sagged, heavy with grief and resignation. He never thought I would stay. He knew me too well to hope. But he had to try. "I love you, Sasha. Promise you'll come back. Please, please come back."

"I will," I said. "I swear I will." He squeezed his eyes shut, then opened them, and I knew that he was seeing me differently now, like someone who would go, not someone who would stay. This was how Thomas got through the bad stuff. He changed his perspective. But he wouldn't forget me. And he would love me. That knowledge lived within me like a brilliant star, and I would carry it with me into the next world, and whatever came after that.

"It's time to go," Juliana said. "I'll take good care of her, Thomas."

"You'd better." He tightened his grip on me. His words said *I'm letting you go,* but his touch still begged me to stay.

"It's all right," Selene said, tugging me free from Thomas's embrace. He released me, his arms falling limp at his sides. "Everything will be all right."

Thomas's hand shot out, but this time he took hold of Selene, his fingers circling her wrist.

"What's that?" he asked, meaning her tattoo, the two overlapping circles glowing in the night. In the near distance, Thirteen Bells sounded thirteen melancholy chimes.

"This is how our journey begins," Selene told him, slipping out of his grasp. "This is the key to the door that leads to my world."

He narrowed his eyes, and I could almost see the tumblers of his brain turning over and over, trying to puzzle something out and failing, to his frustration. Selene touched his shoulder.

"Take care of yourself, traveler," she said. I'd never heard her call him this, never imagined that she would think of him this way, but of course it was one of the things they had in common: they'd both crossed universes to fetch a girl who would save their world. They *were* travelers, both of them, certainly more than Juliana or even me.

Thomas just stood there, staring at the tattoo and her hand on his arm. Then my analogs and I turned and walked into the water, guided by the light of the traveler's mark. As we grew closer, the water up to our knees, I began to see it: the transit. It shimmered like the surface of a soap bubble. Selene stood to one side. After a slight hesitation and a backward glance at Callum, who was standing beside Thomas on the shore, Juliana stepped through and disappeared. The ground rumbled beneath my feet, and then it was my turn. I looked back once more at Thomas, whose face lit up suddenly in understanding.

I thought I heard him cry out, *Sasha, wait!* But the words were washed away by the hush of the waves on the sand, if he even said them at all.

STILL NOT THE END

SEE YOU IN TAIGA

"Clever and exhilarating—each page is a pleasure. I loved the romance and adventure of Sasha's story, and I can't wait for the sequel!"
—ALLY CONDIE, #1 *New York Times* bestselling author of MATCHED

ANNA JARZAB

TANDEM

READ THE FIRST BOOK